WRITTEN IN THE CARDS

ALEXA ASTON

OLIVER HEBER BOOKS

Published by Oliver-Heber Books

0 9 8 7 6 5 4 3 2 1

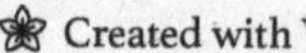 Created with Vellum

PROLOGUE

KANSAS PRAIRIE—SUMMER 1868

Ben Morgan breathed in the hot, still air as his gaze swept over the cloudless sky and flat prairie as he rode toward home from his monthly supply trip. He knew that Eliza would be happy he brought more sugar and coffee than usual, as well as the fabrics and threads her mother sent from Boston. He also carried two letters from her parents and another one from his mother.

They would sit together on the porch after dinner tonight and read these, first to themselves to think on the news shared in them. Then they'd read the letters aloud and talk about their contents. That night, Eliza would carry the letters to bed, slipping them under her pillow as she cried herself to sleep.

Again.

News from home always stirred up his wife. By tomorrow, the fights would begin. They sometimes lasted for days. Ben cursed under his breath, realizing once more what a mistake he'd made bringing his childhood sweetheart to homestead on the flat plains of Kansas after their marriage.

But he couldn't live in Boston—or any crowded city. The war had traumatized him in ways he might never understand. He simply knew he couldn't live in close confines ever again. Like many other soldiers from both sides of the battle, Ben left civilized society to take advantage of the Homestead Act passed during the War Between the States. Now, he farmed his acres. The land would be his free and clear in another two years. He'd built their small house, a larger barn, even the chicken coop.

Ben liked the solitude and quiet of the endless prairie. He enjoyed working with his hands. He could go for weeks and not see another soul and be perfectly fine, just sky and space as his only companions.

Eliza, on the other hand, lived in misery. A city girl from a well-to-do family, she'd let love rule her head and heart. She'd thought moving West as a couple would start their grand adventure of marriage off on the right foot. Little did either of them realize what a fish out of water she would be in their new home.

Reality set in quickly. With no servants to wait on her hand and foot, Eliza became a housewife from scratch, learning first to boil water before trying to add other new skills. She passed for a tolerable cook now, though Ben tired of the few meals she'd mastered. Her attempts to add color to the sod house by affixing magazine pictures to the walls became a disaster. Housekeeping seemed beyond her. The prairie dust settled into everything, from their curtains to their clothes to even the pores of their skin.

Now that she was pregnant after three years of marriage, Ben hoped the longed-for child would be the beginning of a new chapter in their lives. Eliza needed a baby to care for and cherish. Her selfishness and complaints dominated their lives. The woman she'd become irritated him with every passing moment, and he worked hard to hide that irritation.

A baby would be totally dependent upon his mother, and Ben was certain that his wife's maternal instincts could only help their situation. She was the oldest of three girls. He'd seen Eliza mother her two younger sisters over the years. A baby could connect her to those feelings once more.

It was also time to learn how to open his heart and love unconditionally. Maybe the baby would work a miracle on him, too. He'd returned from the war numbed by his experiences. He went through the motions, pretending to be happy to see Eliza and his mother, but a vast emptiness sat inside him. The only feeling he could muster was for Adam. Thankfully, his brother arrived home in Boston alive with all limbs intact. Many of their friends never made it back.

"Please, God. Let the baby make a difference. Let this be a new start for us."

The words, spoken aloud, rang hollow in his ears. Ben might never be the man he was before, the one Eliza had loved. The one she claimed disappeared on the day he marched down Boston Commons to go to war. As a soldier would, he needed to buck up and look ahead. He had a beautiful wife, a baby on the way, and a homestead to be proud of. It was up to him to make a new start with his wife this day. He alone would manage his destiny. He needed to think positive about the future.

Ben put a smile on his face. He urged the horse on as the burning orange sun inched toward the horizon. He would ask Eliza how she felt the minute he arrived, and not grimace if she complained. He would be a dutiful husband, and rub her tired feet and sore back before bed. He promised himself to cuddle her and coddle her. Carrying a baby these last seven months proved hard work. He appreciated her and would tell her to her face.

He spotted their house in the distance and wound up the road. Silence hung like a heavy blanket in the air. No birds sang. Not even a cricket chirped. Ben tensed, sensing something wrong. Eliza usually waited on the porch, ready to greet him when he returned from a supply trip, sewing baby blankets or darning his socks. Her absence troubled him.

Ben got closer and smelled the remains of something burning. He scanned the horizon and realized the barn behind their house had disappeared into a smoldering heap. Panic grabbed him quickly and wrenched his gut hard. Over the last few months, the Indian wars had heated up on the Great Plains. Settlers robbed. Cattle slaughtered.

Or worse.

He spurred his horse to a full gallop and reached the small corral. He froze. Blood seeped into the dirt. His cow lay in scattered pieces, her calf's throat slashed. Chicken feathers dotted the pen and floated in the air. Ben's stomach turned sour even as his mind raced, refusing to form unmentionable thoughts.

He jumped from his horse and ran to the cabin. Eliza liked to leave the door open to catch the breeze as she cooked. Their twin rockers lay broken, scattered in splintered pieces along the porch. He tamped down the fear and dread and stepped through the doorway.

Ransacked. Furniture smashed. Dishes busted. The lone windowpane shattered.

Then he saw her.

Ben walked shakily across the room. His knees threatened to buckle. He bent to Eliza, now a bloody, broken doll. Preserved on her face he saw the horror of her last moments. Bile rose in his throat as his gaze took in what remained of his wife. Then he saw the child in a bloody lump next to her. The savages cut his unborn son from her belly.

He stood, trying to make sense of the scene, stunned, frozen to the spot. It went beyond anything he'd witnessed in the war. A primal scream ripped from his throat, carrying across the empty prairie.

1

NEW YORK CITY—AUGUST 1874

"Hit me again, Maggie! Harder now this time. Don't be afraid, girl. Just haul off and swing."

Maggie threw everything she had into the punch, spinning six-foot Patrick Kelly around as she connected with his jaw. She gave the middle-aged Irishman a satisfied smile as he regained his balance and gawked at her.

"I'm a lefty, Patrick. In case you were wondering."

Her instructor whistled low. "Now, that's a great gift, Maggie, me girl. Lefties be few and far between. If'n ever you're in a fight, you'll have a tremendous advantage over your opponent."

He gave her his charming smile, his blue eyes twinkling. "Go again. Gimme all you've got."

She threw a quick one-two punch with her right leading first, following up with her left.

"I think I would like it better if I didn't have to wear these silly gloves. Don't real men fight with their bare knuckles?"

Her older brother, Marcus, laughed. "Not anymore, Mags. The Marquess of Queensberry Rules have all but eliminated bare-knuckle boxing."

Maggie glanced at where he sat on the loveseat,

sipping Earl Grey tea and nibbling on finger sandwiches. "Who exactly is this Marquess of Queensberry and why did he get to make up these rules?"

Marcus shook his head. "Actually, the marquess merely endorsed the rules, isn't that right, Patrick?"

"Indeed, boyo. A sportsman named John Graham Chambers wrote 'em, but the marquess gained the claim to fame by putting his seal of approval on them. Is it bare knuckles you be wanting to try next?"

Maggie nodded enthusiastically. "I think it would be far more practical to learn how to fight that way, Patrick. When would I ever—if confronted with danger—stop and pull on giant boxing gloves? It's not as if they would even begin to fit in my reticule."

Marcus rolled his eyes. "Simply because you haven't found one large enough yet, dearest sister. Although I would say from last month's bills that you have purchased every size of reticule known to the New York fashion scene."

Maggie snorted. "As if you would begrudge my looking fashionable, Marcus, being the clotheshorse you are. A lady simply must have a reticule for every occasion and I, for one, like to be prepared for whatever social event comes up on my calendar."

"Enough, you two," Patrick ordered. "Let's try it again, Maggie. And remember, if you ever find yourself in a street fight for some daft reason, you form a fist—but don't let your thumb go inside it. Sure as you do, it'd be the first thing you break."

Maggie drew her arm back, ready to show Patrick just how enthusiastic she could be. The drawing room doors opened. She heard the louder-than-usual gasp and cringed.

Aunt Harriet stood in the doorway, disapproval written all over her pinched features. Maggie glanced at Marcus, who'd promised her the old dragon would be gone until nightfall. He shrugged nonchalantly and returned to sipping his tea. Maggie steeled herself to take the brunt of the assault since everything was always her fault and never her brother's crime.

"Good afternoon, Aunt Harriet. I —"

"Don't you *good afternoon* me, Margaret Elizabeth Rutherford. How dare you stand there? My goodness! Are you actually wearing *trousers*? How can you pretend it's a perfectly ordinary afternoon? What on earth possessed you to strap on boxing gloves? And who is this," she raised her eyebrows and sneered, "gentleman?"

Marcus spoke up. "This is Patrick Kelly, Aunt. My boxing instructor extraordinaire."

Patrick bowed. "A pleasure to make your acquaintance, ma'am."

Harriet sniffed. "Well, it's certainly not my pleasure to make yours, sir." She turned back to Maggie. "I am horrified, young lady. Simply horrified. It's the day before your wedding, with a million things left to do. How can you go traipsing about dressed as a man, fighting in a perfectly genteel drawing room? What would your parents think?"

Maggie fought the eye roll that threatened to irritate her aunt even further and went with sarcasm instead.

"Mother died when I was only two, Aunt, so I have no idea what she would think. Papa ignored me for his publishing empire from the time I landed in my cradle. I heard it was something about my not being male, according to servants' gossip. I think he took a general dislike to me since I'm said to favor Mama so much. Therefore, I have no idea what he would think. Knowing him, if he were still alive, he'd enter the drawing room. His eyes would pass over me as if I were invisible. He'd walk to the teacart to snatch a cookie before making a quick departure. He did have a sweet tooth, you know."

Harriet sputtered at Maggie's impudence, finally managing to get out, "You are the most insolent creature! Though I hate to speak ill of the dead and my dearest brother, I do blame Henry for your deplorable behavior. He let you run wild after Rose's death."

"No, Aunt. You are wrong," Maggie said emphatically. "He would have to pay attention to me first in order to let me run wild. We both know he didn't care if I existed or not."

She glanced over at Marcus, ready to drag him into the conversation.

"Now, Marcus, on the other hand, did let me run wild from the time I was small. He allowed me to follow him and his friends about. He's introduced me to all kinds of interesting things over the years. Yet you never seem to blame him. So heap your wrath upon Marcus as the responsible one. He found Patrick for me. He takes boxing lessons from Patrick each week."

Harriet collapsed upon the sofa. "It doesn't mean it's appropriate for you to do so, Margaret. The Rutherfords are one of New York's oldest and finest families. You must act according to your station. And your age. You *are* twenty-three, dear. Not three." She sighed. "I could understand the singing and dancing lessons. Those were a necessity. But the fencing lessons? The shooting lessons? And now this?"

"It's wise for a lady to know how to defend herself, Aunt," Marcus interjected smoothly.

Harriet shot him a look that surprised even Maggie. "You indulge her too much, Marcus. Margaret needs to act like a lady. She should be interested in sewing. Creating menus. Charity work. Like all women of wealth do." Harriet's glare extended to Maggie. "For heaven's sake, you are about to settle down with Richard and be a wife."

Maggie could feel the tightness in her chest starting. In a moment, she'd become short of breath and start feeling that loss of control. She gritted her teeth, determined not to give into it.

She looked over at Patrick, who seemed to have caught her mood. He nodded at her, raising his gloved hands in front of his chest for her. Maggie hauled off and launched a series of hits, each thrown connecting harder than the one before, trying to ease her fears and conquer her frustrations at the same time.

Can I really go through with this wedding?

MAGGIE LOOKED at herself in the full-length mirror. The white wedding dress boasted the popular high neckline made of delicate lace that was removable. Aunt Harriet had convinced Maggie it would give her more freedom to move and be more appropriate for the evening reception. Until then, she found it irritating. And damn hot.

She fingered the white cameo brooch, her most prized possession. Marcus gifted her with it during their trip to Europe last year. Maggie wore it every day to remind her of all they had seen and done. She especially loved Tuscany, with its sweeping landscape and incredible foods and wines. Marcus thoughtfully found a drawing master there, and she'd taken lessons from him, honing her skill.

In France she moved on to paints, enjoying them, but not nearly as much as the charcoal or pen-and-ink sketches. She continued drawing upon their return and thankfully put her talent to good use which no one—not even her brother—knew about.

A knock at the door interrupted her thoughts. Sarah Henry, her matron-of-honor, answered it.

Marcus entered, his dark tailcoat and top hat immaculate. Maggie smiled at him.

"You look more fashionable than the bride," she told him. "All the single ladies of New York will take one look at you and fall madly in love."

He gave her an admiring glance. "Mags, you are stunning in your wedding finery. I adore this cascade of ruffles. And the lace trimming is immaculate. Your dressmaker deserves a bonus for making you look the bride of the year."

"I told her she'd be the most photographed society member of the decade," Sarah said. "The press is already lined up outside, waiting for the happy couple to exit the church. You can see them from the window."

Sarah paused and frowned. "Our bouquets should already have arrived by now. I'm going to check on them and take a peek inside the church. I trust you two will behave." She gave them a wave and left the bridal dressing chamber.

Marcus pulled Maggie to a seat. "I know it's almost time but I have a small present for you." He pulled it from an inside pocket and handed it to her.

Maggie stared at the daguerreotype. "I don't remember having this taken, Marcus. And why would I be wearing such an old-fashioned dress?"

Then it hit her.

"Mama," she whispered.

Maggie studied the picture, wishing she could reach across the years and touch the woman whose portrait she looked at now. Rose Rutherford had a faint flush to her cheeks. A smile, which hinted at knowing some secret, sat on her lips. Maggie's same hazel eyes, a mix of brown and green, stared back at her. Even the copper-colored hair shone softly in the picture. It was as if Maggie looked into a mirror and saw herself.

"Where on earth did you find this?"

Marcus shrugged. "It was among some papers Papa left with his attorney. You so favor her, Mags. I look at this and you. It is as if Mama's come to life again. She always said copper hair ran through her Scots ancestors. I remember being slightly jealous of you when you were born because you shared that with her."

"You remember her much more than I do. I was not even three when she passed."

He nodded. "I was six-and-a-half when the fever struck her. Yes, I do recall her. She loved to laugh. When she got excited or even angry, gold flecks would appear in her eyes."

"Just like me!"

"Yes. You are quite like Mama, Mags." He hugged her. "Having you all these years after losing her was the best compromise possible. It's as if she's always been around, watching over the both of us. That's why I waited until now to give this to you, rather than when I first found it. I thought it would mean more to you on your wedding day."

He squeezed her hand. "Now, place that in your reticule. Mama will walk down the aisle together with us."

Maggie frowned as she put the picture inside her silk reticule and slipped it over her wrist. "I wonder what Mama would make of Richard."

"Oh, Richard's a good sort, you know, if a bit bland. You'll spice up his life, Mags." Marcus's gaze pierced her. "Unless you don't want to."

Maggie bit her lip. "It is what Papa wanted. David DeForest was his best friend, and Bethany has treated me as a daughter while I grew up. I'm very fond of Bethany."

"And David?" Marcus asked. "He is Richard's father."

Maggie wrinkled her nose. "Not so much of David."

"You're not marrying Richard's parents. You're marrying *him*, for better or worse. You *do* love him, don't you? I just assumed since you said 'yes' and finally set the date that you did."

Marcus studied her. "If you have doubts, dearest, don't marry Richard. You don't need to please Papa. He's not here." Marcus took her hands in his. "Please yourself, Mags."

Maggie hesitated. She didn't love Richard. She never had. He followed her around from the time they were children, even though he was two years older than she. She led him into scrapes too numerous to count. Richard was reliable, steady, and oh, so very boring.

Boring could be good, couldn't it? No terrible highs or lows. No drama. Besides, Aunt Harriet might be right. Maggie had been a terror all her life. She did need to grow up and make her own adult decisions.

But wasn't it wrong to marry a man she didn't love in order to please one that never loved her?

Sarah entered the room, bouquets of calla lilies mixed with white roses in hand. "Here you are, Maggie. The church looks beautiful. So many flowers everywhere and packed with people. I can tell no expense has been spared. This is *the* society event of the season."

Maggie took the bouquet. "I suppose it's time."

"Yes. Don't look so nervous. You're starting to make me nervous and I have to walk down the aisle before you and Marcus. Go on, Marcus. Give us our last bit of girl-time. We'll be out in a moment."

Marcus walked through the door, looking over his shoulder at Maggie. She gave him a smile, encouraging him to leave.

Sarah took a quick glance in the mirror at herself, smoothing her hair, and then gave Maggie a long look.

"You are as lovely a bride as I've ever seen, Maggie Rutherford. I hope you and Richard have a happy life together."

"As happy as you've been, Sarah?" Maggie asked.

Sarah shot her a hard look. "Don't judge me, Maggie. Ronald and I suit one another. Besides, many couples lead separate lives. I have time for my baby. Hopefully, there'll be another one on the way soon. I still see my friends and I'm active in charity work. I have a good roof over my head and a closet full of beautiful clothes. What more could I possibly want?"

Maggie thought there had to be more to life than what Sarah described. She didn't want to settle. She wanted *to live*. To have adventures. To see things she'd never seen.

To love and be loved in return.

A sudden knock at the door startled them. Sarah stepped over and opened the door.

"I need to see Miss Maggie Rutherford at once, ma'am. It's an emergency."

"Sir, you have no business interrupting at a time –"

"Let him in, Sarah."

Maggie recognized the voice of the Pinkerton detective she'd hired several months ago. After she and Marcus returned from their extended stay in Europe, Richard seemed frantic to marry her after years of her putting him off. Since she enjoyed the status quo of their close friendship, she found his sudden interest in insisting upon a quick marriage between them a bit strange.

Society thought them a couple. That allowed Maggie to pursue her varied interests without having to fight off potential suitors badgering her with invitations to balls and garden parties. Richard escorted her to all social events, so no line of boring beaux formed at her door.

His abrupt eagerness to marry gave her cause for thought, and Maggie had hired a Pinkerton to get to the bottom of things. Once Aunt Harriet got wind of Richard's wish to formalize their relationship with marriage vows, she conducted the wedding train as if it were a team of runaway horses, galloping to their destination.

Soon Maggie found herself caught up in a whirlwind of activities, from parties to fittings for her wedding dress and trousseau. Hiring this detective became lost in the shuffle. She'd actually avoided thinking about marrying Richard in the midst of everything, concentrating instead on her writing and other interesting activities when she could squeeze them in. Most of her friends were already married, and like Sarah, they led fairly separate lives from their husbands. Maggie assumed she would do the same.

The arrival of the Pinkerton, though, stopped her in her tracks. Being a good judge of character, her ability to read people came in handy. Maggie knew by the look on the man's face that something was afoot.

Sarah exclaimed, "Maggie, what can you be thinking? It's almost time for your march down the aisle! You can't keep half of New York waiting."

Maggie silenced her friend with a glance. "This is important to me, Sarah. Would you please give us a moment?"

Sarah let out a long stream of hot air to express her displeasure and turned sharply. She flounced past the detective and slammed the door as she exited.

"My apologies, Miss Rutherford," the detective said, as he swept off his hat. "My timing is not the best. My father recently passed, up in Boston. I was called away to attend his funeral and settle his estate for my mother and my sister."

He pulled an envelope from his inner coat pocket. "I allowed a colleague to finish compiling my report. He thought it best for me to present it when I returned, due to its extremely delicate nature. When I called at your home just now and found you were at the church, I made haste to arrive before the ceremony."

He handed her his report. "I feel you should read this immediately, Miss Rutherford. Before you take that walk down the aisle." He bowed to her, then turned to the door. "I'll take my leave. Best of luck to you—in whatever course you decide."

Bewildered, Maggie sat, and with shaking hands opened the envelope after the detective left. She skimmed the contents quickly and then read over the report more slowly. Hard up for cash, the DeForests had run up debts all over New York City and beyond.

Richard's father had gambled to the point where it became a sickness. David DeForest's gambling spun out of control, until the fortune he inherited dwindled drastically. It meant Richard and his family urgently needed the money Maggie would come into when she turned twenty-five next year. Although that date was fourteen months away, Maggie knew Marcus would continue her generous monthly allowance until she began receiving her trust fund.

Her mother had thoughtfully drawn up the trust upon Maggie's birth, the money being solely hers and not part of any dowry Henry Rutherford received upon their marriage. Rose Rutherford intended the same for her daughter, to have her own independent means and control of her own fortune.

Richard might love her, but he'd never said the words, either in letters or to her face. Maggie assumed he was primarily interested in what she would bring to the marriage beyond the established dowry. Yes, the DeForests possessed breeding and prestige, but their money was literally gone.

If Richard didn't marry her quickly, the wolves would be baying at the DeForest door, demanding payment. His marriage to Maggie would hold that off, since it was common knowledge she would come into close to half a million dollars in the near future.

She dropped the report on the seat next to her, stunned by its contents.

Marcus opened the door. "The music's started." He held out his arm. Maggie pasted on a smile and walked to him as if in a dream. She slipped her gloved hand through it.

Avoiding Sarah's questioning eyes, Maggie looked around. The detective had departed from the church. Sarah stepped in front of them and they walked down a long corridor in silence. At the end, they entered a magnificent foyer and someone threw open the door. Sarah stepped through and glided down the aisle.

Maggie stood leaning slightly into Marcus for support. Suddenly, the music swelled. He began propelling her down the aisle.

She coasted by a blur of faces. She fought the dizziness with each step. A chill ran through her. Her pounding heart started up, beating more and more rapidly, until she thought she might not be able to breathe.

She flashed back to being locked in the dark pantry and gave a small squeak. Marcus tightened his grip on her and gave her a reassuring smile.

They reached the altar and her brother handed her off to Richard. The groom took her hand to tuck through his arm and frowned.

"A bit cold, Maggie?" he whispered. "I can feel it through your gloves, darling."

She looked at him. Richard's blond hair fell perfectly into place. His moustache was trimmed neatly. She knew his attire to be made of the best silk and wool to be found. He stood tall and assured next to her. He was absolutely perfect.

At least to the outside world.

Reverend White joined their hands and began his opening remarks. Maggie's panic and confusion grew until she visibly trembled. Richard looked down at her with obvious concern. She shook her head and tried to focus on what was being said.

"What's gotten into you, Maggie?" he whispered through the side of his mouth.

"I know you're poor," she blurted out under her breath.

Richard turned to look at her, the shock evident on his face. "What do you mean?"

"I know about your father's gambling."

Reverend White continued speaking, his voice rising above their hushed tones, trying to cover their conversation. Maggie could tell the man of God was perplexed, but he gamely carried on about love and them joining together as one.

"That has nothing to do with us."

"Doesn't it?"

The malevolent look Richard gave her made Maggie cringe. His hand tightened painfully on hers. Gone in an instant was the handsome, dull, mannered gentleman she had known most of her life. Suddenly, Richard loomed large and menacing next to her.

"Don't breathe a word of this to anyone, Maggie. We *will* marry. You *will* be the dutiful wife with a large bank account that will save my family. I expect it. My parents expect it. End of discussion."

His words undid her. Her panic blossomed fully now, her mind racing. She refused to be unhappy for the rest of her life. She was no puppet to dance on a man's string. Marrying Richard DeForest would cause her to wither and die.

At that moment, Maggie caught Reverend White's words, "And if any man has a reason why these two should not be married, you shall speak now or forever hold your peace."

Maggie clawed at Richard's hold on her. She loudly said, "No man—but this woman does."

She turned to face her childhood chum, her groom, the man she thought she'd known. "Richard, I cannot marry you."

Maggie tossed her bouquet aside and rushed back up the aisle. She bolted through the sanctuary. She raced over to the doors. Yanking one open, she hiked up her wedding gown. She galloped down the steps, past the crowd that had gathered, hoping for a glimpse of the happy couple as they left the church. A few newspaper reporters called after her. Maggie ignored them in her haste.

She reached the carriage parked in front of the church, waiting to take the newlyweds to their reception at The Fifth Avenue Hotel. She couldn't afford to have him follow her there. Not now!

The driver leaned against the DeForest carriage, a newspaper in his hand. He gave her a puzzled look and called out, "Where to, miss? Aren't we waiting for Master Richard?"

"Pennsylvania Railroad Station. Hurry. Be quick about it, sir!"

He doffed his cap to her, a wide smile appearing on his face. "With pleasure." The driver helped her up the steps and closed the carriage door.

Maggie collapsed against the velvet seat, her breathing shallow. She swallowed hard, trying to calm her nerves. She shut her eyes and let her head fall back.

What on earth did I just do?

2

SAN ANTONE—JUNE 1875

Ben Morgan entered the saloon. His eyes skimmed the room quickly, sizing up the men present. A gambler needed more than charm and likeability. Keen intelligence was the key to survival. Over the last six years, he'd learned not only to calculate the odds in a card game but also to read his opponents' eyes and their nuances at the table. He honed his intuition until he could spot the biggest fish in the room. He also figured out when to draw and when to fold.

And especially when to leave town.

Introspective by nature before his gambling days, with a great set of math skills in his repertoire, Ben often met with success. Lady Luck played a part, but he took the lessons from his early days of roaming to heart. He played with confidence and dexterity. His hands possessed a skill and grace in their physical movements. His mental skills remained cunning and sharp.

Ben moved to the long bar. He signaled the barkeep and ordered a whiskey. He took the drink in hand and turned to lean back against the polished mahogany, studying the room more slowly now. Scattered games continued at various tables. Ben watched each before choosing the one he would enter.

A sporting gal caught his eye. Dressed in red satin, she stood on the balcony above the room. Coal black hair fell down her back in waves. Ben tipped his hat to her. She gave him a promising smile. Maybe after his gaming tonight, he'd take her for a whirl.

He finished his drink, set the shot glass on the bar, and motioned for another. He wouldn't drink much of this one. Instead, he'd use it more as a prop. Most players didn't trust a man unless he had liquor in his hand. Ben knew alcohol dulled his senses, so he drank sparingly when he played.

He set down his payment and nodded to the barkeep. "Anything you can tell me about the dandy over there?"

The bartender smirked. "That's Jimmy Lonnegan, my friend. Watch him if you join in at his table. He cheats."

Ben raised an eyebrow, surprised not only that Lonnegan's cheating was so well known, but that the barkeep spoke matter-of-factly about it. "How?"

"You name it. Jimmy does it. He's small-time and only cheats about half the time, so most players overlook it."

Ben frowned. His strong sense of right and wrong had led him to lie about his age in order to enter the war at sixteen. In his book, cheaters should never be tolerated, especially when it came to playing cards.

"Why doesn't someone stop him? Or call him out?"

A shadow crossed the barman's face. "Because his brother is Black Tex Lonnegan. That's why. People know better than to cross the likes of him."

Ben nodded. A gunfighter by trade and occasional train robber, Black Tex's reputation stretched far beyond his home state. He was said to be quick on the draw with nerves of steel. Half his gunfights ended with his opponent lying dead in the dirt. The other half got out of town fast before it began and knew never to look back.

Still, it intrigued Ben that Black Tex's little brother thought he could play dirty and hide behind his brother's long shadow. Perhaps it was time someone taught Jimmy Lonnegan a lesson.

Maybe a man who had no fear of dying.

Ben picked up his whiskey and ambled over to Jimmy's table. Three other players sat with Jimmy. One threw down his hand and stood as Ben reached them.

"I'm out, fellas. I figure it's time to find a sporting gal and call it a night."

Jimmy reached over and raked in his winnings.

Ben motioned at the empty chair. "May I?"

Jimmy nodded. "Have a seat, stranger. What do you call yourself?"

Ben used many names as he moved from town to town. It wasn't always wise to spill your name at a game. This time, though, he wanted Jimmy Lonnegan to know who bested him in the end.

"Ben Morgan. What's the game?"

Jimmy shrugged. He brushed his expensive black suit sleeve, smoothing the velvet. Ben noticed the snow-white shirt and fancy brocade vest, along with the large-stoned stickpin that sparkled on the cheater's chest. An enormous gold pocket watch dangled from a heavy gold chain studded with pearls. He seemed a walking advertisement for success.

It made Ben want to take him down even more.

"Poker. You in?"

"I am."

Ben removed his gloves and cracked his knuckles, the only pre-game ritual he participated in. He worked hard to have no tells and show no emotion on his face. Some opponents claimed that ice water ran deep through his veins.

Jimmy shuffled the cards and handed the deck to the player on his left, a sallow-faced balding man. The man cut. Jimmy dealt the cards. The game was officially on.

Ben played conservatively at first, getting a feel for the other players and the cards themselves. He sandpapered his fingertips and wore gloves to protect his fingers at all times unless playing. Gamblers needed smooth hands, soft enough to be able to detect the smallest variation in the surface or shape of the cards.

Too many times card trimmers were used to strip cards, slicing off 1/32 of an inch from cards within the deck. This made certain cards have the faintest of curves, being slightly concave. With a delicate touch, a gambler could tell if the ends felt wide or narrow and know what a card's value was, playing both ends against the middle.

At least Jimmy hadn't doctored the deck in this way.

Each player won a round at first. Then Ben won two in a row. He could feel Jimmy's frustration building. Ben won another—and that was when the younger man made his first move. He had talent. If Ben hadn't watched him so carefully, he never would have seen Jimmy slide a card from up his sleeve, much less take the hand with three kings.

The winning spread evenly again between the four men. A fifth fellow joined them soon after that, his wide girth crowding the other players somewhat. Ben noticed the newcomer almost caressing the cards with his first deal, feeling for any punctured surface that would give away a high card. Ben had done the same when he first shuffled, happy that the deck proved clean.

He studied the cards carefully for any marks as play continued, but discovered none. He was beginning to think that Jimmy wouldn't cheat again, until the latest addition to the table won three hands in a row. This seemed to irk Jimmy, and he pulled blue-tinted spectacles from his pocket, wearing them for the next round.

Ben doubted at least two of the other players even noticed Jimmy's move since they focused so intently on their cards. But the winning man did. He gave Jimmy a frown and then caught Ben's eye.

Ben nodded slightly. He knew Jimmy had pulled out all the stops now. Spectacles such as these enabled the wearer to detect marks made on the backs of cards with phosphorescent ink. The marks would be invisible to the unaided eyes of Jimmy's opponents, but he would know every card they held. It was time to call a halt.

Ben watched cautiously as did the rotund gentleman. When Jimmy turned over four aces and leaned in to claim his winnings, Ben placed a hand over them and stood. "You didn't win the pot fair and square, Jimmy."

"Are you crazy? I won." Jimmy pulled back and tore off the spectacles, waving them wildly. He motioned around the table. "Ask these men. They saw what I turned up."

The large gentleman also stood. "You are a liar and a cheat." He reached over and grabbed the glasses and handed them to Ben.

Ben slid them on and picked up several cards. He

shuffled through them quickly and then gave the spectacles back. The gambler put them on and repeated Ben's actions before taking them off.

"This deck is marked, young man. And you can see the markings with these."

The room grew deathly quiet. Everyone watched for what would come next. Ben leaned over and grabbed Jimmy's sleeve. He fished up it and came out with three high cards.

"I saw him pull a card from his sleeve. And the deck is marked. This man is a fraud."

Sweat poured down Jimmy's brow. "You're wrong. I can explain."

"Did we play with your deck?" Ben asked, looking around at the table.

The other players from the game nodded. "He offered his from the start," the sallow man said.

Jimmy looked around the room, panic on his face. The very air grew ominous and heavy as all eyes stared at him. He shoved the table, turning it over. "You can't do this!"

"What?" Ben asked him. "Declare you a swindler and a fraud? The facts speak for themselves."

"My brother won't let you."

Ben stared at him. "Your brother's not here, son. And who is to say an outlaw and gunfighter like Black Tex would condone cheating? Not even for his little brother."

The heavy player nodded in agreement. "Should we deliver him to the local sheriff, or should we take matters into our own hands?" The man drew a gun and pointed it at Jimmy.

Jimmy wailed, a loud keening of desperation and fear at what would happen next. He dropped to the ground like a limp rag doll. His move embarrassed

Ben. Before he could tell Jimmy to stand up and be a man, Jimmy rolled. In a blur, he pulled a gun and shot the man holding a pistol on him.

Ben reacted with instincts honed by his desperate war years. His gun magically appeared in his hand. A shot rang out and hit the young cheater just as he turned to fire at Ben. Ben spun, narrowly missing the bullet meant for him.

When he straightened, he saw Jimmy dead on the ground. Blood poured from a fatal head wound. Ben averted his eyes and looked to the other player sprawled beside a chair, blood pooling around his prone body.

A wave of dizziness engulfed him. He squeezed his eyes closed as the nausea rose. The sight of blood always affected him this way. Though he'd seen countless dying men during the war, he never got over his aversion to blood.

Suddenly, a low hum buzzed through the saloon. Ben swallowed hard, trying to calm himself. He opened his eyes and saw a man dressed all in black standing in the doorway. Madness gleamed in his eyes. Ben had no doubt he faced Black Tex Lonnegan.

The gunfighter raised a hand. The bar fell silent. The only sound came from a ticking grandfather clock.

"Your brother was cheating at cards." Ben eyed the outlaw with caution. "When we confronted him, he shot a man in desperation and then tried to kill me. He got what he deserved."

A collective gasp echoed throughout the room.

The gunslinger moved a few steps toward Ben and stopped.

"And you deserve worse." Black Tex eyed him with malice. "I intend to skin you alive, the way Injuns do it.

They take their time. After an hour, you'll beg for mercy. After a day, you'll beg for death. But I'll take my time. I can make it last two or three days. It will seem like a lifetime."

A shrill scream filled the air. Ben's eyes flew to its source.

The sporting gal with the ebony hair.

As she screamed, she knocked over a lantern. It sailed through the air and hit a table and then the floor. Flames immediately sprang up, licking the old wooden floor. Another kerosene lantern struck the floor. A scrambling man tried to escape it and caught on fire. His screams sent men running. The crowded saloon became pandemonium.

Ben didn't know if she'd knocked the kerosene lamp over on purpose or accidentally, but the fire and confusion offered him a slim chance for escape. While he was fast with his gun, he would be no match for a professional gunfighter like Black Tex. And he'd decided he wasn't ready for death just yet.

He had to get out. Now.

Fleeing, Ben rushed the opposite direction, up a flight of stairs. He glanced over his shoulder. He saw chaos on the floor below. Running down a hall, he raced into a room with an open window. He climbed out of it, dropping to a wagon below filled with feed. The bags of grain broke his fall. As he jumped from the wagon, he twisted his ankle.

He half-hobbled, half-sprinted down two blocks to where he'd stabled Prince at the livery. He quickly saddled the coal black horse and rode at a gallop out of San Antone without looking back.

3

ABILENE, KANSAS—SEPTEMBER 1875

Ben couldn't believe they'd finally arrived. Eight long weeks on the cattle drive had ended. Wooden buildings of the railhead town of Abilene broke up the endless prairie.

Sid Spedwell, the trail boss, led the herd close to the outskirts of town. He shouted instructions on yarding the cattle. Ben helped drive the animals into a series of pens, where they would wait to be sold and then loaded onto railroad cars in the adjacent rail yard.

Ben dismounted next to One-Eyed John, who rubbed his hands in glee.

"'Bout ready to done be paid, Benny Boy," the cowpoke said. "I want a hot bath and a soft woman." He grinned. "Maybe even two gals."

One-Eyed John had taken Ben under his wing during the monotonous weeks on the trail. He joined up with the herd just outside of Fort Worth, where he'd ridden with haste, trying to escape the long arm of Black Tex Lonnegan. Fortunately, Ben arrived just as Sid Spedwell needed another cowhand. One of the boys took a nasty fall, breaking both an arm and a leg when his horse spooked. Sid got the man the twenty miles to Fort Worth in the back of the cook wagon and dropped him off, but it left them a man down.

Ben figured the drive would be good cover. He doubted Black Tex would think to look for him on the Chisholm Trail, which wasn't used as much the past couple of years since the rise of the Goodnight-Loving and Western Trails. Besides, gamblers didn't get their hands dirty, much less calloused. The towns between Texas and Kansas were few and far between, not on the usual circuit most gamblers played. It would be a different way to pass the time and put distance between him and the notorious gunfighter.

Besides, Ben always made his way near Abilene at least once a year to see his family. His older brother, Adam, ran a small general store in a town less than ten miles from Abilene. Ben enjoyed visiting, but he especially liked spending time with his little niece, Jennie. She'd be five now and looked forward to being a big sister soon. Ben couldn't wait to spoil her and the new baby.

Sid gathered the hands around and doled out the payroll to each. For many of them, it was more money than they'd ever seen at one time. After working the trail, Ben appreciated every dime he received, and thought again how hard these men worked compared to his own life playing cards.

The trail boss pulled him aside. "Ben, as low man on the totem pole, you and Billy Bob need to stay with the herd first while the others hit town. I've already got a buyer lined up so it won't be for more than a couple of hours. Then you can spend that wad of cash to your heart's delight."

"I'll look forward to it," Ben said, as the two men shook hands.

"I appreciate how you joined in fast and worked so

hard. You're a good man, Ben Morgan. I'd have you on my crew anytime, just say the word. You know where to find me if you're ever back in Texas again."

Sid tipped his hat and sauntered off. Ben caught Billy Bob's eye and the seventeen-year-old came over with a big grin on his face.

"Ain't this excitin', Ben? All these cows and the trains and the town waitin' for us to paint it red."

Ben slapped the young man on the shoulder. "All in good time, Billy. Right now, we need to do our last duty to our trail boss and keep a close watch on the herd."

They both climbed on a fence. Ben enjoyed looking at the different men as they drove the herds by, since he'd been with the same outfit for two months. He knew their every story and song.

Suddenly, he spied a woman.

Ben followed her progress across the yard. The subtle sway of her hips drew the eye of every cowboy within a hundred yards. Her chocolate brown dress with its moderate bustle was adorned with a single white cameo pinned to it. Ben found himself salivating as she walked, her hourglass figure curving in all the right places.

Men left and right parted like the Red Sea, allowing her to make her way through the holding yard. As she passed thirty feet in front of him, he could see the milky-white complexion tinged with the color of roses blooming on her cheeks. The sun struck her copper-colored hair and lit it on fire. Ben wished he could unpin her chignon and run his hands through the soft locks.

She looked his direction at that moment. He couldn't control the smile that leaped to his lips. The woman nodded to him, a slight smile on her own lush mouth. He hadn't seen a woman in weeks. Spying this earthbound angel caused a shiver to run through him.

She turned and continued along her way, disappearing into a sea of people. The crowd folded back around her after she passed. His heart pounded from the brief, distant encounter.

Billy Bob punched him hard in the arm. "Damn, Ben. She *smiled* at you. Boy, oh boy. Ain't that somethin'? A purdy lady like that smiled at you! You lucky dawg."

Ben wondered where she came from. Why she was in the rail yard. Who she was. Where she was going.

And how he could find her again.

BEN STABLED Prince and bypassed the rows of saloons, which drew cowboys like a magnet. He entered the large general store across the street. He spent a good portion of his pay choosing new clothes. He didn't want to be clean from a bath and have to put on his dusty trail gear again.

He selected two white shirts, black pants, a black patterned vest, a dark suit coat, and a dark hat. He needed a new pair of boots too. The ones on his feet hadn't been made to withstand the hardships on the cattle trail. Two toes peeped out from his right foot, and a hole had formed on the bottom of his left heel.

He also found a doll that Jennie would love, dressed in red gingham and with hair the color of straw in pigtails. Not knowing if the baby would be a boy or girl, Ben went with a picture book. Jennie would enjoy it now and she could read it to the baby later on.

Ben gathered up his purchases and headed toward the bathhouse. He paid extra for a clean tub of sudsy water, wondering why anyone would settle for the remnants of another man's bath. An hour later after a good scrubbing and tolerating the barber, Ben toweled off and dressed in his new clothes. With his hair cut and the beard gone, save for his usual moustache, he appeared more as the gambler he was. He no longer looked like a cowboy on the cattle trail. Only his tanned face and calloused hands gave away the time he'd spent in the saddle, working the herd.

He needed a drink. To avoid quarrels between the men, Sid forbade drinking on the drive. Ben couldn't wait to calm his thirst with a whiskey, chased down with a cold beer or two.

As he left the bathhouse, he passed the general store again and wandered toward the largest of the saloons. He spied all the signs of civilization in Abilene, including hotels and a bank. He might stay in one of the larger hotels tonight and make his way to Easton first thing tomorrow. It would depend if he could pick up a card game tonight or not. He had an itch that needed to be scratched.

Ben stepped up on the wooden planks that ran along the outside of the saloon and stopped. Standing next to the swinging doors was the copper-haired beauty from earlier that afternoon. She spoke to a cowboy and then waved him off, sending him into the bar with a laugh.

Without thinking, Ben rushed over to her. "What on earth are you doing standing in front of a saloon? Do you realize how rough and rowdy –"

"Oh, there you are." Her hazel eyes twinkled, as she looked at him from head to toe. "My, you certainly clean up well."

Ben stood dumbfounded at the beautiful stranger assessing him like a buyer would a Longhorn steer.

"I've been looking for you everywhere. You'd left the stockyards by the time I headed back your way. I checked the bathhouse, but you hadn't been there yet. I went to the biggest mercantile, but they said I'd just missed you."

She shook her head. "I figured sooner or later you'd make your way to this street so I thought I'd simply wait for you to turn up."

She smiled at him as if waiting for a strange man in front of a cow town bar was the most natural thing on earth for a pretty woman to do.

"You are some crazy lady," Ben blurted out.

The woman chuckled, deep and throaty. He swallowed at the way the sound made him tingle. "You have no idea, sir. My aunt Harriet thinks I went off the rails years ago. But that's another story. I'm here to hear yours."

Ben frowned. "Beg pardon?"

"Oh, I'm making a mess of this, aren't I? Usually, I'm much better organized and certainly display better manners."

She held out a gloved hand to him. "I'm Maggie Rutherford, formerly from New York City. I do detect a hint of Boston in your voice, if I'm not mistaken."

"Yes," Ben admitted. "Boston bred but home is the West now."

"And you just came off the cattle drive. The Chisholm Trail, I presume?"

He nodded, unsure of where their conversation headed.

"Perfect!" she declared. "You are exactly the man I'd like to interview."

"Interview?" He viewed her with suspicion. "What for? Why me?"

She laid a hand on his sleeve. Electricity crackled between them. She pulled her hand away, a puzzled look on her face.

"I, sir, am a novelist. A dime novelist—and a wonderful one if I might say so without seeming to be a braggart. Have you read any Lud Madison books?"

"Yes," Ben said slowly, still wondering about the brief contact between them. "Madison's actually my favorite of the dime novel authors."

"Well, sir." Her hazel eyes sparkled again. "You are talking to Lud Madison in the flesh. Whom do I have the pleasure of speaking with?"

Ben sputtered his name. This heavenly creature wrote dime novels?

Maggie smiled and his heart did a flip-flop. "Oh, dear, I can see I've given you a bit of a start. It's true, though. I *am* Lud Madison. I simply write under a pen name because there are those who deem it unlikely that a woman could write such adventurous tales of the West. I not only write my novels, but I illustrate them, too." Pride was evident in her voice.

"How can I help you, ma'am?" Ben asked.

"I'm doing research for my next novel and I need to talk with someone who's familiar with cattle drives. You caught my eye, Mr. Morgan. I feel you have a story to tell, and I'd love to incorporate some of it into my next book. Naturally, I am happy to pay you for your time."

He had no intention of sharing any of his life's story with Maggie Rutherford, no matter how interesting the fiery redhead seemed. Or how much simply looking at her made his blood boil. He cherished his privacy. He would have to set this lady writer straight and send her on her merry way.

"I'm sorry, ma'am—"

"Maggie. Please call me Maggie. Don't you love how the West is less formal than back East? It is exhilarating." She beamed at him.

"What I mean to say is—"

"Oh, you don't have to tell me, Mr. Morgan. I've waylaid you from your mission. You intended to have a drink and unwind after long weeks on the trail. Well, I know with your fancy new clothes and those rather expensive boots, plus the bath and haircut, you probably have very little of your trail pay left. I can remedy that."

She turned and started to push open one of the swinging doors.

Ben grabbed her elbow, ignoring the heat in the contact. "You can't go in there! It's not respectable."

Maggie's brows rose. "You need a bottle of whiskey, sir, something you sorely can't afford at this point. I aim to remedy that situation. We'll sit. You have your drinks. I'll ask you some questions about being a cowboy on a cattle drive. I'll even pay for a night's rest at a decent hotel."

She tugged and pulled away from him, entering the bar full steam ahead.

A bemused Ben followed her inside. Under his breath, he muttered, "The little spitfire sure has gumption."

4

____

Maggie marched straight to the bar, ignoring the sudden silence her presence drew. Even the piano player stopped mid-note and stared at her. She couldn't help but sashay a bit, enjoying all the male attention. She earned an appreciative wolf whistle for her efforts. That broke the spell and the saloon swung back into life, though Maggie knew she still had the crowd's attention.

She had no intention of staying in the saloon for any length of time. She preferred to conduct her interviews in clean, well-lighted surroundings. This saloon reeked of alcohol, unwashed men, and old urine. Smoke from oil lamps, cigars, and cigarettes hovered in a low cloud. The floor had been sprinkled liberally with sawdust. It must make it easier to clean the long streams of tobacco juice that had missed the spittoons stationed all around the room.

Maggie sensed Ben Morgan behind her. His gaze probably was drawn to her behind. She'd noticed him immediately when she entered the stockyards. What woman wouldn't?

He stood a few inches over six feet, with hair as black as midnight and sapphire blue eyes that sparkled in his tanned face. She'd thought him handsome before, in his dusty trail clothes and heavy beard. After seeing him dressed in decent attire, with his hair trimmed and the beard gone save for a moustache, she admired what she saw even more. Maggie felt quite petite standing next to him. He radiated strength and energy with his broad shoulders, wide chest, and powerful physique.

She withdrew a few bills from her reticule and placed them on the bar. Smiling daintily at the rail-thin barkeep, she asked, "May I have a bottle of your best whiskey? And two glasses to go, please." She batted her eyelashes for emphasis.

"You betcha, ma'am. Anything for you."

The man almost fell over his feet doing her bidding, placing two fairly clean shot glasses and a bottle filled with amber liquid on the bar.

"Thank you so much, sir. Keep the change."

Maggie slid the glasses into her reticule and handed the bottle to Ben Morgan.

"Let's go, Mr. Morgan. We're drawing too much attention here for us to conduct an interview in peace."

She exited the saloon quickly before trouble broke out, assuming Ben would follow. He did, falling into step with her outside.

"We'll go straight to my hotel, The Alamar, to talk. They have a parlor off their lobby that will be perfect for our purpose. You may drink as we speak although if I find you slurring your words, I may have to ask you to abstain further until I am finished with my questions."

Ben latched on to her elbow and Maggie hoped she didn't blush. Every time they had contact, her stomach flipped in a delightful way. She found it a little embarrassing.

And intriguing.

"Do you always get your way, Miss Rutherford?"

"Maggie."

He looked at her steadily with those glowing blue eyes. "Maggie."

"Usually." She licked her lips nervously. "At least my brother, Marcus, would tell you I do. He spoiled me rotten even before I could walk, so I suppose it's his fault that I assume it's perfectly natural to get what I want." She paused. "When I want."

Why on earth had she admitted that?

Ben Morgan affected her in ways she'd never dealt with before. Maggie wasn't sure if she liked it or not. It gave her an out-of-control feeling. Her life in the West centered around her being in total control. No one ever told her what to do or even asked why she acted as she did. She followed her heart.

And she liked it that way.

She gave her most winning smile to the cowboy. "Mr. Morgan, would you please accompany me back to my hotel so we can discuss cattle drives? I promise it will take no more than an hour for me to get the background information I desire. I have the majority of my questions already outlined. It will help me flesh out the details for my new lead character and the nasty antagonist. I will make sure you are set up with a room at The Alamar when we conclude our business." She hesitated. "If that's agreeable with you, that is," she added.

He looked at her with a mix of interest and confusion. She took that as a 'yes' and kept walking. The cowboy began walking along with her again.

"Stay close to me," he warned. "The streets are full of devilry. You've come to a dangerous place, Maggie."

He offered her his arm and Maggie slipped her

hand through the crook. She knew he was right. Cowboys raced horses down the streets of Abilene, letting off steam after coming off the long drive. Fistfights broke out at scattered intervals. Drunken men staggered along, some passing out and falling along the street, where they were generally ignored. Maggie drew a little closer to Ben and smiled.

All these details would make for wonderful narrative in her upcoming book.

Ben, too, would make for a marvelous hero. The minute she saw him, she knew he would have to be her next cover, whether she interviewed him or not. He looked the role of the perfect hero. Maggie couldn't wait to put ink to paper and capture his essence.

As they walked, her heart fluttered more rapidly. It differed from when she woke from a nightmare in a panic or when a situation seemed to close in on her. Those heart palpitations brought a strong nausea. These flutters brought an intoxicating sweetness to them, as excitement built within her.

All at once, she realized the truth.

She was attracted to Ben Morgan.

It made her wonder what it would be like to kiss him. She'd kissed a few men before. Richard a half dozen times over the years, though those kisses were perfunctory pecks on her lips.

An Italian count kissed her when she and Marcus sojourned through Tuscany, but it was fleeting and she judged him to be insincere. Her French drawing master kissed her when they completed their last lesson before her return to America, lingering a little too long for comfort.

But kissing Ben? That would definitely be worth pursuing. She might want to write about romance one day. It only made sense to experience a true kiss. Ben Morgan would make a viable candidate.

She wondered if she would be able to pull off kissing him. Maybe if she got a few drinks in him. At the end of their interview. She could thank him and move in for a swift kiss. That would be the ultimate in research.

"This way," Maggie pointed.

They crossed the street, veering around two different drunks lying in the middle of the dirt avenue. They walked one block over to where The Alamar stood. Ben opened the imposing door and they entered the lobby. Its rich mahogany hardwood floors gleamed under the glow of subtle gas lighting. Scattered arrangements of wing chairs and sofas dotted the lobby's interior.

Maggie still enjoyed a decent hotel. Having been raised in wealth in New York, she was used to a certain standard. Out West, only a handful of fine hotels existed. She'd spent her share in less than humble abodes over the past year. Still, she wouldn't trade this year of her life. She'd traveled extensively, and written and sold two more dime novels in addition to the two she'd previously sold to Rutherford House, her family's publishing firm.

She'd wanted to remain anonymous when she sent in her first manuscript, not wanting to trade on her family name to become a published author. She'd hit upon her pen name, Lud Madison, walking down Madison Avenue one afternoon. The name felt right all the way down to her bones.

Thrilled when she received her first sale notification through a secret post office box address she had rented, Maggie believed her first two books had very good plots. That was why they sold so well. Her last two efforts, though, gave off that whiff of Western authenticity the first two lacked, at least in her mind. Her stories had been solid, but living in the region she wrote about, breathing its air, meeting its inhabitants, gave her the necessary details to capture the feel of a dime novel.

As a result, Lud Madison's star rose. Sales skyrocketed. Maggie breathed a sigh of relief. She hadn't known how long her money would last when she fled New York solely on the profits from her first two books. She didn't want Marcus funding her travels after she ran away from her own wedding. In her mind, it was important to her to make it on her own.

Besides, she couldn't even give her brother an address to write to her since she moved around so much. Once she left New York, the West became her oyster. She soaked up new experiences and adventures as fast as a sponge.

Her publisher, Rutherford House, begged Lud for another book—the sooner, the better. Maggie thought a novel surrounding what happened on a cattle drive and its arrival at a railhead would make for an interesting read. She'd made the trip to Abilene to interview a cowboy fresh off the trail.

"Hello, Sam."

She waved to the desk clerk, a middle-aged man with thinning hair and gold pince-nez who'd been extremely helpful to her already. He had given her information about how and when cattle came into Abilene, and directions on how to find the rail yard.

"Hello, Miss Rutherford. Sir." Sam eyed Ben with interest.

Maggie thought she better arrange a room for Ben now. Abilene seemed rather crowded. Although she knew cowhands couldn't possibly afford to stay at The

Alamar, many of the buyers resided here, according to Sam's information. Even some of the trail bosses would stay a night or two before venturing back south to Texas. She wanted to make sure Ben could be accommodated, and hold up her end of their bargain.

"Sam, would there be another room available, just for tonight? Mr. Morgan here is interested in staying at The Alamar." She was thankful the cowboy didn't look like a typical cowboy, but had dressed more like a gentleman with his store-bought purchases. Prices at The Alamar ran high. Maggie didn't want Sam to know she would be paying for Ben's room. It seemed just a bit forward. She also didn't want the helpful clerk to get the wrong idea about her or her brief relationship with Ben. At least, he looked well-off enough to be paying for his own accommodations.

The clerk frowned. "I don't think so, Miss Rutherford. We're booked solid for the next two weeks since it's prime time for herds to be brought in."

"Do you have someone who could run an errand then? I'd like to help find Mr. Morgan a room while we conduct our business. We'll be in that alcove over there for the next hour or so. It would be desirable for him to have a room once we conclude our interview, if possible."

Sam nodded. "I'll send my boy around. We'll get you taken care of, Mr. Morgan."

"Thank you," Ben replied.

Maggie motioned to the small alcove almost hidden from view. It held a table and two chairs. They walked across the lobby and took their seats. Ben set the bottle of whiskey on the table.

Maggie pulled out a handkerchief and the shot glasses, proceeding to wipe them. "Never hurts to be extra careful."

She poured a hefty amount into the first glass and a normal shot into the second. She handed him the almost overflowing one. She barely clinked their glasses together in order to avoid any spills. "Cheers."

Maggie swallowed her whiskey in one gulp, the liquid burning as it went down to the pit of her stomach. Ben watched in amazement, then shrugged and downed his own.

"Hit me again." He placed his glass on the table.

"One more coming up, sir." Maggie poured him a second drink, worried that he might want to keep the alcohol flowing. She needed to get enough information about the trail from him in order to begin her novel. To her surprise, the cowboy only took a sip and set down the shot glass.

"So, you want to know about cattle?"

"Life on the Chisholm Trail, in particular. What you do on the drive, both in the saddle and when you bed down the animals at night. How many cowboys accompany the herd? What dangers did you face? How long did it take to reach Abilene? Any little facts you think an audience would find interesting."

She leaned over. "Mind you, I don't preach to my readers. It's not as if when they read a Lud Madison book they are attending a lecture. I choose to weave in my tiny tidbits to give my work an air of verisimilitude. The facts merely enhance the plot. Plot and character are far more important, but I do want that believability to be present. The reader learns through osmosis by enjoying the narrative."

Ben took another sip of whiskey. "You accomplish that. I would never have guessed you were a cultured woman from back East. Your books ring true, Maggie."

She beamed at his compliment. "Thank you, Ben. I shall call you Ben since you are finally calling me

Maggie. So plunge in. Tell me whatever you like. I'll take a few notes but I keep most everything in my head. I won't interrupt unless I have a question or don't understand something."

She readied herself, removing paper and a pencil from her reticule. "Start whenever you wish."

He crossed one foot on top of his knee. His hand with the whiskey rested on his thigh.

"Stop me if I bore you," he warned.

Ben thought a moment before beginning. "Cowboys like the Chisholm better than the Western or Goodnight-Loving. The route's flat and open. No hills or wooded areas where coyotes or rustlers can hide. It crosses several rivers, though, and sometimes that causes problems. Steers don't like to swim. And most cowboys don't know how to swim. Plus, there's always a danger of quicksand in the river, which can suck down a man and his horse or group of cattle in the blink of an eye."

He uncrossed his leg and sat back. Maggie could see a faraway look in his eye, as if he relived the drive.

"The trail's about a quarter of a mile wide, like a dusty line as far as the eye can see, moving slow and steady. You have to watch every minute of every day. If the cattle smell water, they get all excited. They want to run fast to taste it, but you don't want them to run too much. They'll lose weight—and that means less money when you get to market."

He grimaced. "The food's monotonous. Some beef spiced with small peppers that have a very hot flavor —called chiles—but mostly beans and sourdough bread. Cookie even made pie with beans. If I never see another bean again, I could die a happy man."

Maggie laughed. Ben already painted a wonderful picture for her. She could see the images he spoke of.

"We came in with about twenty-eight hundred head of cattle, but herds can be as large as three thousand. Takes about eight weeks or so for a dozen men to drive them from Texas to a railhead, be it here or Dodge City or Wichita. We slowed a bit a month in, with some drenching rain and hail after days and days of dust."

"How long do you ride each day?"

"Close to sixteen hours or more in the saddle. You change horses three times a day. Need to keep 'em fresh. You always have to watch for rattlesnakes. And stampedes. I've never experienced one, but they're supposed to be awful. You might want to talk to a hand that has."

He sipped on the whiskey. "The trail boss is in charge. He rides ahead, scouts for water. Pasture. Campsites. Checks the provisions. Keeps records. His word is law. He assigns duties to the men and settles any problems among them.

"Cowboys follow him in pairs, traveling on either side of the herd. The point riders lead the way. Swing riders help turn the herd. You've got flank riders that move alongside. They watch for strays and keep the pace. All these positions trade out to keep things from getting stagnant. Except for drag."

Maggie wrote that word down. "I've never heard that term before. What is it?

Ben shuddered. "That's for the new guys that ride at the back of the herd. You eat a lot of dust being drag, and you ride it the whole way here."

"Sounds like you have experience at that."

"Sure. All cowboys have to start somewhere. What else?"

"What kind of money do you receive?"

"Trail bosses earn over a hundred dollars a month.

They usually make about two hundred and fifty a trip up. Cowboys get about thirty a month and their grub. The cook makes more."

"Really? Why?"

"The best trail bosses know happy men equal productive men, so a cook is rewarded for keeping bellies satisfied. Usually the cook is an ex-cowboy, too broken to ride and rope any longer. Cookie wakes everyone up. Doctors with home remedies. Barbers the men. Even will sew on a button for you."

Ben laughed. "You don't cross his domain. He is king of dry goods, dried fruit, the beans and lard, coffee, and tobacco. Even whiskey, though that's just for medicinal purposes. Drinking isn't tolerated on the trail."

"I suppose that's why so many men head straight for the saloon when they reach town."

Ben finished his drink. "Cookie kept castor oil for being constipated. Liniment oil to rub on sore muscles of men and the horses. He kept a drawer for the trail boss's stuff—his branding book, work papers, pencils."

"Did you see any Indians on the prairie?"

A shadow crossed Ben's face. "Some. From a distance. There's always that fear that they'll attack, so your Winchester is close at hand at all times."

"What kind? Be specific, as I want my readers to know."

"Model 1873. About seven-and-a-half pounds. It's got a lever action."

Maggie nodded. "Yes, I understand that. I've had to learn a lot about guns." She thought a moment. "What about entertainment? Surely after a long day, you don't go straight to sleep."

"Lot of card-playing or mumblety-peg. It's a game where you flip your knife into the ground and try to get it to stand straight up. Mostly, though, it's stories. And music."

"Harmonicas?"

"Yes." Ben pulled out one from his pocket and played a quick scale. "I'd play and One-Eyed John would sing along in a rich baritone. He was so good, no one else would join in."

She jotted the name down. "Could I meet this One-Eyed John? He sounds interesting."

Ben laughed. "He's either stone-cold drunk now or passed out in the bed of a whore. I mean—"

"I know what you mean, Ben. I'm not some greenhorn. I've been traveling the West for a while now."

He looked at her with interest. "Why?"

Maggie considered the question and how much she should reveal. "I wanted to see the places I wrote about. Meet the actual people. Hear their stories. Try to incorporate what I learned into my dime novels."

"What about your family? I'll bet they aren't too happy about you running around unchaperoned."

She shrugged. "My parents are dead. My father wouldn't have cared, even if he were alive. It surprised my brother, but he understood why I came. I needed space. And time. I wasn't quite happy with my life in New York. My earnings as Lud Madison allowed me to head West and see the sights, so to speak."

Ben nodded. "Will you return to New York?"

It was a question she hadn't wanted to ponder. She hadn't really let her thoughts go that far. This past year she'd lived day to day, savoring the small moments. She knew once her birthday came in October and she gained access to her trust fund, she would need to return to New York to meet with her attorney and sign papers. That was a few months away, though.

"I may. I doubt I'll live there permanently ever

again. The West has seeped into my pores some-how. What about you? Will you ever return to Boston?"

"No."

They sat in silence a moment, each lost in his own thoughts, until Sam came toward them and in-terrupted.

"Miss Rutherford. Mr. Morgan. Good, you're still here. My boy's back. He's found you a room. He's waiting on the porch and will escort you over when you finish up your business."

"Thank you, Sam. I appreciate your extra effort," Maggie told him.

The clerk nodded briskly then returned to the front desk. She turned to Ben.

"I believe I have quite a number of useful facts, Ben. I can't thank you enough for allowing me to in-terview you."

She pulled money from her reticule and stood, ready to pass it along to Ben.

"Thank you for your valuable time. This should be more than enough to pay for your room."

Ben rose and waved it away. "The whiskey and company are thanks enough." He corked the bottle and picked it up. "I think I'll take this with me if you don't mind."

"Not at all."

They stood close in the nook, facing each other. Maggie remembered how much she wanted to kiss this man earlier. She'd almost forgotten, losing herself in his stories.

Looking at him now, her lips ached. Her pulse began to race as she stared into his mesmerizing eyes. She was near enough to smell the soap on his skin and the clean cotton of his brand-new shirt. She decided to take a wild chance. She'd never see him again. Why not?

Before she acted on the impulse, he leaned down and pulled her into his arms. His lips grazed hers, softly at first, then they demanded more. She started to ask what was going on and his tongue thrust into her mouth. It began stroking hers, dancing along the roof of her mouth, running along magically, sending chills through her.

She grabbed his shirtfront to steady herself. Her stomach tossed about as wildly as her beating heart. His grasp on her tightened and she melted into his hard, muscled chest. She lost all sense of time.

Then he pulled away from her slightly, their lips almost touching. "Thank you, Miss Rutherford," he whispered. He kissed her again, swift and hard, tipped his hat, and was gone.

She fell back into the chair. Brought her fingers to her pulsating lips. She still tasted his whiskey and something that was simply the essence of Ben Morgan.

Maggie smiled. She definitely needed to do more research on kissing. And she wanted to investigate the possibilities with him.

5

Ben awoke slowly, happy to find himself in a comfortable bed with actual sheets and a down-filled pillow for the first time in over two months. They had made it to Abilene, Kansas. He didn't have to rise at the crack of dawn to wolf down bitter coffee and a quick meal before swinging into the saddle for the day's ride. He wouldn't be breathing in the dust the herd stirred as they moseyed toward Abilene. The physical work of each day on the trail made him remember what farming on the plains had been like.

The years of hard work on his Kansas homestead drifted to his conscience from the distant past. It was something he'd long ago banished from his thoughts. He had loved working the soil with his hands, tending to the small group of farm animals, even building on land that would belong to him free and clear after five years. He enjoyed having a place he could call his own and seeing the fruits of his labor.

But Eliza's death changed all that. Raising a family on his own property morphed into his more recent career of a gambler with wanderlust fever. Over the last few years Ben aimlessly traveled throughout the West, from the Midwest plains to the state of California by the Pacific, and back across to Texas. He looped, swirled, and went wherever the spirit moved him.

Yet he always came back to Kansas.

Adam lived here, his only family since their mother passed a few years back. His brother owned and operated a general store in Easton, about eight miles East of the Abilene railhead. Ben looked forward to his trips there. Easton was the closest thing he could call a home.

After the war, Adam had struck out West, too. He understood how many soldiers would head that way, since he himself survived the horrors of the war. Adam wished to escape the polite society of Boston. Inhabitants there would never understand the men who returned, broken in ways too difficult to comprehend.

While Ben and Eliza applied for land under the Homestead Act, Adam chose a different way of life and built his store. He met and soon married the local preacher's only child, a beautiful woman named Rebecca. Four years Adam's junior, she'd been raised in the West and proved to be resourceful as well as sweet-tempered. Their daughter, Jennie, was their pride and joy. Ben loved his young niece beyond words. He couldn't wait to arrive and see what new mischief she'd gotten into since his last visit.

He dressed and headed downstairs. Though Merchants' Hotel catered primarily to cowboys, he'd landed one of their larger rooms. He knew with all the men pouring into Abilene on a daily basis that he was lucky to have scored such a decent place to spend the night.

Of course, that fell squarely on Miss Maggie

Rutherford's shoulders. Her influence with The Alamar's desk clerk made the difference. Otherwise, he might have slept in the barn with Prince last night.

Ben laughed. Maggie believed him to be an almost penniless cowboy after his spending spree in Abilene yesterday. To think she bought him a bottle of whiskey because she was afraid he couldn't afford it, and even marched into a crowded saloon to do so still amazed him. When he checked out, he found his bill already paid and knew she'd been responsible for that, too.

If only she could have followed him into the bank now. The little dime novelist would be shocked at the amount of money Ben withdrew before embarking for Easton. He retrieved Prince from a nearby livery and swung into the saddle. He wondered what she was doing right now and wished he could see her one more time.

Actually, he wished he could kiss her again.

What possessed him to kiss her in the first place defied reason. He was a logical man. He thought things through before acting. He observed people and situations. He never acted rashly, be it at cards or in his dealings with others.

Yet when it came time to part from Maggie Rutherford last night, he'd behaved in an incredibly out-of-character manner. As he answered her questions about the trail, he studied her hourglass figure and alabaster skin. He wondered what she tasted like. He wished he could see her just before bed, with that mane of copper hair cascading loose and down her back to her waist.

But any male being interviewed by this very attractive woman would do the same. Ben never thought about acting on it.

Until he did.

It probably surprised her as much as it did him. One minute they were saying their goodbyes. Ben was grateful for having spent an enjoyable couple of hours with a pretty woman, especially having just come off a cattle drive full of men.

Then she got this hungry look in her eyes like she needed to be kissed—and he couldn't help himself. Without thinking of the consequences, he simply reacted, pulling her to him and enfolding her in an embrace.

The kiss sizzled from the start, much like the brief contact between them when they'd touched earlier. Ben deepened it on instinct, losing himself in the moment like never before. He didn't know how long it went on. Time stood still.

He didn't know what brought him to his senses. Maybe it was the death clutch as she held his shirt tightly, practically strangling him in the process. But he broke the kiss.

And thanked her...

He almost laughed thinking about that. *He thanked her?* He couldn't remember ever having done that before.

And then he kissed her again. Quick. Hard. Simply because he wanted to. Within seconds, he already yearned to taste that succulent mouth again. He'd heard laudanum could be addictive. He'd put the drug up against Maggie Rutherford's lush lips any day. Maggie's lips? Well, those could definitely be habit-forming.

He thought it best he was leaving Abilene now. If he saw her again, he couldn't say what might happen between them. And if he knew one thing, it was that

Miss Rutherford was an innocent. Oh, she might march into rowdy bars and write about brave adventurers performing feats of wonder but he knew she'd never been kissed like she had last night.

She caught on. Real fast. By the end of that kiss, Maggie Rutherford was teaching him a thing or two. Ben might be a risk-taker—but he definitely didn't want to play with that kind of fire.

BEN RODE into Easton a little after two that afternoon. He saw signs of growth from his last trip eight months earlier. The lone bank looked as though it had built an addition. The Methodist church now had competition from the Baptists across the way.

He headed straight for Morgan's General Store. A sense of pride welled inside him as he saw the store's name etched in gold lettering in the window. A new, larger sign was above the structure. Ben pushed open the door, surprised to see the place void of customers and Adam nowhere in sight. He figured his brother might be unloading a shipment of goods in the back and stepped behind the counter. Pushing the curtain aside, he spied Jennie on the floor.

Sneaking up on her, he lifted her from the waist to swing her up on his shoulders, where she loved to ride around and survey the world. As he began raising her in the air, Ben felt the trembling and turned the little girl toward him. Tears streamed down Jennie's face.

"What's a-matter, Punkin?" he asked, calling her by the special nickname only he used.

Jennie's bottom lip quivered as fresh tears fell. She buried her face in his chest and sobbed silently. Ben brought her close, rubbing her back, murmuring soothing words.

"Let's go find your mama," he finally said, when she seemed to calm. Jennie stiffened in his arms and shook her head violently.

He wondered if she'd done something wrong and was hiding. Time to get to the bottom of things.

Ben looked her in the eyes. "Come on, Punkin. It can't be as bad as you think. Whatever you've done, we'll get it straightened out. You're a good girl, Jennie Morgan. Sometimes, we make mistakes, but we can always fix things right."

He moved to the staircase in the back of the storeroom that led up to the second level where Adam's family lived. As they reached the top, he heard low voices coming from one of the two bedrooms. Since the door was open, he crossed the parlor with Jennie in his arms and entered. He froze in the doorway. Shock hit his system like a pail of freezing water dumped overhead on a winter's day.

Adam lay in the narrow bed, bruised and battered. At least Ben thought it was his brother. One side of his face was mashed into a misshapen mess of dark purple. The other side had long, angry scratches, and pitting as if gravel had been ground into his skin. Bare to his waist, Adam's torso was barely recognizable as human. Ben shuddered to think what lay beneath the quilt that covered his lower body.

He set a wriggling Jennie down, knowing she didn't need to see her daddy like this. The child ran from the room, causing the two adults to turn from Adam and focus on him.

Rebecca sat next to her husband, lines of grief etched into her face. Her hands rested atop one of

Adam's, as if she were too scared to hold it for fear of hurting him more.

A man in a gray suit coat and white shirt stood on the other side. Ben saw the medical bag sitting by the bedside and assumed him to be a doctor.

"Oh, Ben," Rebecca croaked.

He rushed to her side and wrapped her in a bear hug as she rose to meet him. He stroked her hair, closing his eyes, but only seeing Adam's mangled body in his mind.

His sister-in-law pulled back and looked at him a long moment. Ben released her. She turned to the doctor.

"I'll stay with him," the physician said.

Rebecca nodded and took Ben's hand, leading him from the room to the kitchen table.

Ben poured her a glass of water from a carafe sitting there. Rebecca drank slowly. Her eyes closed until she drained the liquid.

She set down the glass and sighed. "I don't know where to start."

Ben took her hand. She sat quietly, gnawing at her bottom lip. Then she drew from some inner strength and met his gaze.

"Jennie got the mumps last month. She lost her appetite. Her fever went sky-high. The swelling came and she was in awful pain."

Ben squeezed her hand to reassure her.

"She got better. The swelling went down. The doctor said she'd be fine, but..."

Her voice trailed off. Ben remained quiet, knowing she'd tell him in her own time.

"She couldn't hear when the fever broke and the swelling subsided, Ben. When she's sick, I always rock her and sing to her. I could tell she just didn't hear me. Dr. Miller said hearing loss happens sometimes with the mumps. Sometimes, it's only in one ear. Sometimes, it's both. Most times it lasts, but he said it might be only temporary."

Ben saw the hopeful look in Rebecca's eyes. Without being told, he knew what her prayers had been for her daughter.

"It's all so new to her. She's just starting to live in a world without sound. She was tossing a ball up and catching it out on the porch while Adam and Morton Joad played a game of checkers. Morton said Jennie missed the ball and scrambled down the stairs to retrieve it from the street."

Rebecca's voice broke. She paused and collected herself.

"Out of nowhere, a runaway team came charging down the street. Morton said they were spooked. Their driver must have fallen out of the wagon. They were totally out of control. Jennie's back was to them. Adam bounded down the steps and pushed her out of the way just in time."

Ben listened to the rest of her halting story, knowing the outcome, having seen what remained of his brother. Adam saved Jennie's life, but the horses and wagon ran over him, crushing him in the process and costing him his own.

"I'd like to spend a little time with him, Rebecca."

She nodded, weeping into a handkerchief.

Ben strode to the bedroom door, dreading seeing Adam again. Dr. Miller stood when he entered.

In hushed tones he told him, "I'm not sure how he's lasted this long, Mr. Morgan. I've given him morphine for any pain he might feel. His spine's badly mangled so I think he's really beyond pain at this point."

The doctor placed a hand upon Ben's shoulder. "I want to go check on Rebecca. She hasn't left his side since the accident happened late yesterday afternoon. With the baby coming soon, she needs to get some rest."

The physician left the room with his medical bag, and Ben walked closer to his big brother. He sat in the chair next to the bed and gently placed his hand over Adam's.

Memories flooded him. He and Adam wrestling. Fishing and swimming together at their grandparents' farm. Digging for buried treasure. Adam putting a frog in the collection plate at church.

Fighting side by side in war. Adam saving his brother's neck on more than one occasion in the heat of battle.

And now this.

Tears slipped down Ben's cheeks and dropped onto the quilt. He didn't know what a world without Adam would be like.

"Ben?"

His gaze flew to Adam's face, where a wisp of a smile sat on cracked lips.

"Adam?"

"Promise," Adam panted.

"Anything," Ben said fervently. "I'd move heaven and earth for you."

"Promise. You. You take care. Rebecca. Jennie. Baby."

"Yes." Ben tried to calm his tone to reassure his brother. "Of course, Adam. I'll look after Rebecca and your children."

Adam sighed. "Love you... little... broth..."

"I love you too, so much." Ben swallowed, fighting to keep control.

"The store. Take care." Adam wheezed.

"Yes, I'll look after the store. Anything, Adam. Stay with us. Don't leave us."

But he did.

6

"Good morning, Sam." Maggie greeted the desk clerk with a smile on her face. "I'm ready to check out if you'd be so good as to prepare my bill."

"Right away, Miss Rutherford. I'll have my boy bring down your trunk." Sam called out instructions to his son and busied himself with the paperwork.

"The stage won't be leaving until noon. Shall I hold your trunk here until it arrives?"

Maggie shook her head. "No, what I need to do is walk over to a local stable and arrange for transportation to Easton. Do you have a recommendation?"

Sam passed her the bill. "Sure do. If you're just headed to Easton, why, I'll have Tim take you there. It's not far at all."

Maggie removed enough money from her reticule to pay for her stay. She added on enough for her trip to Easton and passed it to Sam.

"So, you've finished your business here?"

"Yes, I interviewed several cowboys and a trail boss. I also spoke to a cattle buyer, and even two men who work at the rail yard. I believe I have all the information I need to start my next book."

The clerk gave her a broad grin. "I still can't believe I know the famous Lud Madison." He reached under the counter and brought out a copy of her latest dime novel.

"Would you mind signing my book for me, Miss Rutherford? It'd mean the world to me."

Maggie beamed at him. "Of course." She reached for the fountain pen and dipped it in the inkwell. Opening the cover, she turned to the title page and said, as she wrote, "To Sam, one of my most devoted readers. Enjoy! Lud Madison."

She slid the book back to him. He looked upon it in awe.

"Thank you so much, Miss Rutherford."

Maggie eyed him mischievously. "Keep reading, Sam. You never know when you might appear somewhere in my next book."

He blushed, turning away to clean his pince-nez with a handkerchief. After a moment, he swung around and placed the gold glasses back on the bridge of his nose.

"Ah, here's my boy. Tim, bring Miss Rutherford's trunk over here."

Tim put down her valise and then eased the trunk from his shoulder.

"Thank you, Tim. Miss Rutherford's needing to go to Easton for..." Sam's voice trailed off as he looked at her expectantly.

"My brother's best friend is the sheriff in Easton. He doesn't know it yet, but I'm sure he'll share some stories with me that I can use in my writing."

She thought a moment. "Why, I may even have to write a novel about a Kansas lawman, now that I think about it. Frank is a dear man, and he'd make an outstanding hero." She grinned. "I so enjoy my work."

Tim brought their buggy around, loading her luggage into the rear. He handed her up and they set out in the fine September morning sunshine. Tim was quiet, unlike his talkative father. Left to her own thoughts, Maggie enjoyed the ride. She brainstormed ideas for her cattle drive book, throwing in all kinds of mishaps to cause conflict and adventure. Floods, hail, a tornado, cattle rustlers, Indian attacks—the endless possibilities thrilled her.

The more she pondered, the more the hero in the tale came to resemble Ben Morgan. The man frustrated Maggie to no end. She'd spent more time reliving their kiss than she cared to admit. The fact it occurred so suddenly and unexpectedly made it even more delicious. She would love to explore more kissing with Mr. Ben Morgan, but he'd vanished off the face of the earth.

She'd stopped by his hotel the next morning, hoping to see him, telling herself that she needed to ask him to breakfast to further extend her research. The desk clerk revealed that Mr. Morgan had asked not to be disturbed and no one had seen him that morning. Maggie waited an hour in the lobby, hoping to catch him, before she needed to leave for an interview appointment.

By the time she returned, the clerk informed her that Mr. Morgan had already checked out. He didn't know of his guest's plans or any forwarding address. Though she made inquiries that day and the next as she made the rounds, no one had seen him. Even One-Eyed John, a fellow cowboy with him on the Chisholm Trail, didn't know where he'd gone.

"Benny Boy, he be an interesting one, Miss Rutherford. Joined up with us in Fort Worth, he did. Hands as soft as a baby's behind, but he earned him some calluses along the way. He ain't no stranger to hard work,

I could see that. He sure ain't been on the trail before this time out."

One-Eyed had grinned. "Taught that boy all there's to know 'bout cattle. He be a good rider and fast learner, but I do indeed wonder where he come from. It was like he dropped down from heaven to help us out—then he simply vanished."

Maggie thought long and hard on One-Eyed's words. So, Ben wasn't a career cowboy. He hadn't told her he was, but he gave her the impression that was what he did for a living. He was knowledgeable about what happened on the trail. The experiences he described matched those from others she'd spoken to in Abilene. His size, too, bespoke the fact that he could handle hard, physical labor. One-Eyed's comments about Ben's soft hands gave her pause.

Maggie learned through her travels that gamblers babied their hands. They protected them by always wearing gloves. In many ways, their hands played a large part in their livelihood. Cheating was rampant in games of chance, and a man looked for any advantage he could when gaming.

Unmarred hands could detect all kinds of doctoring of the cards. She had a germ of an idea for a book about a gambler, but she needed to speak to one at length to learn more about cards—how to play, what to look for, and the different ways players cheated. It intrigued her that Ben Morgan might actually be a gambler. That gave him an added air of danger.

And desirability.

They arrived at Easton without incident. Maggie asked Tim to drop her and her luggage at the local sheriff's office and jail. She'd written Frank a month earlier to let him know she'd be in the area. She'd found his reply waiting at The Alamar when she'd arrived in Abilene. He eagerly awaited her visit and knew of a boardinghouse she could stay at while in Easton. Since he hadn't named it, she would find out and have her things sent over there once she knew its location.

Maggie thanked Tim for the ride. She even signed a copy of the dog-eared Lud Madison novel he sheepishly pulled from his pocket. He placed her baggage on the jail's porch and tipped his hat to her, wishing her well in her visit and her next book. She waved goodbye and then stepped out of the bright sunshine into the sheriff's office.

Frank Stansel emerged from the back and looked up in surprise. "Maggie Rutherford. You are a sight for sore eyes!"

They embraced with affection. Maggie knew Frank from the time she could walk. He was a year older than Marcus. She'd trailed after the two boys as soon as she could. She looked upon Frank as another older brother.

"Oh, Frank, you look wonderful yourself. I do believe living out West suits you."

"Come have a seat, Maggie." He led her to a mahogany desk covered in papers. He indicated a chair next to it.

"I'm certain I recognize this desk," she told him.

Frank nodded. "My one luxury I had shipped from home. It's a nice link to the past, but I tell you, Maggie —I'll never set foot in New York again. There's so much space in Kansas. I never feel boxed in. And the people are just right as rain."

"I'm hoping to get Marcus out here at some point."

Frank laughed. "I'd like to see that happen. Visit?

Maybe. I could never imagine Marcus living here. He's too refined. And his clothes are way too fancy."

They both smiled at the idea.

"Marcus does give more thought to his appearance than most men," she agreed. "He's actually running Rutherford House now."

"That's what his last letter said. If anyone can do it, it's Marcus. Smart as a whip. Good with people. Loves to read. I'm sure he's discovering all new kinds of talent and nurturing new, young writers."

Frank brightened. "Say, have you ever met any of them? I mean, with your family in the business and all. You know me. I wasn't much for school and books, but even *I'm* hooked on these dime novels. George Munro. Robert DeWitt. And that Lud Madison. Boy, he can write. He gets his characters in the most impossible situations and then they slip out of them like a greased pig."

Maggie decided to come clean. "Frank. I'm not just on an extended tour of the West to forget my troubles. I—"

He interrupted her. "Now, Maggie, you don't have to tell me the reasons why you're here. I know about you almost marrying Richard What's-His-Name. Sorry, but I never thought him more than a nice—but dull—fellow. He wasn't the one for a spitfire like you. Let's just enjoy a good visit with no thoughts about him."

She sighed. "You're right. I never loved Richard. I doubt he loved me. I figured out in the nick of time I'd rather be free of a husband than spend my life chained to one like Richard DeForest."

Leaning back, she added, "But that's not why I came to the West. I'm telling you this in confidence, Frank Stansel. You're not to breathe a word of this confession to Marcus. I promise I will tell him. In my own time. I just haven't decided when."

Frank looked at her with interest. "You always did have something up your sleeve, Maggie. I'm intrigued. Tell big brother Frank all your secrets."

"I'm Lud Madison."

Frank stared at her. "You're... what?"

"*I* am Lud Madison. I write under that name. I illustrate the books and their covers, too. I sold two dime novels to Rutherford House under my pen name before I ever left New York. No one there—not even Marcus—knows. I fled home at first to escape Richard and the consequences of jilting him at the altar in front of all of New York society.

"Then I realized how valuable this trip could be. I could do all kinds of research. I could talk to actual Westerners. And it's made a difference, Frank. My last two books sold through the roof. People can tell the difference. My writing is stronger. More interesting."

"Well, I'll be damned. Sorry."

Maggie grinned. "Nothing to be sorry for, Frank. But I'd love to interview you."

"Me? Whatever for?"

"You're a lawman in Kansas. All kinds of exciting things happen to lawmen, especially in Kansas—the Indian wars, the railroads, cattle drives. Even the Exodusters and homesteaders. I know you have some stories to share. If you're willing, we can talk like friends about your life, the town, and different crimes that have occurred in your jurisdiction and beyond."

Frank smiled. "I suppose a few of these stories, thinly disguised, just might make it into a future Lud Madison novel?"

She shrugged. "Who knows? Anything's possible."

He talked for close to two hours, sharing all kinds

of tales of life as a sheriff in a small Kansas town. She jotted down a few notes, ready to work in nicknames for criminals he'd locked up and some of their doomed exploits in her future books.

"This has been wonderful, Frank. I'm in awe of what you've accomplished."

"Let me think on things, Maggie. I know I have more stories that Lud Madison might be interested in." He paused. "And then there are the Army stories. You've heard some of them. I may have only served a year and a half before the war ended, but I have a few tales I could tell you about it, as well."

"I'm glad to hear it. Marcus only spent one year in the Army. Papa pulled strings to have him placed far from the action, since Marcus refused to have a substitute take his place. He told me he spent most of his time aiding a quartermaster, counting supplies, and filing reports. It was so boring, he often fell asleep behind his desk, crunching numbers."

"Sounds like Marcus. You know, we really do need to get him out here for a visit. I miss seeing him."

"I wish we could. But seriously? Can you picture Marcus here in Easton? Even in Abilene? He needs fine wine, a five-star hotel, and a valet to help him change clothes three times a day. No opera. No reputable theatre. What would he do?"

"The one thing that would get him out of New York would be wanting to see you, Maggie. The only thing that would keep him out here would be if he met a beautiful woman and fell madly in love. Said woman, of course, refusing to leave her beloved West for the likes of New York. He'd be forced to stay then."

"I don't know if that will ever happen, Frank. Marcus sheds women like a cat sheds his fur in summer. He rarely escorts one anywhere more than three times. He tells me it isn't fair to be seen with them in public more than that because they start getting the idea he might be serious about them."

"Will he ever get serious?"

Maggie frowned. "He's only twenty-eight. Papa didn't settle down and marry Mama until he was thirty-five. Family history says that's younger than most Rutherford men. The longest commitment Marcus has made, other than to his boxing instructor Patrick, is keeping the same mistress for almost a year. Even then, I know he was seeing another one on the side and still escorting a good dozen debutantes to every social event on the New York calendar."

She rose. "I hate that I've taken so much of your time today, Frank."

"Oh, you can see nothing's really happening right now. It comes in spurts. Easton will be quiet as a lamb for days and weeks. Then, trouble stirs. I spring into action like a good dime novel hero would and solve the world's problems." He grinned sheepishly. "Or at least those here in Easton."

Frank stood. "I know we need to get you settled at the boarding house I wrote you about. I should have offered to take you there first and let you wash away the dust from the road. I was just so darn glad to see you."

"I feel the same, Frank. I've been away from home a good while now. Seeing you is the best medicine I could ask for."

"You'll be happy to hear that the Widow Morrow saved a place for you. In fact, her whole place is empty right now. She went over to Chicago to her sister's funeral and won't be back for a couple of weeks. She's staying and visiting family for awhile as long as she's made the trip that far."

He opened his desk drawer and held up a key. "She gave me the key to her place. I even know what room to put you in since she changed the linens for you before she left. You'll have full run of her kitchen until she's back, then look out. That woman's like a general on a mission when she cooks."

"I doubt I'll be here more than a few days at most. Just enough to spend a little more time with you."

"Where are you headed next?"

Maggie laughed. "I have no idea. I just need a quiet place to write. I've got more than one story going in my head right now. Rutherford House is eager for a new Lud Madison tale. I don't want to let my publisher down."

Frank set his hands on her shoulders. "Stay in Easton, Maggie. You're like a breath of sunshine. The Widow Morrow's got no guests. Her place would be as good as any to get your stories down. I can show you all over town, all four blocks of it."

She snorted. "You haven't changed a bit, Frank." She thought a moment. "Before we head over to the widow's place so I can settle in, I'd like to get some writing supplies. You know—pen and ink, fresh paper. It'd be a minor miracle if they had any kind of art supplies. I'd love to work on some drawings for the cattle trail book bouncing around in my head."

He crooked an elbow. "Then it would be my pleasure to escort you to our general store." A dark look crossed his face.

She picked up on it immediately. "What's wrong, Frank?"

He took her gloved hand and pulled it through his arm and led her to the door and out onto the street.

"The owner died a couple of days ago. Funeral was yesterday."

"Was he very old or in poor health?"

"Couldn't have been more than thirty. His little girl went deaf a month ago with a bout of mumps. She was playing in the street and didn't hear a team of out-of-control horses coming her way. Her daddy reached her in time and shoved her out of the way. The team trampled him but good."

Frank shook his head. "Lingered a bit before he died. Doc says even if he'd pulled through, he would've been paralyzed the rest of his life. Maybe it was a blessing in disguise."

"How awful!"

"What's even worse is his widow's about to give birth in the next few weeks. Thank the Lord, Adam's brother had just arrived for a visit. He's going to stay around and run the store. He promised to help until Rebecca gets back on her feet after the baby's born."

"Family is certainly important. I'm so glad I have Marcus to depend upon. Even a thousand miles away from him, I know if something happened to me, he would be on the next train and by my side in no time."

They reached the store and crossed the street. Maggie noted it looked like every general store she'd seen during her travels. Her heart ached for the widow and child who would never know a father.

And the little girl. Poor thing, going deaf and losing her father so closely together. She must feel guilty that she survived the accident that took her daddy.

They walked up the steps. Frank opened the door for her and Maggie sauntered in. As her eyes adjusted from the strong sunlight outside, she looked over to the counter.

Behind it, wearing a black apron over his clothes, stood Ben Morgan.

7

B en looked up, a startled expression crossing his face. Maggie knew her own eyes must be round as saucers at their unexpected encounter. She recovered quickly from the shock of seeing him and greeted him.

"I see you're adding to your resumé, Mr. Morgan. I don't think I pictured you as working in a small town's general store. I do want to thank you for sharing your experiences on the cattle trail with me and for steering me in One-Eyed John's direction. He proved to be a wealth of information. About a lot of things." She paused. "Including you."

Maggie smiled at him, thinking him quite handsome in his starched white shirt and black shopkeeper's apron.

Then, it hit her. Ben Morgan had to be brother to the store's owner. The one who'd tragically lost his life just days ago.

The curtains behind him parted. She saw bits of a stockroom as a woman stepped out, a puzzled look on her face. Maggie noted the sad, tired air about her. Seeing how far along in her pregnancy she was led

Maggie to believe the woman must be the recent widow and Ben Morgan's sister-in-law.

She held out her hand. "Mrs. Morgan, I've just heard about your circumstances. Even though I am a stranger to Easton, I offer you my condolences."

The woman took her hand and Maggie squeezed it. "I am Maggie Rutherford, late of New York, and an old friend of Sheriff Stansel."

"My name is Rebecca Morgan." She looked over at Ben a moment. Maggie read the question in her eyes. "I gather you've met my brother-in-law. And his friend, One-Eyed John, I believe you said?"

Maggie smiled warmly at Ben, hoping to smooth over any awkwardness at the situation. "Oh, yes. Mr. Morgan was quite helpful answering questions I had."

"About a cattle drive." Again, Rebecca looked questioningly at Ben.

"Yes, indeed. I am a writer and had numerous questions regarding cowboys and cattle. Mr. Morgan gave me quite a bit of information about both to help in a book I'm penning."

"Maggie writes dime novels," Frank piped in.

"Hello, Sheriff," Rebecca said, nodding at him. "It's so nice to meet a friend of yours."

"I'd say Maggie's more like family. Her brother, Marcus, is my best friend in the world. I've known her since she was in her cradle." Frank laughed. "Of course, she didn't stay in it very long. Maggie was always following the two of us around from the time she was in diapers."

She held up a hand. "Enough, Frank, or I'll start revealing your darkest secrets. Let me tell you, I know a lot of them."

Rebecca smiled at that comment. Maggie saw how pretty she really was, with her cornflower blue eyes and thick, blonde hair worn in a single braid. She glanced over at Frank and saw him smiling back at the attractive widow.

She knew from her year of living in the West that women were in short supply and didn't remain unwed for long, especially a pretty widow such as Rebecca Morgan. Frank had never married. Maggie wondered if he might be sweet on Rebecca. From their brief encounter, she already liked the widow and thought she'd be a good match for Frank. Maybe Maggie could play matchmaker while in town. The thought helped her reach a decision.

"I'm going to be staying in town for a few weeks," she announced. "The Widow Morrow has a room for me at her boardinghouse and I'll be in residence there." She glanced over her shoulder around the store. "I'll need to pick up some supplies for my visit. Some pens and bottles of ink and writing paper. Drawing paper and pencils and charcoals, if you have them."

"We do."

Maggie looked back at Ben, who had been the one to reply. "I see you've already become familiar with the supplies in stock, Mr. Morgan."

"Ben's been a wonderful help the last few days." A shadow crossed Rebecca's face. "My husband owned and operated this store. His brother has graciously stepped in for a while to manage things."

Ben placed a hand on Rebecca's arm. "I can do a fine job helping Miss Rutherford out, Rebecca. Why don't you get off your feet for a spell?"

"That's probably a good idea. The baby's been kicking like crazy this morning." Rebecca looked at Maggie. "I look forward to spending some time visiting with you, Miss Rutherford."

"Oh, please, call me Maggie."

"Then I shall do so." Rebecca swayed and grabbed the counter. Frank rushed around and wrapped an arm about her, steadying her as he held an elbow.

Maggie hid a smile and decided to embark upon Operation Marriage.

"Frank, maybe you could help Rebecca to a seat and get her something to drink. Even sit with her while I allow Mr. Morgan to help me with my shopping."

"That's a good idea, Maggie. Come on, let's go upstairs and get you off your feet." Frank led Rebecca back through the curtain.

Maggie assumed the family's living quarters were upstairs. She turned to Ben. "Let's get started, Mr. Morgan."

"I thought we were on a first name basis, Maggie." His sapphire eyes blazed as he looked at her. "Especially after..."

She knew he referred to the kiss she'd thought about far too often and felt her cheeks grow warm. "You're right. Ben, it is. I suppose after kissing a man, using his first name shouldn't be such a hard thing to do."

A slight flush crossed his cheeks. She bent and picked up a basket, hiding a smile. "I'll need the supplies I mentioned earlier for my work—the writing and the drawing—and I also want to pick up a few things to eat. Frank and I haven't been over to the boardinghouse yet. I don't know what's in the larder. I can take a few canned goods. Maybe some things like cheese and crackers. Once I've investigated, I'll come back to stock up on a few other items. I've found I need my morning coffee, else I'm a terrible grouch."

Ben came from behind the counter and took the basket from her. "Follow me."

He led her around the store, placing items in the basket, making suggestions, and talking about her research. He asked what she'd learned from One-Eyed and the others she'd interviewed. She found Ben easy to talk to and enjoyed sharing what she'd learned about the cattle business. He brought everything back to the counter and added up her bill and she paid for the items.

"I do want to tell you how sorry I was to hear of your brother's death," Maggie said. "I hope you were able to see him before he passed."

Ben swallowed. "I did. Adam was the best of brothers and the best of men. It was hard seeing him like that, but he was a true hero saving Jennie."

"Frank said she recently lost her hearing."

"Yes. Mumps. Doc said it happens sometimes. She may regain it. She may not." He shook his head. "Right now, she's not talking. At all."

"Since she lost her hearing? But surely she spoke before?"

"Rebecca said she still was speaking after the mumps. Getting a little frustrated by not being able to hear others. They were having a devil of a time trying to explain to her that the mumps caused the problem. She's only five and was just starting to read. It's not as if they could write it out for her." He shook his head. "But after she saw Adam injured, she clammed up. We can't get a word out of her."

"She has to feel terribly guilty about it."

Ben looked at her. "Why?"

"Well, she may feel responsible for her father's death. If he hadn't rushed out and pushed her from harm's way, he would still be alive."

"I hadn't thought of that. I believed she was just sad about losing him and withdrawing into herself. It's hard. Rebecca's trying to deal with the pain of Adam's death while she keeps trying to get Jennie to speak again. Plus, the baby's coming soon. And then there's the store to deal with, too."

"I see you're running it now. Will you stay on?"

Grim determination filled his face. "I feel I should. I made a deathbed promise to Adam to look after things. Even at the end, his family was on his mind. He wanted them taken care of. I can't walk away from that responsibility."

Maggie eyed him. "But staying in one place is not for you."

He took in her words. "How did you know?"

"Just a feeling. Maybe you can stay until after the baby's born. You could hire someone to run the store for Rebecca so she could spend her time with the children. I'm sure you can afford it."

He looked at her with suspicion. "Why do you say that? Remember, you even paid for my hotel room since I spent my trail pay on clothes."

"And fancy ones at that." Maggie hesitated. "I should've known from the clothes you purchased that you weren't a true cowboy."

He started to protest but she cut him off. "I'm not saying you didn't do your job on the trail. In fact, you learned it almost too well. You were full of knowledge so I didn't suspect at first. The more I thought about your manner and the clothes you wore, I realized a cowboy wouldn't have burned through his entire pay for impractical clothes that he wouldn't wear on the trail.

"Then One-Eyed mentioned your hands. How

they were smooth as a baby's bottom. That's when I knew."

Ben eyed her suspiciously. "Knew what?"

"Oh, for heaven's sake. Do I have to spell it out? You're a gambler. I'm sure you're wonderful at it. You're smart, personable, and I assume you read people very well. That's why I'm positive you can afford to hire someone to run Morgan's General Store. In fact, I'll bet you used to send some of your winnings to your brother."

He glared at her. No words came out of those sensual lips that Maggie still wanted to kiss.

"There's nothing shameful in gambling. Is it the life for everyone? Of course not." She studied him a moment. "You're of a certain age. I'm sure you fought in the war. I've met many men who couldn't settle down in one place after that experience. Or men such as Frank, who couldn't stand being cooped up in a big city any longer and came out West seeking solace. There's nothing wrong with that."

She paused. "I think staying here with Rebecca and your niece is a wonderful gesture. Even if it's only for a few months. Both of them can use your strength and support with all they have ahead of them. When it's time to move on, you'll know it."

He mulled over her words. Finally he spoke. "You sound like you know what you're talking about."

"I do. I left New York and came out West for a reason. I keep traveling around, learning, doing, writing. I'll know when it's time to settle down." Maggie wasn't willing to reveal any more about her past.

Frank stepped through the curtains. "Rebecca drank a little tea and has decided to lie down." He looked at the goods on the counter. "If you've finished up your shopping, Maggie, I can escort you to the boardinghouse. Then I'll make sure I get your trunk and valise over there, too."

They said their goodbyes and Frank gathered up the two baskets full of goods. As Maggie stepped through the door, she looked over her shoulder.

"I'll be sure to return your baskets for your next customers, Ben."

She took a few steps before her foot slid out from under her. Suddenly, she pitched forward. She sailed down the steps. She threw out a hand to break her fall and hit the ground hard. The force of the impact bent her wrist backwards.

Pain ratcheted up her arm. Maggie saw a little girl in pigtails standing on the porch, her mouth open in shock.

Frank raced down the steps. "Maggie, are you all right?"

Ben came bounding down the stairs. Before she knew it, he'd scooped her into his arms. He carried her back into the store and up to the family's quarters, setting her down on a mohair camelback sofa, concern written across his brow. For a moment, it saddened her that she wasn't wrapped in his arms longer.

Then the pain hit again—and Maggie cursed.

Ben burst out laughing. Frank had made his way behind them. Rebecca came through a door and stood next to him.

"Please forgive my slip of the tongue," she apologized. "I suppose I've picked up a few colorful words during my travels."

Ben tried to fight the smile that played on his lips. "You look like you're hurting, Maggie. Did you trip?"

"I don't know. I was walking and then I was falling."

"I know what it was," Frank said. "And nobody

needs to get mad." He glanced around. "Jennie must've been playing marbles on the porch. They're scattered all over now and she was scurrying around picking them up as Ben brought Maggie up here."

"She knows not to play by the door," Rebecca said. "Adam and I've told her a dozen times."

"Don't worry," Maggie said. "It was an accident. If anyone's to blame, it's me. I wasn't looking where I was going when I said goodbye."

Ben knelt down and took her wrist. She gasped.

"Better send for Doc," Ben said. "He'll know after examining it if it's broken or not."

"I'll go," Frank told them, gazing at Rebecca. "Would you get Maggie a cup of strong tea? Or let Ben do that and you go find Jennie? She'll be mighty upset and need a little comfort."

"Good idea, Frank," Rebecca said. They both left the room.

Ben looked at Maggie. "I haven't got an inkling how to make a cup of tea other than it involves boiling water. And tea."

She grimaced as she tried to shift her arm in her lap. "Forget the tea, Ben Morgan. What I could really use is a shot of brandy." She thought a moment. "Better make it two."

8

______

Ben walked to the cabinet and opened it. "You have two choices. Brandy. Or whiskey. Dealer's choice."

"Brandy. It's the lesser of two evils."

He uncorked the bottle and poured two fingers into a jelly jar. As he considered the look of pain on her face a moment ago, he added another splash. He sealed the bottle again and replaced it, bringing the drink back to her.

"You aren't going to join me?"

Hazel eyes, tinged with a little gold, beckoned him, but not as much as that lush mouth. He couldn't remember ever wanting to kiss a woman more or wishing he could take down that knot of copper hair. He could almost feel his fingers combing through the fiery tresses.

"No."

He handed her the glass jar. She sipped at the amber liquid. Her eyes closed as she did so. It gave him a chance to study her. It wasn't only her physical appearance that appealed to him so much, although the curves on her petite frame would call out a siren's song to any hot-blooded male.

Ben actually enjoyed her mind. The time they'd spent together that one evening had stayed with him in the days since. Maggie Rutherford possessed a quick wit, a keen intelligence, and the most seductive laugh this side of the Mississippi. He found it odd that he was attracted as much to her mind as he was the rest of her.

And that spelled danger.

He intended to live the rest of his life on his own terms, going where he wanted at a moment's notice. If he had a hankering to play poker in California, he'd leave immediately. If he wanted to feel warmer climes on a whim, he picked up from colder ones and moved on. He would be responsible only for himself.

Never again for another person. Ever.

He'd brought untold unhappiness to Eliza by moving her to a godforsaken prairie, far from civilized society and creature comforts. He refused to be liable for a woman once again. He couldn't bear the thought of making one miserable and uncertain.

The thought of children turned his stomach. Ben still awoke from nightmares of seeing his unborn son lying next to his wife, the brutality of their deaths lingering in his mind. He knew women wanted two things in life—to settle down with a man they could depend upon and to have children.

He was interested in neither.

Maggie Rutherford was all woman. At this point in their brief acquaintance, she seemed much too independent to put roots down in the near future. She certainly didn't seem very maternal. She exuded spunk and an adventurous spirit. She was sowing a few wild oats of her own, but he knew the day would come when she'd long for a permanent home. And children.

He wanted to be long gone when that day arrived.

He looked at the beautiful woman sitting on the sofa. He knew without a doubt that if he didn't get away from her, she would weave a magic spell around his heart. The pull he felt toward her was that strong.

It was bad enough that she'd be in Easton for a couple of weeks writing her next dime novel. At least he'd be busy at the store and probably see her only on the rare occasions she dropped by for supplies.

Ben realized he needed to start making plans for his departure from Easton. He'd stay until after Rebecca gave birth and was back on her feet, but he couldn't be leashed to a small town.

And the temptation of Maggie Rutherford…

Her eyes opened and she handed Ben her empty glass. "Thank you for the medicinal liquid. My belly's got this wonderful glow that's spreading all through me."

She looked down at her wrist with a wry smile. "I can hardly feel any pain."

Ben's eyes moved to her wrist—it was already swelling. He saw the bruising and knew how much it must hurt.

He heard heavy footsteps on the stairs and turned to see both the sheriff and town's doctor enter the room.

"Good afternoon, Miss Rutherford. I am Doctor Albert Miller. Sheriff Staley's informed me about your little mishap. Let me have a look at your injury while you tell me about what actually happened."

Maggie described slipping on the marbles and tumbling down the stairs in front of the store. "I tried to stop my fall but maybe I shouldn't have."

"It's only natural to throw out an arm to serve as a barrier to break a fall," Dr. Miller assured her. "Unfortunately, it sometimes results in breaking an arm or wrist."

"I don't think it's broken," she said. "I broke my left arm once when I fell out of a tree. My collarbone, too. It was the most miserable I've ever been. This isn't nearly as bad as that was."

Frank snorted. "You shouldn't have been climbing that tree to begin with, Maggie."

"Well, you and Marcus did," she retorted. "I assumed it was something that I should do, as well."

The sheriff looked at Ben and the doctor. "Don't feel too sorry for her. She had Marcus and me dancing to her tune for a good two months. We read to her. Played cards and games with her. And I'll even admit to sitting in on a few tea parties with her dolls."

Maggie laughed that rich, throaty laugh that gave Ben shivers.

"You two deserved having to spend all that time with me, Frank Staley." She looked at Ben with a twinkle in her eye. "I enjoyed every moment they waited on me hand and foot."

"At least we taught you how to properly climb a tree after that," Frank retorted.

"You let her climb a tree again?" Ben asked, appalled.

Frank grinned. "You don't *let* Maggie do anything, Ben. She does what she wants. *When* she wants."

"I believe she shared the same sentiment with me when she interviewed me back in Abilene," he replied. "Maggie, you sound like you were a handful growing up."

"My aunt swears I am the spawn of Lucifer and Jezebel."

Dr. Miller cleared his throat. "Despite your interesting childhood, Miss Rutherford, we need to deal with the present circumstances."

Rebecca entered the room, holding Jennie by the hand. "Oh, Dr. Miller, I'm so glad you are here. How is Maggie?"

The physician poked and prodded a few moments. Ben bit his tongue, wanting to order him to back away from her after Maggie's audible gasp but he realized the man simply did his job.

"The good news is the wrist is not broken," the physician announced. "The bad news is Miss Rutherford does have a moderately serious injury."

The doctor faced Maggie. "There are many ligaments which stabilize your wrist joint. One of the most common type of ligament injuries involves the scapho-lunate ligament, which links your scaphoid and lunate bones."

Maggie laughed. "In English, please, Dr. Miller."

"I'm sorry, Miss Rutherford. I tend to get carried away. Basically, I have pinpointed the tenderness and assessed the stability of your wrist. You have either severely stretched or torn ligaments in your right wrist. You will experience pain, swelling, tenderness, and bruising. The looseness of the joint will result in a loss of function.

"This means you'll have to wear a splint for a short while. Not too long, mind you, or muscle stiffness and weakness will result. You need rest and to elevate your wrist above your heart on a pillow, or even to place it along the back of a chair."

"For how long?" Ben asked worriedly.

"A couple of days of elevation. Miss Rutherford should rest her wrist for two to three weeks, and wear a compress with a bandage before trying anything. You may, my dear, wiggle your fingers several times an hour to increase blood circulation. That will help the healing process. It could take anywhere from three to ten weeks to be totally free of pain."

Maggie frowned. "Will there be any permanent damage?"

"If you don't do too much too soon, I don't foresee any. Once the pain leaves and you're able to grip an object, you'll be on the road to recovery. Naturally, it will take time to build your strength back after you are pain-free."

"So Maggie will need assistance for at least three weeks and possibly longer?" Rebecca asked.

"I would say after three weeks, we can assess the situation again and have a better idea of recovery time."

"Then I insist you stay with us, Maggie," Rebecca proclaimed. "I feel responsible for what happened to you."

"What?" Ben exclaimed. "You can't be serious, Rebecca."

"Ben Morgan, I expect better manners from you," Rebecca scolded. "Maggie hurt herself on our property. It's our duty to see to her well-being."

Rebecca pointed to Frank. "You agree with me, don't you, Sheriff?"

Frank tipped his hat. "Ma'am, I've learned never to disagree with a woman." He looked at Ben. "Especially one hell-bent on a mission of mercy."

Maggie interrupted. "It's kind of you to offer, Rebecca, but I don't want to inconvenience you. You already have so much to do."

"Nonsense," Rebecca said. "Ben's running the store. It's time I get off my feet and rest more before the baby comes. Dr. Miller would be the first to second that notion. You'll be good company for me, Maggie.

Besides, you can't stay by yourself at Mrs. Morrow's boardinghouse. You need help dressing every morning. You won't be able to cook for yourself while she's gone. Please. Let us help you."

Ben knew his sister-in-law's tender heart, as well as how much she'd been through in the past few days. Having Maggie here for companionship would help in the grieving process. She'd have someone else besides Jennie to look after.

He glanced at Jennie, who clung to her mother's hand, her eyes wide. Then his niece walked across the room and sat down next to Maggie. She looked up at Maggie with her large blue eyes. Even Ben saw the plea there.

If he knew one thing, it was when to admit defeat. The Morgan women had ganged up on him in a fight he wasn't willing to enter. His heart raced faster than a locomotive about to jump its tracks.

Ben glanced at Maggie. "I guess we're delighted to have you as a houseguest. Indefinitely. I hope you'll stay as long as you'd like."

Maggie's smile lit up the room.

9

The doctor attached a splint to Maggie's wrist to immobilize it for the next few days. Those gathered watched the process in fascination. Jennie, in particular, seemed captivated by what the physician did with the items he took from his worn leather bag.

It reminded Maggie of when she, Marcus, and Frank played 'sick patient' twenty years before. Maggie always insisted she be the doctor, though the boys agreed that women never became doctors in real life. She remembered tending to pretend broken bones, sprained ankles, imaginary cuts, bruises, and the inevitable sore throat.

The latter always ended with Cook providing hot broth or tea for the patient. If he recovered quickly enough—and Maggie demanded he do so by the count of ten—all three were rewarded with tea cakes and milk. Perhaps she could play the game with Jennie over the next few days to help pass the time.

Dr. Miller said, "I think Ben should run downstairs and bring up some patent medicine for you, Miss Rutherford. You need to rest a good long spell. In fact, I'd like you to sleep through the night. A patent medicine will help do that."

Maggie laughed. "I know there's enough alcohol in most patent medicines to ensure that happens. I've never used one before but I hear they're very strong."

"You mean you haven't tried any of Dr. McBride's *King of Pain*?" Frank teased. "I've seen the advertisements. It promises to cure cholera, diarrhea, headache, earache, toothache, colic, and a bad cough."

"Don't forget back and side pain, asthma, heart palpitations, liver complaints, and rheumatism," added Rebecca. "We sell enough of Dr. McBride's cure-all in the store for me to have that label memorized. You'd be surprised at how many people buy patent medicines. His has been a best seller for us since it came out five years ago. It's an item we always keep in stock."

Dr. Miller shook his head. "It's best used as a sedative. Frankly, I wish I'd thought of slapping my own name on a label and proclaiming all the wonders that *Dr. Miller's Medical Magic* might cure."

He turned to Maggie. "The *King of Pain* will make you drowsy and numb your wrist pain, Miss Rutherford. Most patent medicines contain at least fifteen percent alcohol."

"If it doesn't cure you, Maggie, at least you'll feel better," Frank chimed in. "I'll make sure to bring your valise and trunk over so you'll have what you need when you do wake up."

Frank looked at Rebecca. "If you wouldn't mind, I'd like to stop by tomorrow and check up on Maggie. Make sure she's keeping out of mischief."

"Why don't you come to supper, Sheriff? A man's got to eat and you can visit with Maggie at the same time."

Maggie noticed the slight flush creep up Frank's neck and realized that her friend might already have feelings for the new widow. Frank seemed very solicitous toward Rebecca. They both seemed comfortable with each other.

Although Rebecca only recently lost her husband, a Western woman alone didn't stay that way long, whether for her personal safety or financial reasons. Rebecca would also have her children's welfare to consider. Maggie wondered how willing Frank would be to accept the coming baby as his own, as well as sweet little Jennie.

She glanced at the young girl sitting beside her on the sofa. Jennie appeared to be a miniature version of Rebecca at that age, with the same blonde hair and blue eyes. Her head turned to each person that spoke. Maggie felt sure Jennie was trying to read their lips and follow the conversation.

"Don't mind if I do," said Frank agreeably. He leaned down and kissed Maggie's cheek. "Take care, Maggie Moon, and get lots of rest. I'll see you tomorrow."

"I look forward to your visit, Frank. Remember to start thinking about those war stories for me," she reminded him. "That could be an entirely different book."

"I'll walk you down, Frank. I need to get the *King of Pain* for Maggie," Ben said, leading the way to the door. "I also need to return to work. I hope I haven't missed any customers."

"I'd like to get some food in you before you drink the medicine, Maggie," Rebecca said. "It'll do more good if you don't take it on an empty stomach. Dr. Miller is right. It's very strong."

Rebecca thought a moment. "We had chicken for dinner. There is plenty left over for supper. Let me fix you some of that."

Soon, Maggie dined on cold chicken and green beans, washing it down with lemonade. Ben gave her a hefty dose of *King of Pain*. Between it, the brandy she'd consumed earlier, and a full stomach, she could hardly keep her eyes open. Rebecca showed her to a room.

"This is Jennie's, but she's been sleeping with me the last few nights."

Maggie saw the anguish that flickered across Rebecca's face and realized that the two had slept together ever since Adam Morgan's death.

She looked down at Jennie, who'd trailed them like a shadow, before speaking slowly and clearly so the little girl might be able to understand her. "Thank you for letting me stay in your room, Jennie. I appreciate it. Just let me know when you want it back and I'll be happy to go stay at Mrs. Morrow's boardinghouse."

Jennie smiled shyly and took Maggie's hand, squeezing it briefly.

"She's certainly taken to you," Rebecca said. "I think it'll do both of us good to have your company." She looked down at her daughter. "Let's leave Miss Maggie alone now so she can get some rest. I'll help you clean up any missing marbles in a few minutes but first I need to help Miss Maggie into bed."

Maggie protested but Rebecca insisted. She even brought in one of her own nightgowns. "You need to be comfortable, Maggie. Wearing a corset and bustle aren't any way to get the rest required."

"While I do wear bustles, I'll admit to you that I gave up wearing a corset shortly after I came out West." Maggie grinned. "It has been the most liberating feeling in the world. You'd think I was able to vote or something else so invigorating."

Rebecca sized her up. "If that's your figure without a corset, I'll bet you turned even more heads with one back home."

She shrugged as Rebecca helped her undress. "Not really. I was a bit of an odd duck, at least as far as New York society was concerned. Don't get me wrong. I was invited to and attended all the right parties. I don't think many men gave me a second glance. My tendency to pursue things that interested me put more than a few off. I did have a beau for many years that escorted me to functions so I was considered off-limits in the minds of most."

Rebecca's eyebrows shot up. "What of this beau now? Is he waiting for you back in New York?"

She sighed as she slipped beneath the covers, her eyelids drooping. "That is definitely a story for another day."

MAGGIE CAME TO, groggy, not sure where she was or even the day of the week. Her eyes opened slowly to darkness. Deep panic set in instantly. She started to scream.

Suddenly, strong hands rested on her shoulders, shaking her.

"Maggie! Wake up! Wake up!"

Hysteria rose in her, swelling like a river overrunning its banks, spilling out in all directions. She tried to speak. Terror forced her voice away. She began shaking violently. Tremors rocked the narrow bed.

"Maggie. It's Ben. I'm here with you. I won't leave you. You're all right. You're fine now."

Strong hands kneaded her shoulders, bringing her comfort. "You just had a nightmare, Maggie, but you're good. I'm letting go of you. Just for a moment. I'm going to light a candle and make the darkness go away. You'll be fine. I'll be right here."

The hands left her shoulders, leaving an immense void. She sucked in a breath, drowning in dread.

A match scratched and gave off a small bit of light. A hand attached to the match moved. She heard the wick catch fire. Hope sprang within her. The hand adjusted the kerosene lantern to a full glow. She saw Ben blow out the match and turn toward her.

The door opened. Rebecca looked in, worry on her features.

"Maggie had a bad dream," Ben said. "She's shaken but I'll stay with her. Go back to bed, Rebecca. If Jennie wakes up and you're gone, she'll be terrified."

"Of course." Rebecca smiled reassuringly at Maggie. "Let me know if you need anything."

Maggie nodded mutely, still unsure if she possessed a voice anymore.

The door closed and she glanced at Ben. He pulled up a chair next to the bed and took one of her hands in his.

"You're ice cold." He stood and pulled the quilt up over her, helping her adjust her injured wrist back to where it rested atop a pillow.

"Just breathe. I'm here."

They sat in silence several minutes, Ben's eyes never wavering from hers as he continued to hold her hand. Maggie gulped air down at first. Then as the moments passed, her breathing calmed. Finally, she spoke.

"I'm sorry."

He shook his head. "No need to apologize. Those patent medicines can do some crazy things to your brain. Between taking that and being injured, no wonder you had a bad dream."

"It wasn't a nightmare, Ben."

He looked at her quizzically. "Then what?"

"I'm afraid of the dark. Literally. Like a child."

He nodded. Maggie appreciated that he didn't appear to be judging her.

She explained. "I've always gotten a little discombobulated at strange surroundings. So waking up here, especially after taking the medicine, would have confused me. But I sleep with a candle every night. I've had to since I was five. You saw what happened because I didn't."

"What frightened you then?"

She paused, gathering her thoughts. "I loved playing hide and seek when I was a little girl. I never tired of it. Marcus, Frank, and I would play over and over. Even though I was younger by four years, they both admitted I always did a better job of finding the best places to hide.

"Until one afternoon." She trembled and Ben laced his fingers with hers. Comfort washed over Maggie like warm sunshine. It gave her strength as she spoke.

"Our butler warned us never to play in the basement. It was off-limits, no questions asked. It was dank. Dark. A little scary. All kinds of things were kept down there—old furniture covered in ghostly sheets, trunks with long-forgotten clothes—that kind of thing. Cook stored all her canning in a room with rows and rows of shelves. I vaguely remember big barrels and bins, so I'm sure things such as flour and sugar were kept there, as well."

Maggie sighed. "Normally, the door remained locked and that kept temptation away. But one day, I saw it ajar. I'm sure a servant had gone down there and hadn't come back up yet. A candle was burning at the foot of the stairs. My curiosity got the best of me and I ventured down the stairs."

"Were you afraid?"

She thought a moment. "I don't think so. I think I was more scared of being caught by a servant than any actual fear of the basement. I wandered around a bit, able to see in the dim light from a few high windows. Then I went into the wine cellar, which was a separate room with its own heavy door. My father collected wines so it was cavernous, row upon row of bottles."

Maggie shivered at the memory. "I explored a while longer and then a mouse ran over my foot. That scared me so I ran back to the door. Only it was closed and locked. Probably by the same servant. I know the first footman used to go down to bring up wine for dinner every evening. He might have been in the cellar when I entered and we missed each other completely."

Ben increased the pressure on her hand. It was gentle yet firm. It gave her the confidence to keep speaking.

"They didn't find me until the next day. No one thought to look in the locked basement, especially since we were forbidden to play there. Marcus said they nearly tore the house apart, and let me tell you, it's quite a large house. He even had the servants look outside, in the gardens and beyond, in case I'd broken the rules and left the house to hide."

Ben's thumb rubbed in a small circle, soothing Maggie, calming her.

"Frank brought his parents over to help look. He and Marcus blamed themselves for challenging me to always up the ante and find an even more difficult and impossible place to hide."

Ben frowned. "What about your parents? You've mentioned your servants and Frank's parents in the hunt—but not your own."

Maggie bit her lip. "My mother died of a fever when I was two. I don't really have any true memories of her. My father? Well, he couldn't be bothered with such childish nonsense. Marcus told me later that Father refused to join the search. Instead, he locked himself in his library with a glass of port and a good book."

She smiled weakly. "The story of my life. Father was disappointed when my mother produced a girl instead of a spare to go with the heir. I rarely saw him and when I did? He ignored me. I'd rather have been proclaimed a nuisance. Instead, I was pushed aside or neglected."

Maggie shook her head at the memories. "The nanny was fired without references. That didn't bother me since she rarely paid any attention to me. She always pawned me off on Marcus so she could lie down because of her frequent headaches. I think back now and realize that she was a closet drinker. I'm sure she spent most of her afternoons in a stupor.

"Being a male, Marcus had my father's ear. Soon after this incident, my brother demanded that our aunt Harriet, newly-widowed, come live with us and care for us. Marcus was leaving his tutor for boarding school soon, and he wanted to make sure I was cared for properly."

"This is the same aunt who proclaimed you the spawn of Lucifer and Jezebel?"

She laughed. "Well, she *is* my father's sister. That side of the family is a cold lot. Aunt Harriet did her best, considering all the trouble Marcus and I gave her over the years."

"Do you ever have nightmares of it?"

Maggie frowned. "Not really. But the experience left me with an utter fear of the dark. I remember when the faint light faded from the windows high above me. I'd already beat on the door, hollering for someone to come get me out. Then, the dark came. It was so black that I couldn't see my hand in front of my face. No one found me. Terror set in as the mice scurried. I screamed until my throat was raw and no sound came out."

Ben squeezed her hand. "Well, Maggie Rutherford, you seem one of the bravest women I've ever known in our short acquaintance. You have a great spirit and enthusiasm about you. The fact that you need a candle to sleep with shouldn't trouble you in the slightest."

"Thank you for saying that, Ben. The fear is something that will most likely stay with me the rest of my life, according to more than one doctor. It did lead to something else, though."

"What?"

"When I get terribly upset or feel cornered or filled with fear, I panic. An actual, physical fear runs through my body. I get light-headed and shaky. My heart races. I can't seem to catch my breath. It doesn't happen often but when it does, I am a physical and emotional wreck."

"When was the last time it happened, Maggie?"

"On my wedding day."

10

Maggie awoke to warm sunshine filling the room and the smell of bacon, which made her stomach growl. She felt refreshed, her wrist stiff but stable. She wiggled her fingers as Dr. Miller had recommended. She discovered them able to move with no problem as she looked around the room. A quilt hung neatly folded across the back of the chair next to the bed. A light tap on the door caused her to smooth her hair. She hoped she looked somewhat presentable.

"Come in," she called and the door opened.

Rebecca entered bearing a tray, Jennie fast on her heels.

"Good morning, Maggie. I hope you slept well after your bad dream."

"Yes. I'm sorry I disturbed you. I hope Jennie didn't miss you."

Rebecca set the tray on the table next to the bed and ruffled her daughter's hair as she sat. Jennie crawled up into her mother's lap. "No, she was fast asleep when I returned. I hope you didn't mind Ben sitting with you through the night."

She started. "Ben stayed here all night?"

Rebecca nodded. "He insisted on sleeping in this chair next to you, just in case you needed anything. I guess it was a good thing he was nearby when you awoke in unfamiliar surroundings last night."

Maggie reached for a piece of crisp bacon. "I'm famished."

The thought of Ben Morgan holding a vigil by her side intrigued her. She hadn't expected him to do such a thing. It assured her that deciding to stay in Easton and accept Rebecca's invitation had been the right move. She was more than curious about the gambler-turned- cowhand-turned-store worker. She wanted to study him carefully over the next few days.

And not just because of a book she might write.

"Frank brought your luggage over. It's resting in the corner. If you'd like, I can hang a few of your gowns in the wardrobe." Rebecca smiled. "Frank actually built that wardrobe, as well as our table and chairs."

That surprised her. "I never knew Frank to be so handy."

"He says he started whittling in the Army. That hobby grew into creating simple furniture. Easton is a pretty quiet little town. He works on pieces at the office when he has nothing else to do. I'm sure everyone within five miles has something Frank has made."

Maggie finished her bacon. She started in on a bowl of steaming oatmeal. "I'm glad to see Frank's adjusted so well to small town life. New York is quite different. I do worry about him out here so far from family, though. Alone. I wonder why he's never married."

Rebecca shrugged. "Who knows? Maybe he's never found the right woman. There aren't as many to choose from when a man travels this far out. I can't think of any women in Easton that aren't married other than the Widow Morrow." She paused. "And myself."

Maggie saw tears brimming in Rebecca's eyes and took her hand. "I am so sorry for your loss, Rebecca. It seems you built a good life here with your husband, starting up the general store. Having children. I know you'll miss him terribly."

Rebecca took a handkerchief from her pocket and brushed away her tears. "Adam was such a fine man. Strong yet kind. He never said a harsh word about anyone. He was always willing to lend a helping hand to those in need."

"I know it's early yet but have you decided what your plans are for the future?"

Rebecca brushed her lips against the top of Jennie's head. "Honestly, I haven't wanted to think about it these last few days. I want to focus on having a healthy baby. I thank the Good Lord that Ben happened to make one of his infrequent visits when he did. He's been more than willing to jump in and run the store for now."

Jennie began wiggling. Rebecca helped her down and looked her in the eye. "Go play with your doll, sweetheart. I want to visit with Maggie a little more."

The girl nodded and skipped out the door.

"You're doing exactly the right thing," Maggie told her. "Getting her attention and speaking directly to her. We had a maid who was deaf. I learned to make eye contact with her and speak slowly and clearly. She could read lips and almost always picked up on what I said to her."

"It was such a blow when she lost her hearing. Dr. Miller said it might return but I'm not hopeful. Then her father dying, too? My poor baby girl has had a tough time."

"Keeping things as normal as possible will be the best medicine for her," she assured Rebecca. "I'm sure when the baby comes, Jennie will be a wonderful big sister. You'll probably get more help than you need."

"I'm sure you're right." Rebecca sighed. "Is it wrong of me to wish for a boy? I really didn't care before now, but with Adam passing, I'd love to have a little boy who looks just like his father. He would be such a sweet reminder."

"You'll be happy with the baby no matter what the gender is, Rebecca. And when the time comes, you'll make the right decision about your family's future."

"I'd like to stay in Easton and keep running the store if I could. I'd need help, though. I couldn't manage on my own with two little ones. I know Ben won't leave me high and dry. He'll make sure things are settled here before he takes off again. Wherever that might be."

"Ben doesn't have a home?"

Rebecca bit her lip. "Not anymore. I'd rather not gossip about Ben's situation, though, if you don't mind."

"I understand he's a very private man." Maggie put down her empty bowl. "I'd love to get dressed now and I definitely will need help with my rat's nest of hair. Are you up for the task?"

Rebecca stood and smiled. "I couldn't think of anything else I'd rather do. Thank you again, Maggie, for agreeing to stay. I've missed having a close female friend. My sister and I were only eleven months apart and we were thick as thieves growing up. We both married about the same time, but she moved to

Cincinnati with her husband shortly afterward. We exchange letters but it's not the same."

"I, too, am happy to make a new friend," Maggie told her. "I appreciate you allowing me to stay with you. I've traveled over a year now from place to place. It's nice to be in one spot and share a conversation with another woman."

Rebecca removed Maggie's brush from her valise. "Shall we get started?"

"You are a brave woman, Rebecca Morgan."

OVER THE NEXT FEW DAYS, Maggie's life quickly fell into a predictable pattern. Rebecca helped her dress each morning. Together, they would breakfast with Jennie. Ben rose earlier to eat and was already on duty at the store.

She spent the mornings playing with Jennie, sometimes with dolls at a tea party or playing mamas and babies. Jennie never spoke but Maggie continued to address the small girl directly and chattered throughout their play. She hoped that one day soon Jennie would begin talking again, despite her hearing loss. Dr. Miller had told Rebecca that it might take time for Jennie to speak again because of the double trauma of losing her hearing and her father so closely together.

After all of them shared the noon meal, both Rebecca and Jennie would lie down for a nap. In the two weeks Maggie had lived with the Morgans, she noticed how much larger Rebecca's belly grew and how hard it became for her to get around. Maggie helped with whatever chores she could do with her left hand but suggested to Ben that he hire someone to do some of the heavier housekeeping, such as the laundry.

Afternoons, Maggie spent down in the general store, seated on a stool behind the counter. She loved engaging the citizens of Easton in conversation as they came in for a bit of shopping and gossip. She got to know many of the townspeople living in the small community. When things slowed, she would scribble away on her current story or work on drawings for the book.

Her favorite times came when she and Ben talked. At first, he'd been reluctant to interrupt her work. She got the conversation going by asking him a few questions about a cowboy's life on the cattle trail. She tried to glean those small details from him that would lend her novel the air of verisimilitude that added polish to her work.

As she parted the curtains one afternoon and entered from the storeroom, Ben finished stocking some canned goods on a shelf and smiled at her.

"You got a letter from Rutherford House, Lud. And a heavy package that accompanied it." He indicated where the two rested on top of the counter as he joined her behind the counter.

Maggie laughed. "Yes, I had Frank forward them my address since I'd be staying in Easton awhile."

He started to pass the envelope to her and stopped. "Would you like me to open it for you?"

"Thank you. Although I've learned to live one-handed, there are still certain tasks that I find difficult. At least I hurt my right wrist. If I hadn't been able to write or sketch with my left hand the last two weeks, I might have lost my mind."

He pulled a letter opener from under the counter

and slit the envelope open, removing the single page from inside and handing it to her.

She skimmed the contents and burst out laughing. "It's from my brother. He's never written Lud Madison before. Only my editor, Archibald Posty, has. Listen to this."

My DEAR MR. MADISON,

My name is Marcus Rutherford and I am head of Rutherford Publishing House. I am eagerly awaiting the next Lud Madison novel, as I am one of your biggest admirers. Mr. Posty assures me that you have a work in progress and will deliver it to him shortly.

I would like to add to the ease of this process by bestowing upon you a gift from your publishing house, which I am told is now revolutionizing business and soon the publishing world. You may have heard of this new invention. It is called the typewriter and has been available for a few years.

It is the creation of a Mr. Sholes and Mr. Densmore but they have sold the patent to an acquaintance of mine, a Mr. Remington, he of firearms and sewing machines fame. Mr. Remington's engineers have tested and improved the device, which will now go on the market in final form.

I am sending you posthaste one of these so-called typewriters, with the instructions on how to use the machine. Once learned, I am assured it is a simple and easy process in which to write more quickly. Mr. Remington seems to think that it will become the rage with all authors.

I hope this letter finds you in good spirits and busy in completing your latest tale. Rutherford House is happy to partner with you now and in the future.

Yours truly,
Marcus Rutherford

. . .

MAGGIE SQUEALED WITH DELIGHT. "I've seen this contraption demonstrated when I was in Denver this past spring. The man's fingers flew over... oh, what is it called? A keyboard, I think. He punched keys marked with letters of the alphabet and they struck a piece of paper. The words formed along a line almost by magic. It was amazing!"

"Then let's open the parcel and see it for ourselves."

Ben used his pocketknife to open the box. He extracted the typewriter, a small pamphlet that accompanied it, some black ribbons in cases, and a ream of paper.

"It's heavy," he told her. "It would be bulky for a woman to carry, much less travel with."

She struck a pose with her good left arm, flexing a muscle. "I am stronger than I look, Mr. Morgan. I've had actual boxing lessons from an Irish brawler. I could probably take you on and knock you down before you knew what hit you."

Ben's lazy smile warmed her inside, all the way down to her toes. "You are a constant surprise to me, Maggie Rutherford."

They unfolded the instructions and she read them aloud while he affixed the ribbon in the prescribed manner. He then loaded the typewriter with a piece of white paper that sat upon a roll. They took turns striking the keys, marveling at the words that appeared upon the page. The pamphlet illustrated how certain fingers were designated to strike individual keys.

"Once the pattern is learned, this will be a remarkable way for me to write my novels," she commented. "I'll have to come up with stories at a faster rate but that won't be a problem at all. I have so many ideas that run through my brain now, I sometimes have trouble getting them all down on paper."

"You can type out your ideas, Maggie, as well as your novels. That way you won't lose any of them."

She beamed at him, elated at the idea he proposed. She wished her wrist would be healed immediately so she could teach her fingers to dance across the keyboard. Nothing would make her happier than quickly setting down all the storylines that skittered through her head. Nothing.

Until Ben leaned over and kissed her.

Then her idea of happiness took a seismic shift.

11

B en kissed Maggie without thinking. One minute they played with the newfangled contraption, both delighted at the way words quickly appeared upon the blank page. It seemed natural to suggest she use the typewriter to capture her ideas for her dime novels.

That's when his world changed.

He looked down and saw her smile. That radiance washed over him. Instinctively, he wanted—no, needed—to be a part of her happiness.

His mouth came down on hers. His hands rose to cup her face. A little gasp of surprise squeaked out, but her lips softened under his. What started out as gentle soon became demanding, as his need rose. He wanted to drink up every drop of sunshine that was Maggie Rutherford. His fingers moved to her neck, stroking the smooth alabaster skin, drawing her closer as his hands slid to grasp her shoulders.

Ben slid his tongue inside her mouth, exploring, tasting, an urgency pushing him. No coherent thought formed as he felt his pulse race. Time ceased to exist. His past forgotten. Only this moment, this present, was real.

His hands slid down her arms slowly, wishing they caressed bare flesh instead of the silk material of her dress. Then he reached her wrists, and she flinched.

Their eyes flew open. He saw her hazel eyes more green than brown now, with tiny flecks of gold dancing in them. Her mouth, a pout of rosebud, trembled.

He checked his passion as his eyes dropped to her wrapped, injured wrist. He lifted it gently, stroking carefully above it, not wanting to break off contact with her.

"I hope I didn't hurt you," he said softly.

"No." Her voice was a whisper.

"I've wanted to do that ever since... well, ever since the last time. Back in Abilene," he admitted.

"I've wanted you do to do that," her lips turned up in a satisfied smile, "every time I've laid eyes on you," she answered.

He slowly rubbed his thumb along the edge of the compress around her wrist. "How does it feel?"

"Much better. I think Dr. Miller erred on the side of caution. It's stronger every day. I think within a week, I'll be back to normal."

Ben heard her words but watched the pulse in her throat jump as she spoke.

"A gentleman would probably apologize right about now for taking advantage of you." He stared into her eyes, seeing the flicker of desire still smoldering.

"But you're no gentlemen."

"No."

"Then I guess–"

A bell tinkled as the door to the store opened. Ben released Maggie's wrist.

"Why, hello. You're Adam's brother, aren't you?" A

stout women with iron gray hair assessed them with eyes that Ben thought didn't miss much.

"I don't believe I know you, young lady." The woman smiled. "Unless you're the sheriff's friend, Miss Rutherford. Although I didn't see any sign of you back at my house."

Ben placed the woman with her last remark. "Yes, I'm Ben Morgan. And you're Mrs. Morrow, the lady who runs the boardinghouse."

"One and the same. I just returned from Chicago. Been visiting family and came in on the noon train to Abilene today." She frowned. "So, Miss Rutherford, where have you been staying? I told Sheriff Staley which room to put you in. Obviously, that didn't happen."

The widow harrumphed. "Men never seem to listen. Mr. Morrow was always bad about woolgathering anytime I spoke. I had to tell him something a good three or four times before I was certain he heard it. God rest his soul."

Ben winced, guilty for feeling happy that Mr. Morrow had escaped his wife's clutches, even if it was to an early grave.

"I had an accident and injured my wrist the day I arrived in Easton, Mrs. Morrow," Maggie told the woman. "Rebecca Morgan was kind enough to ask me to stay with her. She's looked out for me and helped me with daily tasks such as brushing my hair and buttoning all those cumbersome buttons that seem to grace women's fashions these days."

"Tsk-tsk, that just won't do, Miss Rutherford. Rebecca will be giving birth soon and needs her rest. I am perfectly capable of taking care of your needs. There's no need to inconvenience the Morgans anymore."

She looked at Ben. "Young man, you see that Miss Rutherford's things are gathered up and have her trunk brought over to my place. We'll head over there now."

Ben saw Maggie was a little flustered by the take-charge widow and intervened. "I know Miss Rutherford would like to thank my sister-in-law for all that she's done for her. A friendship has sprung up between them and they've become quite close these past couple of weeks."

He looked over at Maggie. "Rebecca's napping with Jennie now, isn't she? And wasn't the sheriff coming over to supper to visit with you and the rest of us?"

"Yes, Frank is coming tonight," Maggie agreed quickly. She looked back at Mrs. Morrow. "Maybe I could arrive after breakfast tomorrow. That way you'll have time to have everything ready."

"Nonsense, child. You have your supper like planned, and then Sheriff Stansel may escort you home to me once you've said your goodbyes. Now, let me get a little shopping done. I've been gone a few weeks and I need to restock my larder."

"I'll get a basket for you, Mrs. Morrow," Ben told the woman. "We'll get you fixed up in no time."

MAGGIE LEFT the store and went upstairs to the family's quarters. Although Mrs. Morrow had applied strong pressure to her, reluctantly convincing—if not downright ordering—Maggie to move to the boardinghouse, she knew the widow was right.

After all, hadn't this visit with Rebecca lasted almost three weeks now? Maggie didn't want to take advantage of the friendship that had sprung up between them. Rebecca needed to put herself first for once. She should have as much rest as possible before the baby came. Maggie didn't want to impose on her new friend any longer.

Upstairs, she found Jennie sitting at the table, turning the pages of a picture book. Maggie pulled up a chair next to her and faced the small child.

"Hello, Jennie. Would you like me to read the book to you? You can watch my lips and see me form the words. You're such a big girl now. I'll bet you already know how to read some of the words."

Jennie nodded, smiling shyly. She pushed the book closer to Maggie.

"Let's start at the beginning." Maggie flipped back and opened to the title page. She glanced at the name and then looked Jennie squarely in the eye.

"*The Story of Little Red Riding Hood.*" She paused. "That's the name of your picture book."

She turned the page and looked back at Jennie. "Oh, look. Little Red Riding Hood looks an awful lot like you."

Jennie smiled again and nodded. She leaned closer to Maggie and touched the drawing of Red Riding Hood.

Maggie took that as a good sign. She knew how desperately Rebecca wanted to hear Jennie speak again. Maggie knew the girl could, but she also understood how the trauma of losing her hearing and her father back-to-back might have affected her.

After her own experience of being locked in the wine cellar, she didn't speak for over a week. At first, she had no voice. The hours spent screaming in terror robbed her of it. Once it returned, Maggie feared speaking. If she decided to talk, she knew they would

ask her about that night. She refused to think about it
—so she didn't talk about the basement or anything
else.

Finally, Marcus cajoled a few words out of her.
Maggie remembered it involved bribery and a handful
of peppermints. She never could resist a peppermint,
and her older brother was clever enough to figure out
how to pull her from her shell by using the candy.

Maybe once she built more trust between her and
Jennie, a similar solution might work.

They finished the book. Maggie closed it and set it
on the table. She took Jennie's hand in hers, making
sure the girl watched her lips.

"Jennie, I'm going to go stay at Mrs. Morrow's for a
while."

The girl's eyes welled with tears. Maggie leaned
over and hugged her tightly.

"I plan to come see you and your mama every
single day. I need to get settled in somewhere else before your little brother or sister arrives."

She stroked Jennie's flaxen hair, so smooth and
baby-fine to the touch. "This will give you and your
mama special girl-time together, just the two of you.
She's going to depend upon you an awful lot once the
baby comes."

That comment made Jennie smile widely. Maggie
hoped she would continue to hold Jennie's trust and
be able to pull her from her silent world.

"What have you two been up to?"

She turned and saw Rebecca had risen from her
nap. Jennie scrambled down and collected her doll.
She sat on the floor playing with it while Maggie informed Rebecca of Mrs. Morrow's visit. She stifled Rebecca's protests about the impending move, assuring
her they would still see each other every day. The

older woman lived less than half a mile's walk from the general store.

"We have grown far too close, Rebecca, for you to think you'd be rid of me so easily. I promise to visit every day. I'll still be in town for a few weeks while I'm finishing my manuscript and the accompanying illustrations."

Rebecca sighed. "I know when Mrs. Morrow's mind is made up, there's no changing it. How is your wrist doing?"

"As I told Ben earlier this afternoon, I think it's ever so much better. It's been frustrating to be one-handed but at least I didn't injure my dominant hand. If I'd had to stop writing and drawing for the duration, I might have gone *'round the bend*, as our cook used to say."

Rebecca groaned. "Oh, what a luxury to have a cook. Do you miss living a life full of servants and wealth, Maggie?"

She had shared some of her background with Rebecca, though not any details about being a runaway bride.

"Not really. I've always been self-sufficient and wanted to do everything myself. I had a nanny when I was young, and then a governess who eventually oversaw my studies. I constantly battled them both, fighting for every inch of independence I could find."

She smiled at the memories. "Both of them took my being left-handed as a personal affront. They each tried to break me of writing left-handed, until they realized that no one really cared. Marcus had been forced to change to doing everything right-handed when he was a child. My father insisted upon it. I'm grateful he didn't care enough about a girl to intervene.

"And I was headstrong enough to challenge him if he'd tried to. But enough of that. We need to see to supper. You know Frank has proven partial to your stew and potatoes."

Rebecca laughed. "Frank Stansel is partial to food. I've never seen a man who could put away as much as he does in a single meal and never look as if he's gained a pound."

The women busied themselves preparing supper. Frank arrived like clockwork. She hoped he would find an excuse on a regular basis to keep stopping by to see Rebecca, even with Maggie being gone to the boardinghouse. She knew her friend still mourned the recent death of her husband, but Frank was the best of men. If he and Rebecca eventually paired up, Maggie would be more than pleased.

They enjoyed a lively meal full of entertaining conversation. Ben even pulled a harmonica from his pocket when he told a story about songs on the cattle trail. He played them a mournful sounding tune that he insisted helped to calm the cattle at night.

Frank volunteered to help Rebecca clean up so Maggie would be free to gather the last of her belongings. Ben had already taken her trunk with the typewriter inside it over to Mrs. Morrow's. He offered to carry her valise and escort her to the boardinghouse. Maggie agreed. She hugged Rebecca and Jennie, while Frank promised to stop by mid-morning to see her.

"Remember, we still need to get some more examples down of different crimes and punishments in the West," he told her. "Stealing a horse back East might be a misdemeanor but it's a hanging offense out here. A stranded man without his horse faces too many dangers."

"I love how you say *we*, Sheriff," Rebecca pointed

out. "It sounds as if you're helping Maggie to write one of her dime novels."

Frank blushed. "Well, I'm not much of a writer."

"He does have a way with the facts, which I can work into a compelling narrative," Maggie added. "Frank is a good judge of character. He sizes up people and situations well. I have several pages of notes based upon his recollections already. I'm sure he'll expect me to dedicate a half-dozen or more books to him with the wealth of material he's given me. Not that I've dedicated my novels to anyone, so far."

"Is that unusual?" asked Ben.

She laughed. "It's not as if Lud Madison can name people in his dedications. I toyed with the idea of dedicating my first novel to my brother—no names mentioned, of course—but it seemed a bit awkward. I didn't think it very sporting to simply make up imaginary people and have Lud dedicate his books to them. When my editor has inquired, I've brushed it off as Lud not being very sentimental in that regard. He hasn't pressed me on the issue."

"Do you ever think you'll reveal your true identity and write under your own name?" Rebecca wondered aloud.

"I think the time has come to let Marcus know the truth. As far as the public goes? I don't think so. The books sell exceedingly well under a man's name. I don't want to tinker with success. I certainly don't want to hurt my sales. I've been able to live on my own this past year, supporting myself with the income Lud has generated."

"We better get going, Maggie," Ben said. "Otherwise, the Widow Morrow might come looking for you."

She wished everyone a good night and promised

to stop by and take her noon meal the next day with the Morgans. Ben claimed her valise. They made their way down the stairs and out to the street.

He offered her his arm and she slipped her good hand through the crook. They began walking down the dirt road of Easton's main street. The sun slowly dipped below the horizon, the end of the September eve bringing a slight coolness to the air.

Their silence seemed more companionable than awkward to her. She'd never been as comfortable with a man as she felt when she was near Ben Morgan. Her heart ached. She wouldn't be in close proximity to him anymore. Of course, she would stop by to visit with Rebecca and Jennie.

Maggie sighed. She feared the loss of those long afternoons she and Ben spent together in the general store. Sometimes they'd talked about all kinds of things. At different times, they each worked in silence, happy in one another's company.

Maybe it was time she faced reality. At some point, either she or Ben would leave Easton, he to return to his nomadic life, while she...

What will I do?

She had traveled far and wide for over a year now. She felt at home in the West. She realized while she might visit New York upon occasion to see Marcus and his eventual family, she would never choose to live there again.

Despite the fact that she enjoyed her own wanderings and hoped to continue to see different parts of the West, she pined for a home.

Easton felt like that home.

Would the town feel the same once Ben moved on? She doubted it. Yet Maggie knew a time was coming when she wanted to put down roots of her own. Easton might be as good a place as any. She was already getting to know people in the small community. She had Frank and Rebecca as friends. Abilene offered some bigger city conveniences. There were trains to Chicago or New York from the railhead.

She decided to carefully consider her options in the next few weeks. She would try to remember not to factor Ben Morgan into any eventual decision she made.

They arrived at a white clapboard house, two-storied and neat as a pin. A row of flowers grew near the steps leading up to the porch. Ben escorted her up them and set down her case by the door.

"You said on your wedding day." His gaze searched hers.

Goose bumps popped up on Maggie's arms. "My wedding day?"

He nodded. "That first night. When you woke up in the dark and screamed. We talked about how you always needed a light to sleep. You said whenever you got scared or felt cornered, you got all panicked. I asked the last time you'd felt that way—and you said on your wedding day."

Ben studied her a long moment. "Are you married, Maggie? And do you love him still?"

12

Ben needed to know her answer. The more time he spent with Maggie Rutherford, the more he felt their lives intertwined. In a few short weeks, he knew more about her than anyone he'd ever known.

And he loved her.

That scared him beyond words.

He never intended to get close to another woman, much less fall in love. But there was a powerful draw to Maggie that mere words couldn't describe. He felt whole again around her, whole and healed. His damaged heart, ripped to shreds by Eliza's death, suddenly knit together as never before.

He loved Maggie's mind and heart, her spirit and soul. She seemed as necessary to him as the air he breathed. Each time he saw her, he wanted to kiss her senseless.

And more.

But she'd mentioned her wedding day. Exhausted by the turmoil of the day—her injury, ingesting the strong patent medicine, awakening in terror in the dark, sharing her traumatic experience as a child—Maggie had fallen into a deep sleep.

She never referred to her wedding after that. Ben,

too much of a coward, couldn't force himself to bring it up. It had eaten away at him, even as he'd kissed her today. The kiss was so right. Or he wanted it to be. For him to even consider doing it again, much less even toying with the idea of a future with this woman, he had to know the truth.

She burst out laughing.

He took a step back. Was she making fun of him? Anger poured through him at being the butt of some sick joke.

She touched his arm. "I'm sorry, Ben. Truly, I am." She wiped at her eyes and grew serious. "No. I'm not married. I never have been."

"But—"

She waved a hand in the air. "Oh, there *was* a wedding day. There was a church full of New York society people and a groom waiting at the altar."

Confusion filled him. "What happened?"

"I couldn't do it. I knew it was what I was supposed to do. My fiancé's father and mine had been best friends all their lives. They wanted a marriage between us from the time we were in the cradle. But me? I panicked. I walked down that aisle with all those people looking at me and everything closed in on me. I was suffocating."

Ben nodded. "What did you do?"

"I had to get out of there. I literally ran back up the aisle. I ran to the West. I ran for a new life. I didn't look back. And here I am."

He started to smile. He could see her bolting for freedom. It was just like her.

Maggie sighed. "So yes, I had a wedding day. But no wedding."

Relief ran through his veins. Before she said another word, he latched onto her and kissed her hard.

He kissed her deep and long and with a passion that flared out of control.

He would've gone on kissing her. Until a whack landed on his head. Twice. And then a smack hard on his shoulder.

He tore his mouth from hers. "What the hell?"

He saw a broom coming at him. It struck him hard in the back before he could utter another word. He released Maggie and saw the Widow Morrow on the other end of the broom, swinging it like the Archangel Michael swinging his sword.

Ben couldn't believe they'd been so rudely interrupted. And by a broom! He instantly knew Maggie could and would make good use of this bit of nonsense in a scene for one of her books.

"No spooning on my porch, young man! I have a reputation to maintain. I run a respectable business. Now, git!"

Mrs. Morrow looked at Maggie. "Inside. Now. And take your case with you." She glared at Ben. "I said, *git!*"

Ben hid a smile and tipped his hat. "Evening, ladies." He hurried down the steps, chuckling all the way home.

MAGGIE ROSE the next morning when she heard Mrs. Morrow stirring. She dreaded facing the woman after last night's episode.

Fortunately, Mrs. Morrow couldn't have been nicer to her. She helped Maggie dress, complimenting her on both her sense of style and color of hair.

"My, this copper is a beautiful shade, Miss Rutherford. Makes me long for the days when my own hair was dark and sleek. Things change as you age."

"Please, call me Maggie. Everyone does. And thank you. My mother's hair was also copper, though my brother tells me hers was slightly redder than mine."

"You don't remember her?"

"No, I lost her when I was quite young. I do have a picture of her. It's one of my most prized possessions."

She went to the bureau and handed over the daguerreotype that Marcus gave to her on her wedding day.

"My," Mrs. Morrow cooed, "she is a beauty. You're so like her, dear. Come sit. I'll braid your hair and coil it up for you."

She let the older woman fuss over her. Mrs. Morrow brushed out Maggie's hair, plaiting it before twisting it up and pinning it securely.

"Oh, that looks lovely." She turned her head to see the full effect in the mirror. "Thank you so much."

Mrs. Morrow smiled. "I'm sure Mr. Morgan will think so."

She blushed. "About last night."

The widow waved a hand. "Not to worry, dear. I was quite the belle in my time. Beaux to my left and right. Then Mr. Morrow stole my heart. Now, mind you, he knew how to pay a compliment, but he was so absent-minded. I had to stay on him all the time, God rest his soul."

The older lady brightened. "You have to leave them wanting more, Maggie. I heard you two arrive and watched you out my window. My, you were putting on quite a show. That Mr. Morgan is a fine-looking man but he needed to mind his P's and Q's.

Don't worry. I think he'll still fancy you. Despite my broom separating you two."

Maggie laughed. "Are you trying to couple us together?"

Mrs. Morrow tilted her head. "I didn't think so. I thought the sheriff was sweet on you, him being so particular in trying to set things up here for your visit. I felt certain you'd be Mrs. Frank Stansel by the end of the year before I even met you."

"Oh, no." The thought had Maggie chuckling. "Frank has known me since my birth. He's as much a brother to me as Marcus, my own flesh and blood. Marcus's and Frank's friendship goes back to when they were in their own cradles. Our fathers were friends as boys. I was eager to visit Frank here in Easton while I traveled but there's no romantic attachment between us."

"So, he's a sort of big brother to you?"

"Yes, ma'am. He'll even be by to check on me this morning to make sure I've settled in properly."

"Then let's get some breakfast in us. I'll put extra biscuits and coffee on." Mrs. Morrow winked. "I'm known across three counties for my biscuits. I'm sure Sheriff Stansel will make room for a few when he visits."

The women breakfasted on eggs and bacon. Maggie ate three of the famous biscuits, proclaiming them light as air.

She worked on her drawings for a couple of hours at the desk in her room, until Frank arrived. She heard his voice when he called out a greeting. She assumed Mrs. Morrow sat on her front porch awaiting him. Maggie came down the stairs as the widow ushered Frank into the kitchen.

"I've plenty of biscuits left from breakfast, Sheriff."

Frank swept off his hat and greeted Maggie. "Morning, Maggie. Mrs. Morrow is trying to ply me with biscuits. Shall I take her up on her generous offer?"

"Only if you partake of the rhubarb jam with them. Or the strawberry rhubarb. Both were excellent choices, though I'd lean toward the strawberry rhubarb if I were you."

They settled at the table. Frank gobbled biscuits down as if there were no tomorrow. When he finished, he suggested they return to the jail and continue with Maggie's research.

"That way, you can walk over for lunch with the Morgans after we finish up. Mrs. Morgan told me last night that you were expected and she wouldn't take no for an answer. I guaranteed her you'd show up."

They told Mrs. Morrow goodbye and set out for the jail, passing the time with small talk until they arrived. Maggie took a seat in front of the desk. Frank sat behind it, stretching out his legs. He propped them, crossed at the ankles, on top of the desk.

"Let's talk about gunfighters, Frank. I've heard tales of some. Surely you know of real men who make their living in the profession. I have an inkling of an idea for a story about a gunfighter and his one true love."

Frank nodded. "Met some. Arrested a few. Most professional gunfighters work in four states—Texas, California, Missouri, or here in Kansas. Or else you can find them in three territories—Colorado, Oklahoma, or New Mexico. That's where the most shootings occur. They're loners, mostly."

"Is it true that many of them were once lawmen? Or they become lawmen?"

"Some have served the law. Others might have

once been cowboys, soldiers, miners, bounty hunters, or were one-time ranchers. I arrested one that was a butcher and another who claimed to be a buffalo scout for the railroad at one point."

"What makes a man want to kill for a living?"

He shrugged. "Who knows? I'm sure if you talked to ten of them, they'd each have a different story. Some do it for adventure. Some might've fallen on hard times. Others? They're just mean sons-of-bitches." He stopped for a moment.

"Don't you know any decent men who are fast with a gun?" she asked.

"Not really. You might've heard of Billy Brooks. I met him when he first came to Kansas. Used to drive for the Southwestern Stage Company when they went through Newton. When Newton incorporated and started a police force a couple years back, Billy got himself appointed as town marshal, mostly because everyone knew how ornery he was. But I guess it didn't suit him. I heard he turned to the outlaw life. Gunfights. Stealing horses. Got himself arrested near Caldwell last year. Some vigilante group took him and two others from the jail and invited them to a necktie party. That was the end of old Billy."

Maggie shuddered. "It's hard to believe civilized men would take the law into their own hands like that instead of allowing the accused to stand trial."

"Sometimes people think the law takes a little too long. You've been here a while. You know the code of the West. It's part chivalry, part common sense, and part vigilante no-nonsense."

Frank placed locked fingers behind his neck. "You've probably heard stories of Wild Bill Hickok. He's starting to make a name for himself."

She nodded. "I talked at great length to Sam, the

clerk at The Alamar, when I was staying in Abilene. He told me Wild Bill started out as a Kansas homesteader before the war. Afterwards, he was arrested and then acquitted of murder. He became town marshal in Abilene four years ago. Sam said an incident occurred, which led to Mr. Hickok leaving town, but he refused to elaborate on it."

Frank guffawed loudly, slapping his thigh with his hand. "I'll bet he did. Only because I like you will I tell you this story, Maggie."

She sat up expectantly, her pencil poised above a piece of paper, ready to take notes.

"Two men operated the Bull's Head Tavern in Abilene. They painted a picture of a bull on the side of their saloon as a way of advertising. Trouble was the regular citizens of Abilene took offense to all of the large, erect equipment the bull had. They demanded Marshal Hickok do something about this travesty. Bill requested the fellows change their picture. The owners refused."

Maggie gasped. "To flaunt such an eyesore? That's appalling, Frank."

"Well, old Wild Bill altered the picture himself, according to those in the know. Not long after, Phil Coe, one of the Bull's Head owners, wound up pulling a gun on the marshal. Wild Bill killed him. He caught a glimpse of someone else he thought was charging him. He turned and fired two more shots. Killed an Abilene special deputy. Poor guy was just coming to Bill's aid."

"Oh, my goodness. What happened? I know Marshal Hickok is no longer in Abilene."

"The town council relieved him of his duties shortly after the incident. Seems this wasn't the only questionable action Bill took while serving as town marshal. There was talk of other suspect shootings and misconduct. Bill left town. I have no idea where he went. Knowing Bill, he'll turn up somewhere."

Maggie furiously jotted down bits of the story. "Oh, Frank, I owe you plenty for sharing so much with me."

He swung his legs back to the floor and stood. "I have an idea. You might want to examine some of the wanted posters that have come through."

He opened the top left drawer of his desk and pulled out a stack of flyers. "Why don't you take these with you and study them for a day or two? You might find something of interest and be able to use it."

"That's a wonderful idea." She slid her pencil and paper into her reticule and reached for the wanted posters. "I never thought to use these as a resource."

She flipped through them quickly, cringing as she read phrases of crimes committed. The sketches that adorned most every poster left her with a sick feeling.

Standing, she told Frank, "I'll definitely look over these and return them to you soon." She checked the watch pinned to her blouse. "It's about time for me to go over to Rebecca's."

"I'll escort you there."

Maggie started to protest, knowing there was no need since the general store was so close, but she realized it gave Frank a good excuse to catch a glimpse of Rebecca.

"I'd appreciate that."

They walked a few blocks and entered the store. Maggie saw Ben helping a customer. She and Frank headed to the counter where Rebecca sat on a stool, frowning at a ledger.

When she caught sight of them, Rebecca smiled. She came around the counter. "I'm so glad to see you,

Maggie. I know it's only been since last night but it seems an eternity."

Maggie set down her reticule and the stack of flyers. The two women hugged.

"It's certainly nice to see you, too, Frank. Are you going to be staying for the meal, as well?"

"I hadn't planned on it."

"Well, there's plenty, so please don't hesitate," Rebecca assured him. "I fried up some pork not an hour ago. I have a pot of fresh green beans and new potatoes to go with it."

"Sold!" Frank proclaimed. "A single man is smart enough never to turn down home cooking."

"Let's go upstairs, Rebecca, and get the table set," Maggie told her friend. She glanced at the open ledger. "I'll gather your things and bring them up."

"Let me help you up those stairs," Frank said, gently taking Rebecca's arm.

Maggie watched them head back through the stockroom. She slipped the flyers into the accounts ledger and picked up it and her reticule with her good hand.

The bell tinkled with the customer departing and Ben joined her. "Mrs. Smith comes in to look at fabrics or buttons at least three times a week. I'm sure Adam was lucky to ring up a sale from her once a month."

"Some women need time before they make up their minds."

Ben gazed at her steadily. "You don't seem to be one of those women."

"No," Maggie said softly. "I've always been one to know what I want fairly quickly. Marcus always says I'm the more decisive of the two of us."

"Shall we go upstairs?" Ben asked. "Let me take

that for you. That book is heavy and your reticule looks full."

She handed him the account book but it slipped from her grasp. It fell to the floor, the wanted posters spilling on the ground. "I'm so sorry, Ben. I can be clumsy."

"It's not your fault—you're still operating with one hand." He bent to retrieve the papers. "I'll have these up in a jiffy."

Maggie watched him gather the flyers. Suddenly, Ben stopped dead in his tracks. He lifted a page, looking at it carefully.

"Frank is letting me borrow his wanted posters. I'm going to review them and see if they have anything I might be able to use." She paused. "See anyone you know?"

Ben shook his head and continued to collect the flyers. He stacked them together.

"Here you go." He handed them to Maggie. "I'll carry the ledger if you'll take the stack of criminals in hand."

The poster on top was the one that had caught Ben's attention. She looked at the picture of the wanted man. He was a known gunfighter, Black Tex Lonnegan. He possessed cold eyes, a cruel mouth, and was responsible for more than a score of killings.

Maggie wondered how Ben knew the outlaw.

13

Maggie perched in front of the small mirror, admiring her appearance much like her best friend, Sarah Henry, once had on Maggie's wedding day. She often teased Sarah for being overly vain as they grew up, while Sarah accused Maggie of never worrying about what she looked like.

For the most part, Sarah was right. It wasn't that Maggie never bothered with her appearance. She liked shopping for pretty clothes and enjoyed wearing them, especially if she could find the perfect reticule to match her ensemble. She always made sure her hair was neat and tidy before she went down for breakfast.

However, Maggie rarely looked at herself or gave her appearance a second thought once the day started. As long as she wore the appropriate clothes for any given situation, she'd rather revel in the experience of that situation—not fret over what she looked like during it.

Marcus had told her she should take a man's attitude when it came to clothing. *"Before you depart, do your utmost to look your absolute best. Then, totally forget about your appearance."* She worshipped her brother and so his word became law. She focused on going, doing, and seeing things. She preferred to live in the moment, rather than worry about what she looked like—or what others thought about how she appeared.

Tonight proved the exception to that steadfast rule.

She reached for a pair of emerald earbobs and attached them. They complimented her rich hunter-green dress. Both brought out the green in her eyes. She noticed her face flushed and knew it was from anticipating the excitement of the evening.

Maggie opened a pot of rouge. Her complexion didn't need any heightened color. She did dab a smidgeon onto her bottom lip and spread it accordingly, before mashing her lips together to even out the color. She stared at herself, pleased with her reflection.

She shook off a sudden onset of nerves as she thought about what might occur on this late September eve, the last Saturday of the month. Maggie closed her eyes.

She might dine with Ben Morgan.

She might dance with Ben Morgan.

If her luck held, she definitely planned to kiss Ben Morgan. More than once.

A knock at the door brought her out of the sweet reverie. She stood and went to the door. As she opened it, Mrs. Morrow bustled in.

"Oh, my. Maggie, you absolutely glow in that gown!" Her landlady exclaimed. "How is your wrist?"

She glanced down, happy to see no bandage, only two gold bracelets adorning her arm. She'd gone for several hours a day this past week without the dressing, slowly exercising the joint back to full strength.

"It feels wonderful. Almost decadent to be sporting bracelets and not some medical dressing."

"You did well dressing yourself," Mrs. Morrow said. "You even placed your cameo perfectly. I see you've left your hair for me to do."

"If you wouldn't mind. You arrange it so artfully. I'm afraid that's not a feminine skill I possess."

Maggie seated herself as Mrs. Morrow took up the brush, pulling it through her hair in long strokes.

"It's almost a shame to put up these copper tresses. They're so pretty. Ah, I know just the thing to do." The older woman hummed under her breath as she twisted and pinned. Within minutes, Maggie beamed at the results.

"I declare, Mrs. Morrow, you could style even Queen Victoria's hair. Who knew a talented woman such as yourself lived on the Kansas prairie? I believe you could move to New York City tomorrow and be gainfully employed as an artist of hair to the most famous women residing on Fifth Avenue."

The landlady beamed at her words. "You are too profuse in your praise, Maggie, but I'll accept your compliments all the same."

A loud knock at the front door sounded. Maggie rose from her seat.

"It sounds like our escort to the barn supper and dance has arrived."

Mrs. Morrow smiled. "Then let's go greet him."

The women went down the stairs and found Frank standing on the porch. He whistled his appreciation as he swept off his hat and bowed.

"I will be the talk of the town, accompanying two of the most beautiful women in Easton."

"Sheriff Stansel, I'm glad you recognize that you

are a fortunate man. Wait a moment while I organize my potluck dishes from the kitchen."

As Mrs. Morrow walked away, Frank called out behind her, "I hope that includes a good amount of your biscuits."

Maggie beamed at Frank. "You certainly clean up well. It's been a while since we've danced, hasn't it?"

Frank nodded. "I still possess two left feet but I hope you'll do me the honor of a dance."

"Is there anyone else you might be interested in dancing with tonight?"

He looked steadily at her, his lips pursed wryly. "I never could keep a secret from you or Marcus. I suppose you've noticed my interest in the Widow Morgan."

Maggie took his hand and gave it a squeeze. "Rebecca is a wonderful woman, Frank. She'd be lucky to have you in her life."

He placed his hat back on his head. "I haven't wanted to say anything to her. I know it's only been a few weeks since Adam passed. She's all wrapped up in getting ready for the baby. Maggie, I can't help but want to take care of her. She's sweet as the day is long. She's got a wonderful sense of humor. That little Jennie already tugs on my heart, too."

"What about the baby?" she asked.

"What about it?" Frank paused. "Oh, I understand. I'm not jealous that it's another man's child. Adam Morgan was a fine, upstanding fellow. I considered him my close friend. But he's gone. Rebecca and the children are here. They need someone to look after them. I want in the worst way to be the one who does that."

"I think you'll know when the time is right to make

your feelings known, Frank. Trust your instincts. They've never let you down before."

He nodded. "You're right. As usual. Don't let that go to your head. Speaking of your head, your hair looks really nice, Maggie. That's a pretty dress, too."

"What? Praise from Frank Stansel, the man of few words and even fewer compliments? You've even promised me a dance. Why, this is a red-letter day!" she teased. "I may have to include it in my next book."

Before Frank could retort, Mrs. Morrow called out for his help. Soon the three of them bounced along in the buggy, the women protecting the food they carried as Frank managed the reins. They arrived at the Creamers' property fifteen minutes later, surrounded by others arriving for the evening's festivities.

Frank helped the two women from the vehicle, insisting he carry in the apple pie and sponge cake, while they brought the rest.

As they walked into the large red barn, Maggie saw several people she'd met at the general store. She waved to some and promised to catch up with others after she set down the two baskets of biscuits. Ethel Creamer motioned them over to the tables, directing where to place breads, vegetables, meats, and desserts in various groupings.

"Thank you for inviting me this evening," Maggie told Ethel, a broad-hipped woman with a kind face and curly brown hair.

"You're part of Easton. Of *course* we invited you."

"I've never attended a barn supper and dance before," Maggie confided. "I'm looking forward to it."

"I notice you aren't wearing your bandage," Ethel said. "I didn't know you'd already healed up. I would have also invited you to the quilting bee these last two days, while the men harvested the corn crop."

"I noticed the corn as we pulled up outside. Will it be placed inside the barn once the dance is over tonight?"

"Yes, indeed. The local men have been gathering on farms in the area to help with the fall harvesting. That will continue for another week or so. The custom in Easton has always been to celebrate at the midpoint and again at the end of the season. The women usually hold quilting circles to pass the time in-between feeding the men each day."

"Well, I've only taken my dressing off a few times before tonight. This will be the first true test to see how well I've healed." Maggie leaned over and lowered her voice. "Frankly, I couldn't have done much at the quilting bee even if I had the use of both hands. I'm afraid when it comes to sewing, I'm all thumbs."

Ethel giggled. "You aren't the only one, dear. You're still welcome to come anytime. You can be one of our readers. Those who aren't quite as talented in the sewing department often read aloud or help prepare food. I've heard you're a writer. I'm sure the group of ladies gathered would love to hear one of your stories."

"Then I shall plan on it. I might even read you a snippet of my latest work in progress and get your opinion on it."

Ethel said, "I see George motioning me over. I swear that man can't be left unsupervised for two minutes. They call women the weaker sex. Hmph!" Ethel set off in the direction of her husband, promising to speak to Maggie later.

"I see you made it."

She turned and saw Ben standing in front of her. His dark black hair was neatly combed, while his sapphire blue eyes twinkled in amusement.

"Good evening, Ben. You look very nice." She couldn't help but notice how handsome he appeared in the snow-white dress shirt, black string tie, and dark wool suit.

"You stole the words right out of my mouth. You're a sight in green, Maggie, but then again, you look breathtaking in a dress of any color."

Her lips turned up in a smile. "Are you flirting with me, Ben Morgan?"

His crooked smile made her swallow hard as he looked at her. "I just might be, Maggie Rutherford."

"Hey, everybody! Can I have your attention?"

She saw George Creamer waving his hands. The large group quieted down as the middle-aged man thanked everyone for all their hard work over the last two weeks. He talked about bringing in the fall harvest around their community and promised them a night of fun and relaxation as their reward. They'd continue the harvesting process the next week.

"It's time to eat our fill and dance the night away," George concluded. "Have at it. There better be at least two of Mrs. Morrow's biscuits still left by the time I go through the line, else the party's over."

Laughter filled the barn as the older children scampered across the barn to begin going through the line. Mothers gathered their younger children who needed help. Those two groups were allowed through first. Then the other adults fell into line behind them.

"I've been looking forward to this all day," Maggie told Ben as they walked to the end of the line that had formed. "I hope the tables don't collapse under the weight of so much food."

"Don't eat too much."

His sudden wink made her laugh. "Really? Why not?"

He leaned down, his lips brushing her ear as he whispered, "Because I plan to dance with you all night long, Maggie Rutherford. My hand in yours. Your body close to mine. I want you light on your feet. I intend to dance you out the door and kiss you in the moonlight."

He stepped back and kept his gaze straight ahead.

Her stomach exploded with butterflies. How could she eat even a bite of supper now?

14

Ben piled his plate high. He filled it with chicken, beef, pork, an assortment of vegetables, and several slices of bread. By the time, he reached Mrs. Morrow's indescribable biscuits, the only room left was in his mouth.

Maggie punched him in the arm. "Ben Morgan, you did not just pop that entire biscuit into your mouth."

He chewed thoughtfully, enjoying every bit of its flakiness. He nodded at Maggie, who couldn't keep the smile from her face as he reached back and grabbed another one.

"It looks like the whole town of Easton turned out. I really like George and Ethel," she said. "They seem so kind and hard-working."

Ben swallowed. He looked around as they made their way to a table. All at once, he felt a sense of community. What would it be like to be a part of this group for a lifetime? He tried to picture Eliza here. Her image faded before he could sharpen it in his mind. He focused harder on the memory. All he could remember was a vague picture of her seated in her Boston home, serving tea, chatting with her sisters.

Eliza, as a young girl, and not the woman he'd married.

Why couldn't he picture her anymore? Or in this life on the plains? His heart told him it was because Eliza never really belonged here.

Frank motioned them over, and Ben followed Maggie to the table. He wanted a life with this woman. Yet it made him feel disloyal to the blurry image of his wife, gone now for years.

That frustrated him. Maggie Rutherford possessed everything he wanted in a woman. She was bright, quick-witted, compassionate, and had a wonderful sense of humor. He admired that she'd made her own way, supporting herself with her writing.

Yet something held him back. He couldn't commit to her or settling down, here in Easton or anywhere else, no matter how perfect it all seemed. He'd promised himself long ago that he'd never devote himself again to one woman and one place. Had what happened before hurt too much for him to contemplate that kind of life again?

He vowed to live in the moment—enjoy this night, each dance, holding her close. Savor a few stolen kisses. Then he would move on. He had to. Roaming ran through his blood now.

He decided that after tonight, his priority would be to find someone to run his brother's general store, maybe even purchase it outright. Rebecca said she wanted to hire a clerk to help run the store so she could retain ownership. Ben doubted she'd find a taker under those circumstances. Rebecca needed to sell the store.

It was too much a reminder of Adam and the life they'd shared. Ben would stay long enough to help build Rebecca a house. She had roots in Easton, and her family would lose their residence once the store sold. At least the sale would leave her with a solid nest egg, and he would always be sure to provide for them beyond that.

He'd asked Rebecca once, shortly after Adam's death, if she thought about returning to her parents. She strongly vetoed the idea. She wanted to stay where she'd created a life with Adam and made friends. She wanted to be near his grave and take the children there to honor and remember him.

As he ate and listened to the table's conversation, he glanced at Frank Stansel. Whether Rebecca knew or not, Ben figured that Easton's sheriff would be her next husband. Ben saw the stolen glances and longing on Frank's face. He knew the man would bide his time before he spoke his mind.

In fact, he might need to encourage Frank to make a move and declare his feelings. Ben's mind would be much more at ease upon leaving Easton if he knew things were settled between his sister-in-law and the lawman. Whatever happened, Adam's family would be in good hands. Frank Stansel was as solid as they came, well-respected, and entertaining as all get out. Rebecca and the children would be safe, protected, and loved. Ben couldn't ask for more than that.

He finished up his dinner. He studied Maggie, her cheeks flushed, a glow about her as she partook in the conversation at their table. He wished they'd met in a different time and place.

Donald Smith, the local blacksmith, joined their table with his wife, Frances. They soon enlivened the conversation as they talked about moving here from Pennsylvania and raising six children. Donald pointed out several of his boys playing tag.

"I have to keep my eyes on them all the time. Even

in my sleep," Frances said. "The two girls are easy but I had the four boys in five years. What a time that was. Fortunately, the girls are older than my boys. They've been wonderful little helpers to me."

"I think of the energy I use up playing with Jennie. Adding five more to the mix? Especially boys?" Ben shook his head. "My mother only had Adam and me to care for. She always said that we were good as gold but we were still boys. I sometimes wonder how she managed to raise us and keep her sanity with all the mischief we got into."

Rebecca rubbed a hand over her swollen belly. "I love having a girl but I pray this one's a boy."

She smiled at Ben. He hoped she got her wish. He wondered if she would name the child after Adam if it were a boy.

"Well, boys will be boys," Frank noted. "You don't hear talk of women being criminals. Boys just seem drawn to trouble. Hey, did anyone hear about The Alamo being robbed last week in Abilene?"

"Isn't that the large saloon on Cedar?" Maggie asked. "The one that boasts of an orchestra and every gaming table known to man?"

Frank nodded. "That's the one. Someone took all the money in their safe last week and also stole several cases of liquor. The town marshal figured out that two cowpokes fresh off the cattle trail from Texas did the looting. They had the gall to set up a little booth next to the rail yard. They sold shots of whiskey to men coming straight off the cattle drives. Doing a heck of a business before the cowboys could even get into town."

"I'll bet that was popular," Ben said.

Frank chuckled. "Cowboys started arriving drunk at the bathhouse and the local saloons. They raved about Abilene's hospitality and the impromptu bar. The marshal investigated and figured out the situation. He made the two cowpokes return the remaining alcohol to The Alamo, as well as the money they stole, plus enough to cover the bottles they'd already sold."

"Is this as serious a crime as stealing horses? Robbing a saloon of its liquor and money?" Maggie asked. "I would think with the profits made from alcohol, their punishment would be severe."

"Nope. The problem was solved," Frank informed them. "The marshal shut down their little business. The Alamo got back what was missing and even the profits the two men made from their sales. The owners actually came out ahead. No charges were brought against the two. They were merely escorted from town and told never to return."

"That's preposterous!" proclaimed Maggie. "Those men stole. They lied. They were cheating—"

Ben placed a hand on her shoulder. "Calm down, Maggie. Let's go get us some dessert. I know you have a sweet tooth. I think I hear a slice of Rebecca's apple pie calling your name. Frank's already finished his piece of it."

She huffed in exasperation as everyone laughed. "I suppose I still have a little Yankee sense of justice in me." She shrugged. "I think I'll simply put it in one of my books. People believe I make up such outrageous things. If only they knew half of what I write is the gospel truth."

Ben led her to a table bountiful with desserts. He chose not only the apple pie but also put a mound of peach cobbler on his plate.

"I'm not sure you'll be so light on your feet after this meal," Maggie teased him.

"I'm not one to pass up dessert. But don't you

worry—I'll out-dance everyone here tonight. Count on it."

They rejoined their group and he added, "I'm spoiled by all this home cooking. I'm usually not in a place long enough to enjoy getting any."

He spooned a bite of the apple pie into his mouth and smiled. "Rebecca, you've outdone yourself with this pie. It's the best you've ever made. You're a wonderful cook. Isn't she, Frank?" Ben looked across the table.

Frank patted his gut. "I second it. Maybe I should get seconds of it myself, if you'll excuse me."

Ben noticed the musicians setting up as he finished his cobbler. He saw two fiddles and a banjo.

"I should've brought my harmonica," he said.

"Where did you learn to play?" Maggie asked.

"In the Army. A guy in my regiment played one. He taught me." He paused, a wave of sadness flooding him. "He was wounded at Walkerton. It was a gut shot so he knew it was fatal."

"I'm sorry," she said, sympathy filling her face.

He cleared his throat. "He gave me his harmonica and wished me better luck than what he'd had. Pressed it and a letter to his sweetheart in my hand. I always think of him when I play."

"What are some of your favorite songs?"

"I'm partial to *Amazing* Grace. I also like *Clementine* and *She'll Be Coming 'Round the Mountain*."

"I enjoyed the tunes you played us after dinner that night," Maggie said. "The ones you learned out on the Chisholm Trail."

"One-Eyed John taught me several. He was a good man. Hard worker." Ben glanced around. "Looks like they're clearing the tables for the music and dancing to begin."

"Let's help them." Maggie rose and started gathering empty dishes.

He and the other men moved the tables and benches to make room for dancing.

Frank came over and told Maggie, "Remember, I've claimed a dance. I always have one in me before I step to the sidelines for the night."

A surge of jealousy rushed through Ben. He tried tamping it down, telling himself it was only Frank, and that he and Maggie were childhood friends.

Maggie glanced over at Ben and Rebecca. "Frank is about as poor a dancer as I've ever had the misfortune of partnering. I'm sure somewhere out there is a worse dancer, but I haven't met him yet." She rolled her eyes. "I hope my toes will survive this night."

Ben's jealousy cooled at her comment, aided by Frank's sheepish grin.

"Come on, Maggie. Let's do this." Frank led her to the center of the room.

He and Rebecca watched as the pair stumbled along to the music. Ben saw the wistful look on Rebecca's face. "Are you all right?"

Her eyes brightened with unshed tears. "Adam loved to dance but I never cared for it. I would dance once for his sake. He'd laugh at me and tell me I had no rhythm."

"I didn't know that," Ben said. "We didn't do much dancing in Boston."

"Oh, Adam loved a good barn dance. After we wound up dancing our one song, I'd excuse myself and sit. Your brother would dance with every lady present after that. He didn't want anyone being left out as a wallflower. I enjoyed watching him have a good time."

Ben squeezed her hand. "You'll have good times again, Rebecca. Count on it."

"I know. I realize I will move on, but a piece of my heart will always belong to Adam."

The song ended. Maggie and Frank returned.

"I hope I didn't embarrass you too badly, Maggie. I think I only stepped on your toes twice."

"I'm fine, Frank. You just warmed me up. I'm raring to go."

"Then I'll keep Rebecca company since I've done my duty. We'll sit and enjoy the music." Ben watched Frank lead Rebecca over to a bench set against the wall.

Maggie looked expectantly at him. "Ready to give this a whirl?"

They danced to three songs in a row before she declared she was out of breath and needed some punch to revive her. He returned with the punch and saw that Jennie stood with Maggie. The little girl's eyes were wide with excitement.

"Let's you and me go show everyone how it's done, Punkin." He picked up his niece and took her to the middle of the floor. He released her so that her feet rested atop his. He beamed at the joy on her face as they danced.

Once the song ended, he returned her to Rebecca. Jennie scooted up into Frank's lap. Ben walked back to Maggie, who'd finished her punch. He took her hand. "Ready for another round?"

They danced to *Camptown Races* and then *I Dream of Jeannie with the Light Brown Hair*. As he'd planned, he guided her out the open barn door into the cool September night. Stars sprinkled the night sky. They came to a halt under a scraggly tree, away from everyone else.

"You're the prettiest lady I've seen, Maggie Rutherford."

She blushed at his compliment. "Are you sure you're not a ladies' man?" she asked lightly.

"Not really." He grew serious. "Maggie, I can't guarantee you anything. I don't know where I'll be six months or six years from now. But we have this moment. Right now."

"Then don't waste it."

15

Ben's mouth came down and touched hers. The kiss was sweet and long. It caused a yearning to rise in Maggie. Gently, he urged her lips apart, his tongue gliding along the seam of her mouth. She answered him in kind, tasting what was his essence, inhaling the scent that made him Ben.

His arms came around her. He pulled her close. She rested her hands flat against his broad chest, the muscles tensing at her touch. Her fingers tingled with the heat of his body and the pounding of his heart below them.

She knew this couldn't last. What sparked between them was raw and real, but nothing permanent would occur. That thought didn't stop her. She wanted to live for this moment, this now, for this man here at her fingertips. His mouth beckoned hers, as their tongues mated in a ritual as old as time.

He deepened the kiss. She clutched his shirt tightly, hanging on for the wild ride of passion rolling through her. The music fled. The darkness around them was forgotten. Only here and now were meant to be.

He pulled his mouth from hers, his breathing

harsh. He trailed soft butterfly kisses along her cheek to her ear. A frisson of pleasure swept through her when his teeth found and tugged on her earlobe. Something built in her. Her breath quickened. Her pulse fluttered.

His hands spread wide on her back, dropping to her waist and below. They cupped her bottom and brought her even closer against him. She gasped as the pleasant tingling grew. It started to spread through her as he stroked her with his hands and nibbled on her neck.

Then his hands came to her waist and after lingering a moment, he released her. The heat from his mouth was torn away. Desolation whipped through her as he took a step back. The desertion felt like a betrayal.

His eyes glittered, desire heightened in them. His voice was low as he reached and took her hand.

"I had to stop. If I didn't..." His voice faded.

Her chest rose up and down quickly. She tried to calm her breathing. She blinked rapidly to keep tears from forming and spilling down her cheeks.

"Maggie. I want you. As much as any man has ever wanted a woman." He ran a hand through his thick, dark hair. "But I respect you enough to stop. I thought we could enjoy a few playful kisses under the moonlight and—"

"I understand." Maggie swallowed, restraining the emotions dancing through her. "You don't have to say another word." She glanced around and saw a bale of hay nearby. "Would you at least sit with me a while?"

He nodded. They moved to the bale and sat, so close their hips touched. He took her hand and entwined his fingers through hers. No words were necessary between them.

She focused on their joined hands and realized she'd fallen in love. Ben Morgan might be a gambler and wanderer who'd never settle down, but he was a gentleman. She needed a little quiet time with him. Just the two of them. In silence.

Together.

Her thoughts wandered. She didn't know how long they sat under the stars. She forced herself not to think of tomorrow and the tomorrows after that when he would be gone from her life. She lived in this moment, relishing the feel of his fingers entangled with hers, their shoulders touching. She focused on how she felt. She committed to memory this slice of her life.

She would write about tonight, keep a record of this moment. In the years to come, she would take it out and re-read it a thousand times.

"Ben? Maggie? There you are."

She looked up and saw Frank standing before them, a panicked look on his face.

"We need to go. Rebecca's going to have the baby."

Maggie scrambled to her feet. Ben followed suit. They found Rebecca inside, a slightly dazed look on her face, talking with Dr. Miller and Mrs. Morrow.

"It is a few weeks early. Two to three, I'd say. Under the circumstances, I expected this," the physician said. "Let's get you home. A second baby doesn't wait around to be born like a first one does."

Rebecca smiled half-heartedly at Maggie and Ben. "Sorry to cut your evening short."

Ben placed an arm around her. "I'd much rather go home and meet my new niece or nephew than dance."

Maggie warmed at Ben's thoughtful words to his sister-in-law. Yet it also brought a renewed sadness.

Rebecca having the baby moved Ben one step closer to leaving. Maggie forced the thought from her mind. She needed to concentrate on the situation at hand, not moon over something that hadn't yet occurred. The group moved outside. She held Jennie's hand, not wanting the little girl to get lost in the shuffle. Frank agreed to drop Mrs. Morrow off at the boardinghouse since it was on the way. He'd take Dr. Miller a few doors down to pick up his medical bag before they joined the others back at the general store.

"Why don't you let Jennie stay the night with me?" Mrs. Morrow suggested. "We can walk over in the morning after breakfast and meet her new sibling."

Rebecca thanked Mrs. Morrow. She and Maggie set off for home with Ben.

In the wagon, Rebecca leaned over and murmured, "I was worried with all Jennie's been through how she'd handle the trauma of me being in labor." She screwed up her face and then breathed quickly in and out several times, panting like an overheated dog. "Ooh, that was a doozey."

Maggie linked her arm through Rebecca's. "You'll be fine. I won't leave you for a second."

"I know." Her friend grimaced. "It hit hard last time but not nearly as quick. Dr. Miller warned me a second baby comes faster than the first."

"I'll get you home in plenty of time," Ben said. "Why, you may have this one so fast that Maggie and I will head back to the barn dance. We'll probably miss only half a dozen songs at most."

He winked at Rebecca, who threw a hard elbow into his side. He grunted and both women laughed.

Ben moaned. "You've injured me for life."

Rebecca snorted. "The weaker sex is by far the

stronger, Ben Morgan. That's just one puny elbow in your ribs. Try going through childbirth."

"No, ma'am, thank you all the same. God knew what He was doing when He set it up for women to be the bearer of children."

They arrived at the general store a few minutes later. Ben assisted Maggie from the buckboard. He turned and then lifted Rebecca into his arms. She was in visible pain and moaning loudly.

Maggie's heart did a flip-flop once again at his kindness. She watched Ben sweep his sister-in-law off her feet and carry her inside. She quickly hitched the horse to the railing and followed them upstairs.

Rebecca began barking orders. Maggie thought she must sound like the drill sergeant Frank had served under during the war. He'd entertained her with stories of the man, acting out situations that caused her to laugh herself senseless.

She stifled the laughter that bubbled up so she wouldn't hurt her friend's feelings. Maggie and Ben scurried around, boiling water and gathering plenty of clean towels. Dr. Miller arrived in jovial spirits. He declared birthing babies his absolute favorite thing to do.

Maggie noticed that Frank looked a little green around the gills. She pulled him aside. "You don't have to stay, Frank. You got Dr. Miller here in plenty of time. Your job's done for the night."

"I want to be here," Frank confided. "I need to know Rebecca and the baby will be all right."

"You'll be good company for Ben. I'll keep you two posted on her progress."

She joined the doctor in Rebecca's bedroom. Rebecca held out a hand for her to take. Maggie discovered that her friend had suddenly gained the strength of ten men. Since she was just now out of the compress from the wrist injury, she hoped the bone-squeezing grip Rebecca had on her wouldn't reinjure her, much less break any bones.

Something between a groan and a scream poured from Rebecca at an ear-piercing level. Maggie's thoughts flashed immediately to Mrs. Morrow's foresight in having Jennie accompany her back to the boardinghouse. Maggie wished she were with them right about now. She had never witnessed a birth before and wasn't sure if she wanted to at this moment.

Yet a short time later, Rebecca was all smiles. Dr. Miller assisted Maggie in washing the baby. She wrapped the infant in a flannel blanket and held the small bundle close for a moment before Rebecca beckoned for her to come back to the bed.

She placed the baby in Rebecca's arms. Her friend's hair had come loose during the birthing process, so Maggie brushed the blonde curls, smoothing and spreading them about Rebecca's shoulders. She also wiped Rebecca's face with a dampened cloth.

Dr. Miller gave a few instructions to both women and then proclaimed, "My work here is done. I'm heading home for a celebratory brandy."

Maggie escorted him to the outer room where Ben and Frank both anxiously paced. They stopped cold in their tracks as she and Dr. Miller entered.

Smiling at the two men, she announced, "Rebecca is ready to see you now. Follow me."

Dr. Miller waved and said, "I'll let myself out." He paused and observed the two men. "Put smiles on your faces, gentlemen. You both look like death warmed over. You haven't done any of the work tonight. Rebecca is full of happiness. You should be, as well."

He took his leave as both men glanced at each other and then back at Maggie.

"Is she really fine?" Ben asked.

"We thought she was dying," Frank added. "I've never heard such awful noises coming from an animal, much less a lady like Rebecca."

Maggie put a hand on her hip. "Men!"

She turned, opened the bedroom door, and walked through it. The room was bathed in soft light from candles.

Rebecca sat serenely in the bed, her new child mewling softly in her arms. She motioned to the men, who hesitated in the doorway. "Well, don't just stand there. Come meet Charles Adam Morgan."

16

Ben couldn't believe how much time and effort it took to care for a baby. Rebecca was up all hours of the night with little Charles, or Charlie, as they all called him from the start. She named the child after her older brother who'd died in the war. The two of them had been close.

"Adam and I spoke often of naming a boy after Charles," Rebecca told them that night shortly after the baby was born. "My brother and my husband will now live on through this little man. My sweet Charlie."

He found solace in the fact that the infant was a male. He was proud that Rebecca used Adam's name as the child's middle one. She reassured him on several occasions that Charlie would grow up knowing everything she could tell him about Adam. Her husband's picture was prominently displayed on the mantel. Charlie even visited his papa's grave when he was only a week old. They also had a long talk about her family's future.

"Rebecca, I'm not sure if we'll be able to find someone to merely help you run the store out here in Easton. If it were in Abilene proper, where there's a larger population to draw from, I don't think we'd have as much of a problem."

He paused, waiting to be sure he had Rebecca's attention as she cooed over the baby. "For someone to do so much work, he'll want to make it his own. Leave his mark on things."

"I'll tell you now that I tend to agree with you." She looked up at him. "I'd wanted to keep the store in the family so Charlie and Jennie would have a legacy from Adam. I realize I don't have the time to be as active as I'd like in keeping the business not only going, but thriving. If it were only Jennie, that wouldn't be a problem. With the baby now, I have to realign my priorities. He does take up quite a bit of time."

"Would you like me to pursue finding a buyer?" he asked.

She nodded as she smiled down at Charlie. "Yes. Selling is what's best. Adam and I built up a small nest egg for a rainy day. Between that and what I will make on selling the store and its inventory, we can be comfortable in Easton for quite a while."

She stopped and swallowed, as if something pained her. "Ben, I want to ask you something. I don't want to hurt your feelings because I know how much you loved Adam, but I also have to think about my future and the future of our children."

He looked at her steadily, suspecting what was on her mind. "Go on."

"Big city life isn't for me. It's certainly not where I want to raise my children. My sister offered to have us move to Cincinnati and live with her family. I'd prefer not to do that."

"Is there anyone else?" Ben asked. "Another member of your family you'd rather live with?"

"I'm sure you're thinking of my parents. I don't think that's a good idea. Mama is someone who fusses too much over me. She'd treat me as if I were still a child if we moved in with them. And Daddy? I love him with all my heart. He's a good man and an excellent preacher, but he is very old-fashioned and quite austere."

"I see."

Rebecca stood, bouncing Charlie as she moved around the room. "I want my children to be able to laugh. To enjoy life. I want to teach them right from wrong. To love one another and others around them. But I don't want religion crammed down their throats day and night. The way I was raised."

"Adam wouldn't have liked that," Ben said.

She eyed him carefully as she continued. "I know. It's what would happen if I moved back in with them. Papa is controlling and very, very strict. He thinks life is all about rules and regulations. There's no such thing as an exception. Mama would smother me and the children."

"I understand," he said.

She smiled at him. "I don't think I was my true self until Adam came along. With him, I felt free as a bird to be the best me I could be. We lived. We laughed. We loved. We learned. Together. That's not the kind of marriage my parents have. I don't want to go back to that house with no way out."

She handed Charlie to Ben. He looked down at the baby, in awe of his tiny perfection.

"I want the best for Charlie. For you and Jennie, too. So if staying in Easton is what you want, we'll make it happen. I do think we should go ahead and start building a house for you, though. You won't be able to live above the store after we find a buyer. The new owner will want to move in, especially if he has a family that needs to be settled."

"That's the other thing I wanted to speak with you about," Rebecca said. "I've lived out West my entire life, so my sensibilities are grounded in reality. I know with your Boston upbringing that you may think a bit differently from me on certain matters."

"Like what?" he asked.

She sat, leaning forward, hands folded neatly on her lap. "Women are scarce here. A single woman is in high demand. I've known women who married less than two weeks after they've buried a husband, before he's even cold in the ground. I not only wish to remain in Easton, Ben, but I plan to remarry."

He tensed at her carefully chosen words and tried to still the anger drumming within him. His heart told him that Rebecca would do the right thing and not be disloyal to Adam's memory. He himself had already thought about her situation and knew what she would reveal next even before she said it.

She stood and looked him squarely in the eye. "I'm going to marry Frank Stansel. I don't love him. Yet. But I think love will grow between us. Frank's never married. I'm not sure why. I don't know if there's a girl back East that broke his heart. I'm not sure exactly why he came to Kansas and landed here in Easton after the war."

"You could ask Maggie," he said. "She knows him better than we do."

"Frank's a good man," Rebecca said. "A much better man than most. He's kind and considerate. Steady as a rock. He was a good friend to Adam and he's been the same to me since Adam's death. Frank needs a family. I've got a ready-made one for him."

He nodded. "I do think Frank has feelings for you."

"I agree. I've felt him looking at me lately. I've enjoyed spending time with him since Maggie's been here. Having her nearby has been the perfect excuse for him to come around often. I think my future lies with Frank. I don't know how soon or when that future will begin, but I needed to share with you what's on my mind. You're my family, Ben. You'll always be family. I wanted to make sure this was fine by you."

He smiled down at Charlie, who now slept nestled in his arms. Already he could see from the baby's mouth and chin that he would favor Adam. "Do you think Frank will take to another man's children?"

"I do. If I didn't, then he wouldn't be the man for me. I believe he's smart enough to understand how I'll always love Adam with a part of my heart reserved for him alone."

She sat again in her chair. "So, as far as starting to build us a house? Let's hold off on that, Ben. If I plan to be with Frank, I'd like his input on the place that we make our home. Let's concentrate on finding a buyer for Morgan's General Store. And yes, I'll insist the name remain the same as part of the sales agreement. I want to walk by with Jennie and Charlie and be able to point out to them the place their daddy built from scratch. I want them to take pride in what Adam accomplished."

"They will. And I think you won't find a better man than Frank Stansel."

Rebecca stood. "I think that Frank will make a wonderful father. To them and any children we might have together. He's been such a pussycat with both of my kids. I think it only right that he has some of his own, as well."

Ben admired his sister-in-law so much in that moment. She'd started a new life with the love of her life.

They'd created a wonderful foundation in Easton, with the store and Jennie. Yet that practical Western woman in her knew when it was time to lay sentimentality aside and do what was best for herself and her children.

"Frank's going to be a lucky man," Ben said and grinned. "Even if he doesn't know it yet."

BEN DECIDED to go into Abilene the next morning. He asked Maggie to watch the store for him. She was only too happy to help if he would post a letter for her in return.

"I'm going to put some advertisements into various newspapers," he said. "Rebecca's decided that selling the store would be best. A new owner will free her up to concentrate on the children without having to worry about inventory, ordering goods, and billing people. She can be a little tender-hearted. I know the bill-collecting end of things is a little tough on her."

"She told me she's ready to stay in Easton. Even after the store sells," Maggie said. "I guess she'll need to find a new place to live."

"About that." Ben paused. "How much has she told you regarding her future plans?"

She smiled widely. "You mean that she aims to make an honest man of Frank Stansel?"

"I guess you know after all."

Maggie sniffed. "Of course I know. We have no secrets between us. Rebecca and I are best friends for life now, as close as sisters ever could be. I'm glad she finally told you what's been on her mind." She paused. "You know, she still loves Adam."

"I do. But I understand her reasoning. I couldn't

ask for a better man to help raise Adam's children than Frank. He has a good heart. I wonder when he'll figure out that his future's already been planned for him."

She waved a hand in the air. "Oh, there's no need to bother him with those kinds of details just yet. When the time is right, either he or Rebecca will make their move."

"I agree. Thanks again for watching the store this morning."

He climbed into the buckboard and asked, "Can you think of anything else I might be able to pick up for you while I'm in Abilene?"

Maggie scrunched up her face in thought. Ben found her totally kissable in that moment but he kept his distance. He hadn't touched her—much less kissed her—since the night of the barn dance two weeks earlier. He decided he needed to put some distance into their physical relationship. He didn't want to break her heart upon leaving Easton. Seeing that Rebecca would be settled sometime in the near future, Ben realized his days in Easton were numbered.

Still, he'd visited with Maggie plenty of times. She came over to spell Rebecca from a crying Charlie or even work with Jennie. The two of them read together. Maggie had taught Jennie her letters and started helping her spell one-syllable words such as dog and cat. The more time Ben spent around Maggie, the harder he knew it would be to leave when that time came. He'd cut out anything physical between them as a way to start distancing himself from her.

So, first things first. He needed to find a buyer for the general store. He'd make sure Rebecca's personal life was in order. Then he needed to get back to business.

Gambling.

Funny, but he hadn't missed it nearly as much as he would have thought. Ever since he'd played his last hand in San Antone, cards had been the last thing on his mind. When he headed quickly out of town and joined up with the cattle drive just outside of Fort Worth, he didn't give gaming a thought.

Life on the cattle trail proved to be hard work, with sixteen- to eighteen-hour days. Although he was weary to the bone at the end of each day, the hard labor left him with a satisfaction that gambling never had. The same thing applied to running the general store in Easton. He took naturally to talking with the customers, learning their buying habits, anticipating the needs of the town as he placed orders for new merchandise.

In a short time, he inserted himself into the tight-knit community and found he really enjoyed being a part of it. Yet in the back of his mind, the image of Black Tex Lonnegan still lurked. How could he forget the gunslinger when he'd spied that wanted poster that Maggie borrowed from Frank? His blood froze as the picture of Black Tex peered back at him.

He'd quickly glanced over the contents of the poster, noting how many men Lonnegan had killed and the other crimes he'd committed. Lonnegan wanted him dead. Ben had no doubt in his mind that the gunfighter would continue the hunt until one or both of them were dead.

Black Tex was the kind of man that would see himself as an avenging angel. He'd bring justice down upon the head of his brother's murderer. All Ben had done was call the man out for cheating and then defended himself when the younger Lonnegan almost shot him dead.

Black Texas Lonnegan would shoot to kill first. The criminal would be hunting for Ben in bars and saloons or anywhere gaming tables existed. Going on the cattle drive was the last place the gunslinger might have looked for him. Even if Lonnegan had, Ben made sure to go by a different last name when he signed up with the trail boss.

He'd used his real name here in Easton. He had no reason to think Lonnegan would come to a small speck that barely made the Kansas map. Besides, everyone in town knew him as Adam's brother so a false name wasn't possible. Ben didn't want any wind of his being in Easton to reach Lonnegan. He couldn't risk putting Rebecca and the children in harm's way.

He certainly didn't want Maggie in the line of fire. Men like Black Tex Lonnegan wouldn't hesitate to use a loved one against Ben.

By God, Maggie *was* a loved one. The copper-haired beauty with the warm smile and womanly curves had become everything to him. Though he'd abruptly brought any kind of physical relationship to a halt, he yearned with every fiber in his being to love every inch of Maggie Rutherford. He would move heaven and earth for her.

Even die for her, if the need arose.

And Lonnegan, if he learned that, would use Maggie to make Ben pay. Then the criminal would use up Maggie herself, taking the light out of her eyes and the goodness from her soul.

He knew in his heart that to keep those he loved safe from harm's way, he had no choice except to leave Easton. He could support himself gambling as he journeyed out as far West as California. He might settle down to a quiet, solitary life. Under an assumed name. Farm a little. Raise some animals. Live off the land. Send money and letters back to Easton when he could.

He pictured himself going into a town. Maybe even a large city, such as San Francisco. He'd go to a bookstore and peer through the window, spying the latest Lud Madison dime novel on display. He'd venture in and pick up a copy, smiling to himself as he bought it because he knew the author. He'd take it home and pore over it, reading it again and again, hearing Maggie's voice in every line. He knew he would weep. For the missed opportunities. For having to leave the love of his life behind.

He shook himself from his reverie. Fortunately, Adam's horse seemed to know the way to Abilene, for he found himself almost there.

Ben's heart sank. The next time he came to Abilene, he'd catch a train and walk away from Maggie Rutherford.

For good.

17

Maggie typed *The End* and pulled the page from her typewriter. She couldn't believe she'd written her latest book so quickly. Of course, using Ben Morgan as inspiration for the dime novel's hero and cattle-drive boss spurred ideas left and right. She actually wound up trimming parts of the story, but she knew she could use those ideas in a future book.

She rotated her wrist clockwise and then counter-clockwise a few times. She had adopted the practice since the dressing came off and her wrist seemed good as new. She thought not having to write out the entire manuscript in longhand helped the recovery process. Her hand always cramped when she went on a writing spree in the past.

This time, she'd done the first half of the story by hand, and then typed the rest, once Marcus' gift to Lud Madison came in the mail. She knew her editor in New York would not only be grateful to see a manuscript completed this fast, but ecstatic that at least the typed portion of it was entirely legible.

Maggie never had the patience to work at her penmanship as most girls did. Archibald Posty sometimes struggled with her words on the page. Still, the editor usually interpreted correctly what she had written. She was certain he chalked up the poor cursive to being a man's handwriting.

That caused her to chuckle aloud. She wondered what Marcus would think when she revealed to him that Lud Madison was actually his little sister. At least she knew from his letter to Lud that Marcus deemed himself a fan of the dime novelist.

She thought about the letter she had Ben post in Abilene a few days ago. In it, Maggie told her brother that she'd halted her travels for a while and was visiting at length with Frank. She wondered if Marcus would make the connection that Lud Madison was also staying in Easton. She doubted it, deciding that her brother merely wrote Lud the letter. He didn't actually address the package to the author in Easton. His very efficient assistant would have taken care of that detail.

In her letter, Maggie had asked Marcus to come to Easton for a visit and to bring their attorney. Today's birthday was different from all those that came before it. In the back of her mind, Maggie christened October fifteenth of eighteen seventy-five as her own personal independence day.

The day she came into one hundred thousand dollars.

Rose Rutherford brought quite a fortune into her marriage with Henry Rutherford. This money had pumped up Rutherford House, allowing it to become one of the premier publishing houses in the country, as well as extending and modernizing the Rutherford mansion in Manhattan.

Still, Rose's father permitted his only child to keep control of a considerable amount of money, a sum that Henry Rutherford never touched. Their attorney,

Dudley Simpson, explained to Maggie over the years that her mother established a trust for her daughter upon her birth. Maggie would take control of the funds upon her twenty-fifth birthday.

And yet when she awoke this morning, she didn't feel any different.

She took pride in having supported herself this past year, with no help from Marcus. The income she earned as her alter ego gave her enough to live comfortably. She didn't have a clue what she would do with such immense wealth once it came into her possession. She also knew there had to be extensive paperwork to sign, and legal jargon that Mr. Simpson would interpret for her.

So, she'd asked Marcus to bring the man to Kansas with him. She knew they could take care of all the legal procedures and then send the lawyer back to New York. She wanted Marcus to stay a little longer. She missed her brother terribly. He would enjoy visiting with her and Frank. She couldn't wait to introduce him to everyone in Easton.

Once he was here, she would confess to Marcus that she was Lud Madison. She couldn't wait to see the look on his face.

Maggie placed the last manuscript page at the bottom of the pile and stretched her arms over her head, yawning broadly. She shifted in the chair, suddenly conscious of the garter pistol she'd slipped into her boot this morning.

She reached down and hiked up her skirt so she could see the small derringer poking out of her boot. While journeying throughout the West, Maggie wore the pistol for protection. Small in size, it contained ammunition for only two shots. The sporting gal she interviewed her first month during her travels insisted Maggie purchase one immediately.

"You never know when you might need it, honey," the painted lady told her. "The West is a wild place. You're zigzagging all around on your own, from what you say. Just make sure if you ever have to use it that your target's in close range. The short barrel makes it handy to conceal, but it's not accurate from a distance."

Maggie assured the woman she would purchase one that day and wear it. She had kept her promise every day, until the accident in Easton. With her wrist banged up, Maggie couldn't put on, much less pull off, her boots. She went back to wearing a more ladylike shoe. She simply carried the pistol in her reticule.

Under Frank's supervision, Easton seemed as safe as any place Maggie had visited. Eventually, she began leaving the derringer in her drawer at the boarding-house. Now that she could once again manipulate her boots without help, she felt almost naked without the gun. Today, she'd decided to start wearing it again.

You never knew when trouble might strike.

BEN OPENED the general store an hour early. A crowd would be expected over the next few hours. Frank had warned him that people would be coming from at least two counties over for the annual Easton Shooting Match. They'd likely want to stock up on supplies before or after the competition.

He let in the group of shoppers waiting at the door. They filled the place on this Saturday. He was thankful that Mrs. Morrow had volunteered to watch Charlie and Jennie so that Rebecca could help him at the counter. Maggie also circulated around, assisting customers in finding everything on their supply list and pointing out additional items she thought they might need.

Ben smiled as he watched her in action. He figured sales would double with her useful advice. Women took to her suggestions with thoughtful nods. Men practically drooled as they placed goods she recommended in their baskets.

Frank poked his head in the doorway. "Contest starts in fifteen minutes, so finish up, folks. You can always come back to shop. After my victory, that is."

The sheriff grinned broadly and tipped his hat before exiting the store.

"Frank's won the shooting match two years running," Rebecca informed Ben as he tallied a column of numbers. He quoted the total price due to a tall farmer in bib overalls.

The farmer paid and said, "Sheriff Stansel's the best shot I've ever seen. Me 'n' the missus wouldn't miss the shooting contest for the world." He nodded his thanks, gathered his supplies, and left.

Ben asked, "Who won previous contests before Frank?"

Rebecca laughed. "Frank started up the competition. He arrived in Easton three years ago last month. He started the shooting match three weeks later. People already look forward to it every year. It's mushroomed now. You'll see a few booths set up outside, with women selling everything from quilts to homemade pies and jars of jellies. George Creamer brought a few ponies last year and gave children rides for a penny. Three of Donald Smith's boys sold penny candy the first year. They decided they could make more money another way last year."

"Sounds like those boys got into some mischief."

She chuckled. "They bought several pies from women selling them and then took turns allowing other boys to smash pies in their face. For a price. They made good money until their mama heard about it and rounded them up. Who knows what those boys will get into this year?" She sighed. "I don't envy Frances having six children."

"What does it take to enter the shooting match?" Ben asked. "I was a fair shot in the war. I still carry my Colt from that time. I might be able to give Frank a run for his money."

Before he received an answer, shoppers swarmed the counter. Ben and Rebecca quickly added up prices and received their payment from the customers. Then in the space of five minutes, the store went from packed to deserted.

Maggie strolled over. "I'm glad business was booming."

"Thanks for your help," Rebecca said. "You really know how to push merchandise. How you got rid of that ugly dish set is beyond me. I'm grateful I don't have to look at it anymore."

Maggie shrugged. "My brother will tell you that I've always been able to sweet talk people. Do you mind if I head over to the match now?"

"Go ahead. We'll be right behind you. Don't let Frank start without us," Rebecca teased.

Maggie exited the store and Ben took a deep breath. "I suppose it'll pick back up once the contest ends?"

"Yes, but I think we've handled the worst of it. I'm going up to get Mrs. Morrow and the children. If you'll place the money in the safe, I'll lock up when we leave."

"That's actually where my Colt is. I wanted to keep it far from Jennie's curious hands. I know you've taught her not to touch guns but I've left it in there all the same. I'll retrieve it and see you out front."

Rebecca headed upstairs while Ben pulled the morning's take from the till and set it inside the safe in the storeroom. He removed his Colt revolver. The time to wear it again had arrived. The slow pace of Easton had lulled him into complacency. He knew his days here were numbered. He might as well get used to his holster and gun once more.

He strapped on the holster and checked the gun. He had come down late at night and cleaned it once a week so that the mechanism was in working order. He slid the revolver in and took a deep breath. Ben decided that he'd do his utmost to best Frank Stansel today. He was a much better shot than he'd let on to Rebecca. Even though Frank was the reigning champion, Ben felt he could take the sheriff. It was partly to make sure his skills were in shape.

But mostly to impress Maggie Rutherford.

He knew it was foolish but he wanted to squeeze a last little bit of attention from Maggie. He ached every time he looked at the woman. It took everything in his power not to sweep her off her feet each time he saw her. The urge to kiss her senseless grew stronger by the day, even more so since his lips hadn't brushed against hers in fourteen days now.

Not that he'd been counting.

Ben headed out and followed the crowds toward the edge of town. He spied Maggie's copper hair shining in the sun under her smart hat and went to join her. Her hazel eyes sparkled with what could only be mischief. He wondered what she'd been up to in the short time since they'd parted.

She greeted him and shivered. "I guess the Indian summer of the last few days is gone." She tightened the cream-colored shawl around her. "I think the temperature's dropped a good twenty degrees from yesterday."

Ben heard a crinkling as she moved. "What's that noise?"

Maggie bit her lower lip and opened her arms. Ben saw a number written on a piece of paper that was pinned to her dress front. "I decided to enter the shooting contest."

"Good Lord, Maggie. Why'd you do a thing like that?"

She frowned at him. "Ben Morgan, are you one of those men who think a woman's only good for baking and birthing babies?"

He cocked his head. "I didn't say that. Don't get your feathers all ruffled over nothing."

She sniffed. "You didn't have to. You're Boston-bred, even if you live in the West now. I've always found Boston men to be particularly pigheaded."

"I thought you were from New York."

Her lips turned up in a half-smile. "That doesn't mean I haven't known a few Boston men in my time."

Jealousy flared through him at her words. "I'm as open-minded as the next man, Boston or otherwise."

"But you don't think I should enter the shooting contest, do you?"

Without warning, Maggie reached over and yanked Ben's revolver from his holster. She spun, twisted, and twirled it like lightning before holding it up to study.

"A Colt Army. 1860. Single-action. Six-shot weapon. Has a rear sight that's a notch in the hammer but you can only see it when it's cocked. Accurate up to seventy-five yards. Maybe a hundred—but only if you're a really good shot."

She whirled it around again and slid it back into Ben's holster before he could react. Then she gave him a blazing, wickedly sinful smile that made his heart lurch.

"You are a woman with many secrets, Maggie."

She tossed her head, her hat tilting slightly askew. "You've only scratched the surface, Ben Morgan. Now, why don't you go sign up and see if you can best me? It's two dollars to enter." She motioned him away with her hands. "Shoo. Hope you're in time. I'd love to see another couple of bucks added to my prize money."

Not one to back down from a challenge, Ben nodded curtly at her. After asking a few people where to go, he made his way to the registration table. He plunked down the entry fee and signed his name on the sheet of paid contestants. Glancing over it, he noticed Maggie was the only female entrant.

An hour later, the field winnowed to Morton Joad, Frank, Maggie, and Ben. Morton was more lucky than smart, and at eighty yards and a wind that increased by the minute, he bowed out.

Frank made his shot and then passed the silver-plated Colt Peacemaker over to Maggie. They'd shared the gun throughout each round. Ben knew this model had more power and was less likely to misfire than his own weapon, which was over a decade older. The Peacemaker's range of a hundred yards would best him if the contest went on much longer.

And it did.

Both Ben and Maggie made the ninety-yard shot, but Frank missed. The crowd gasped in surprise that the previous champion fell. Ben proved unsuccessful when five more yards were added. All Maggie needed to do was make her shot.

She stepped up confidently and shouted, "Move it back five more."

Dr. Miller hesitated. Maggie stood her ground. Finally, the physician acquiesced to her demand.

Maggie raised the Peacemaker with her left hand, aimed, and fired.

18

"That was a victory for all women, Maggie."

Maggie squeezed Mrs. Morrow's hand. "Thank you for the compliment. I hope all the females in Easton know they share a little bit of this victory with me."

Frank shook his head ruefully. "I always knew you were a better shot than me. I hoped you'd have an off day, especially with the wind picking up halfway through the competition."

She looked around. "It's died down now. And the sun's come out again, warming things up. This Kansas weather is so unpredictable."

"I'll take this over all the snow we'll see in a few months' time." Rebecca bounced Charlie in her arms.

"You knew Maggie could shoot well?" Ben asked.

"Maggie pretty much does everything well." Frank grinned at her, and she gave a small curtsy. Jennie watched her and then imitated the gesture, as those gathered around laughed.

"Maggie did everything Marcus and I did, growing up. She was a scrawny little thing but she never gave up. We had riding and shooting lessons. Maggie trailed along until the instructors let her try. She also took dancing and music lessons. Marcus and I stayed far away from that. The three of us even wound up taking fencing from some crazy Frenchman."

Frank brightened. "Remember when you took your foil—or was it your saber?—and tried to slice the buttons from Denby's jacket?"

Maggie laughed at the memory. "Denby was—is—our family butler. I wanted to show off a bit," she explained. "Poor Denby barely knew what happened. One moment his jacket was buttoned properly, and the next..."

"A few buttons did plop to the ground," Frank finished. "I still remember the look of shock on his face. He never lost his temper, though."

Frank raised his eyebrows, and in a haughty British accent proclaimed, "Miss Margaret, please assist me in collecting my buttons. Remember that you've added to Mrs. Smith's workload with your actions today, as she will have to sew these on to my coat again."

Maggie added, "I learned my lesson that day. Mrs. Smith actually made me sew the buttons back on. I hated sewing. I'd rather be running or reading or doing a thousand other things." She smiled. "I still hate to sew or do any kind of needlework to this day."

"Well, today is your day, Maggie, as the champion shooter of Easton," Rebecca proclaimed. "How do you plan on celebrating your victory?"

She glanced around at the crowd of people and the activity in the streets. "What I'd really like is a little peace and quiet after all the noise of shooting for so many rounds."

Ben spoke up. "I feel exactly the same way. Since the weather's warmed up a little, how would you like to take a drive?" He stopped and looked at Rebecca.

"Oh. Maybe later. We probably need to head back and open the store again."

"Nonsense," Rebecca said. "Most everyone is standing about visiting now. I can handle any shoppers that come by if Mrs. Morrow won't mind coming with us and watching over the children while they nap."

"I'd love to, dear." The older woman leaned over and kissed one of Charlie's fists. "I can't seem to get enough of this little man."

Frank took Jennie's hand and offered Rebecca his arm. "Then I'll escort all you lovely ladies back to the store. If I'm in your company, it'll cut down on the catcalls and cutting remarks tossed my way."

Rebecca took Frank's arm. "Would a slice of peach pie help you deal with the criticism and loss of your title?"

Maggie saw Frank's eyes light up at the prospect of pie. "Save the reigning champion a piece, Rebecca. I'll stop by for it after our drive."

She and Ben strolled down the street together and caught up with Morton Joad to let him know they were taking Prince from his stables and one of Joad's carts from his livery for a drive.

He pumped her hand enthusiastically. "Never saw a woman who could shoot like that, Miss Maggie."

She smiled broadly. "You should see me box."

Morton's mouth fell open. "You're a boxer?"

"Well, I took boxing lessons," she said modestly. "I haven't had the need to put my knowledge into action but you never know. A lady needs to always be prepared."

Morton wagged a finger at her. "You are a dangerous woman, Maggie Rutherford. Remind me to mind my P's and Q's around you."

Ben soon had Prince hitched to a buggy. He took a blanket sitting on top of a bale of hay and tossed it in the back. "A cool front may move in with the way the weather's been acting lately. This might come in handy."

They left town driving east. Ben pointed out that the western road to Abilene might be more active so he would take the opposite way. "I'm like you. A little peace and quiet is what the doctor ordered. I hope we don't see another soul for miles."

Maggie pursed her lips, trying not to laugh. "Sounds as if you've missed a little sleep lately."

"That's just the half of it." He let out a rush of air. "Charlie's up all hours of the day and night. I thought babies were quiet little things. Just sat there and gurgled and cooed and slept most of the time. Not our Charlie. He's noisy and constantly needs something. I didn't know a little fellow like that could take up so much time and energy. He's not even a month old yet, and the center of attention and main topic of every conversation."

"Imagine what he'll be like when he's walking and talking."

He paused. "You know all this. You've stopped by quite a bit to visit Rebecca and spend time with Jennie since his birth. I honestly don't know how you're getting your book writing done."

Maggie beamed. "I finished my latest work in progress yesterday. The writing, the cover, and all the illustrations. It was my present to myself."

"Present?" He turned and looked at her. "Maggie Rutherford. You've been holding out on us. Was it your birthday?"

"Yes," she admitted. "I've never really gone overboard in celebrating one. Oh, Mrs. Smith would always arrange to have Cook make a cake for me. But my father didn't really acknowledge it. Or me, for that matter. He was one of those men who felt any female child was a waste of space."

"Then I'm sorry," Ben said softly. "My remarks about you entering the shooting match must've stung doubly because of his treatment of you."

She blinked rapidly, willing no tears to be shed over memories of her father or his lack of interest in her. "It's all behind me now. Marcus more than made up for any inattention." She brightened. "My brother will be paying a visit to Easton shortly. I haven't seen him in over a year, plus he'll be delighted to catch up with Frank. They are brothers of the heart if not in blood."

"Then I look forward to meeting him."

They rode in companionable silence for a few miles. Maggie sensed that this might be the last time she would be alone with Ben. Would Marcus even arrive in time to meet him?

A cool breeze suddenly whipped up, chilling her. Maggie pulled her shawl about her. "Seems like we've hit that cool air from this morning again." She glanced up at the sky and sniffed the air. "It's darker now. I think those are rain clouds gathering up ahead."

He gazed toward the horizon. "You could be right. Might be time to head back." He slowed Prince from his trot and turned the cart so they could return along the same route.

As they drove toward home, she looked over her shoulder. The sky darkened and then turned green as thunderclouds blocked the weak sunlight. Then without warning, the wind died. An eerie silence blanketed the day.

Ben pulled up on the reins and stopped the buggy. "Do you hear that?"

No sound carried on the prairie. No birds sang. No crickets chirped. It was as if nature held its breath.

She shivered. "It's so strange. Ouch! My ears!"

He grimaced. "Mine, too. They're popping like crazy. The air pressure's dropped. Do you feel the difference?"

She nodded, holding her hands over her ears. "What could cause something like this?"

Dust whirled about them as the wind picked up again. The rain began in earnest. One minute, only a few drops hit. Seconds later, the rain pelted them with tremendous force.

He reached back and yanked the blanket forward. He tossed it into Maggie's lap. "Put this over you. It'll offer some protection."

She shook open the blanket and pulled it over her head. The sky darkened to a greenish black now. More than rain chilled her. She looked behind them and caught sight of a funnel cloud forming in the distance.

"Ben, behind us!" She pointed as hail started peppering them along with the rain. Other clouds quickly moved toward the funnel-shaped one.

"Dammit! It's a twister."

She heard as well as sensed the rushing air about them. She'd listened to tales of twisters—violent, destructive, whirling winds that progressed in a narrow strip over land. They could wipe out everything in their paths.

"We've got to take cover," he hollered as the noise picked up. "Over there! The Rucker place."

Maggie looked to her left. She saw a small barn and even smaller house sitting about a quarter mile off the road. She recalled Rebecca telling her that Mrs.

Rucker decided to leave the homestead just before the barn dance in September. Her husband's death earlier in the summer, along with her two daughters being grown and gone, convinced the widow to move to Abilene to live with her sister. No one had bought the property in the short time it had been vacated.

Ben pulled up on the reins and jumped down from the buggy. He motioned Maggie over as he quickly loosened a nervous Prince from the traces. She flung the blanket off and joined him.

"It's faster to ride. We don't have much time."

He leaped on the horse and lifted Maggie up in front of him. He kicked the skittish horse. They took off, flying across the empty crop land. They reached the barn. Maggie slid off the gelding. Ben jumped down and took tight hold of the reins. She lifted her skirts and ran to throw open the door to the abandoned barn. She glanced over her shoulder and saw the funnel cloud growing closer.

They entered the dim barn. Ben hurriedly led his horse into the small, single stall and shut the gate. They both surveyed the interior. They needed to find a more secure place to take shelter. If the tornado turned this way, the entire barn could be lifted from the ground in a single swoop, killing them in the process.

"The root cellar!" Maggie shouted over the howling noise of the wind and rain beating on the roof. "Rebecca said that Mrs. Rucker always talked about putting her vegetables there to keep them from spoiling in the summer and freezing during winter. Her canning, too. It's got to be big enough to shelter us."

"Should be next to the house. In the ground," Ben yelled. "Let's go!"

They ran from the barn toward the house. The sky darkened to look like night. She spied the wooden door and grabbed his hand. "I see it!" she cried.

They made their way to it, while the wind threatened to bowl them over. Ben leaned down and flung back the door. He reached inside. "Ladder's here. Climb down. Fast!"

Maggie looked into the black hole. Her insides tilted as if she were a rag doll. Sweat broke out along her hairline. She froze, still as a statue.

Ben yelled something at her. She turned to look at him.

"I can't. Go. Down there. No."

He glared at her. "Do not put a spoke in this wheel, Maggie Rutherford. This is do or die—and I don't plan on us dying today."

Her teeth chattered, banging together like a boy pounding a drum. Blood rushed to her ears. Nausea punched her gut. Dizziness exploded inside her head at the same time.

Suddenly, his arms wrapped around her like a vise. He propelled her closer to the blackness. She squeezed her eyes shut. She couldn't bear to keep them open any longer. He hoisted her down. She fell to her knees on cool, damp earth.

The trap door clanged shut, the reverberation echoing in her mind. She hunched on the ground, whimpering. Her eyes flew open unwillingly. Darkness filled the small space even as the space in her chest shrank. She couldn't breathe. Couldn't speak.

She would die here in this darkness.

And Ben would never know she loved him.

19

Ben bounded onto the ladder and scrambled down a couple of rungs. He pulled the door shut and found a bolt to slide across it. He prayed it would hold as he scrambled down the few remaining steps of the creaking ladder. The pungent scent of fresh dirt rose around him. He reached out, totally blind in the darkness. He touched Maggie's skirts. He moved closer to her, finding her crouched like a small kitten, all tucked up in a tight ball, her limbs bundled under her, bustle high in the air.

"Maggie," he whispered. "I'm here." He hesitated a moment. Then he stroked a hand along her arched back.

A strangled sound emerged from her, half gasp, half choked. In an instant, it hit him.

She was terrified of the dark.

He thought back to when she'd injured her wrist her first day in Easton. She'd awoken that night in a dark, strange room and screamed. It was the most blood-chilling sound he had ever heard voiced by a human. He'd tried his best to comfort her. She'd revealed to him how she couldn't sleep without a candle ever since she'd been accidentally locked up in her family's cellar overnight.

Now they found themselves in the same situation. This time she was an adult.

Still, he could only imagine the fear tearing at her. She'd explained how she panicked in the dark. Severe physical symptoms tore at her body until she couldn't even breathe.

A keening noise suddenly filled the small space. The wail pierced his soul in its mournful terror. Instantly he leaned over her, his body a protective shell. She began rocking, swaying back and forth, and he moved with her. The motion became more violent and Ben knew he needed to contain her.

He wrapped his arms around her and somehow lifted her, falling back. He scooted to the closest wall and leaned against it. He spread his legs wide and slipped her between them, then twisted and pulled her closer until she rested within his arms.

She clawed at his shirtfront, burying her face in his chest. Her nails dug into his flesh. Sobs poured from her. He rocked her as if she were Charlie, murmuring soothing nonsense to calm her as the wind howled above them.

The door to the root cellar vibrated and pulsed. It began flapping wildly. He held Maggie tightly, knowing he would do whatever it took to protect her. The wind continued to roar like a caged lion, the rain punishing, the noise deafening. How long it went on, he couldn't say. He continued to cradle her, whispering to her, reassuring her they would live.

Then a calm descended, quick as a match blown out. He knew they'd ridden out the raging storm. Together, they had lived through a Great Plains twister.

He took a deep breath and released it slowly. He began to stroke her hair.

Her hat, long gone, allowed him to do so unhindered. He found that pins fell as he pushed his fingers deeper, massaging her scalp, comforting her as best he could. The long tresses fell about her. Ben leaned in and inhaled the lilac scent they bore.

Her mouth found his.

His body trembled as the hunger and heat took hold of them. Everything around them ceased to exist. What was important was her touch, her taste, the feel of their tongues dancing faster and faster, spiraling out of control.

His arms tightened around Maggie as her nails dug deeper into him, raking down his chest. His mouth moved to her neck. The sweetness of it created a raging need in him. He kept his right arm snug around her waist as his left came around, brushing her breast, then kneading it.

She moaned, this time in pleasure. He worked a few buttons of her blouse loose. His fingers slid inside and rubbed the soft flesh.

She drew a sharp breath and whispered his name. She released his shirt. He sensed her fingers unbuttoning the rest of her tailored white blouse. She wiggled in his lap. A soft curse passed her lips. He realized what she wanted and helped lift her blouse from her skirt. He slid it off her shoulders and down her arms.

He tossed it aside. His lips dropped to her collarbone, planting delicate kisses. She fumbled with his shirt buttons. He allowed her to do so. He cupped her face in his hands. He kissed her deeply, then heard her sigh. Cool air hit his chest when she fanned open the shirt.

Ben broke the kiss long enough to shrug out of his shirt and quickly returned to her mouth. His hands cupped her full breasts. Her chemise stood in his way. His thumbs circled her breasts, the nipples standing at attention through the thin material.

"Ben Morgan, get this detestable chemise off me now," she growled. "Rip it if you have to!"

He chuckled low and did her bidding.

His mouth searched in the darkness. He found her nipple, his tongue encircling, teasing. Her hands crept into his hair and clutched it. She pulled him nearer to her. She gave that throaty laugh, the one he loved to hear. He pictured her, head tossed back, smile wide.

"Ben?"

He heard her voice but couldn't stop himself. The velvet skin under his hands was smooth as silk. He kissed one breast thoroughly, then the other.

"Ben."

Her tone was more insistent now. He broke away and ran a lazy tongue up her neck to her mouth. He needed another taste and kissed her hard, knowing he needed to stop soon before things went beyond his control.

"Ben!"

He broke the kiss.

Maggie's fingers dug into his shoulders, her face an inch from his. "Something's roiling inside me. I'm fluttery. I can't breathe. There's a throbbing that's building. I need something but I don't know what. You do. So, do it."

"No."

She was a virgin. Their time together had come to an end. He refused to use her and then leave, the way so many men would have done.

Her grip tightened on him. "Don't leave this as unfinished business between us, Ben Morgan." Her voice broke. "Please. Don't."

"Maggie, I—"

"Don't Maggie me," she snarled. "I know what I'm asking. I want this, Ben. I *need* this. I want *you*. On those nights, years from now, I want to remember this moment, this now, this time. That it was ours. It belonged to *us*. No one else."

She leaned in and brushed her lips tenderly against his. "Please. Love me, Ben. Give me a memory so strong I'll never forget you."

And so he did.

MAGGIE'S EYES SLOWLY OPENED, as if she'd been drugged with too much laudanum. Lethargy weighed down her bones. A delicious warmth encircled her.

Then she realized that she lay in Ben's arms. They nestled together. Her backside pressed against his front. His arm rested around her waist, holding her tightly to him.

The silence enveloped them, as did the dark. Her mouth opened, no sound coming out. Her lips curled in a smile. She wasn't afraid. She lay on the ground. In the dark. And no fear ran through her. She sighed happily.

"You're awake."

"Mmm." It was about all she could manage.

He turned her toward him and kissed her. The kiss was long and full of a wistful yearning. She understood.

And it didn't bother her. At least not yet. Every limb in her body oozed satisfaction. Ben Morgan not only was heavenly to look at, but he'd proved to be an excellent lover. She wished they had more time together but she also understood his need to move on to a new place.

She experienced that same need to escape her life in New York. She'd felt trapped, as if she'd go semi-crazy. Her new life as a Western woman allowed her to be in charge of herself and she cherished that independence.

"Thank you," she said, when he ended the kiss.

"You're welcome," he replied softly.

"I'm not afraid anymore."

"I'm glad."

"You did that for me. I'll be eternally grateful. You'll never know how wonderful it is to find the fear gone. Vanished. I don't know if I'll ever be afraid again."

He chuckled. "Of course, you will. Mrs. Morrow will go on the warpath about something. That's always something to fear. You might cross a rattler and have a close call. Your editor might not like your next book. There'll always be something to fear, Maggie. You know now that you can conquer those fears."

He squeezed her hand and sat up. "Might as well see what damage the twister did."

She heard rustling and knew he was dressing. She wondered how much time had passed after they fell asleep making love.

Love.

She wished she'd told Ben she loved him, but she sensed he wouldn't cotton to those words. Love meant promises—and staying around to keep them. She knew he could do neither. Because of that, she'd held her tongue and luxuriated in the sensation of him inside her, of their joining together as one.

She doubted she'd ever do something like this

again. She couldn't imagine feeling the same way toward any other man as she did Ben.

That was fine. She was a self-reliant woman. She would continue to make her own way in the world. Even if that world was one without the man she loved.

She heard a shuffling and the stairs creaking. He unbolted and pushed back the trap door. His low whistle told her things weren't as they left them when the door closed them inside the root cellar.

"Roof's gone and one side of the barn." He paused. "The rest of the barn actually looks like it is still standing."

She heard the relief in his voice.

"I'm going to see if Prince survived. If I can get near him after him being spooked in the worst way, I'd like to try and ride him back to town if we can."

She found the wadded up chemise and wrapped what was left of it around her. She assured herself that no one would expect her to look as if she'd stepped off a band-box after surviving a twister. She placed her blouse on top, fastening the buttons and tucking it into the waist of the skirt she still wore, along with her boots. They'd been in too much a hurry to rid her of those in the dark.

Yet, Ben had taken his time with her, slowing their pace when she wanted to race. He helped her relish the new feelings and sensations. She moved toward the short ladder and climbed from the cellar.

The buggy hadn't survived the storm. Ben mounted the horse and pulled Maggie up in front of him. They rode about three miles until they came to the outskirts of Easton.

Or what was left of Easton.

20

Maggie's heart hurt as Ben stopped the horse. Neither of them spoke as they stared at the rubble in the moonlight. Small to begin with, only half of the town remained.

"Looks like the twister swept in and veered off there."

Her gaze followed the direction he pointed. The East side of the main thoroughfare had been totally destroyed. She drew a quick breath.

"How many have been killed? And who? Oh, Ben, I can't stand to think of it."

"Don't go there, Maggie," he warned her. "We don't know if anyone's been hurt, much less killed. Keep your head."

She glared at him. "Are you made of stone, Ben Morgan? Look at the damage that tornado caused. You have loved ones in this town! What if..." She choked on the words.

He gave her a squeeze. "No one knows that better than I do," he said quietly. "I've lost family before. It tears me up inside to think it's happened again. But we don't know anything yet. Hope for the best."

And prepare for the worst, she thought.

He flicked the reins and the horse started up again slowly. As they came closer, dread washed over her as the path of destruction became clearer. No smithy stood on the edge of town to greet them. It and the livery were gone, as if the two buildings never existed. Scattered fragments of rock were all that remained of Frank's jail.

Maggie dug her fingernails into the palm of her hands. *Not Frank*, she thought. *Please, God. Not Frank. Not Rebecca and the children. Please.*

Ben led the horse over a couple of silent blocks. No movement. No living person greeted them. Maggie burst into tears when she saw the general store still standing. His arm tightened around her waist and she heard his sigh of relief.

He dismounted and held his hands up to her. He pulled her from the horse and hugged her to him.

"Thank God!"

They turned and saw Rebecca leaning out the upstairs window. Tears streamed down her face. She ducked back inside. Within a minute she ran from inside the store to greet them, crunching along the shattered glass lying in the street. She threw herself at them. They clung to each other in relief.

"The children?" Ben asked. "Frank?"

"Fine, they're fine. We're all fine." Rebecca wiped at her eyes with the apron she wore around her waist. "We've been so worried about the two of you. Where were you when it struck?"

"Near the Rucker place, heading back toward town," Maggie told her. "We took shelter in the root cellar. It was a little cramped. The smell of fresh soil will never be as sweet as it was today."

Rebecca hugged her again. "I had awful visions of you being blown away. I've heard tales of cattle being lifted into the sky and dumped miles away. Plows and cows, too."

"That may have happened to the buggy I rented. We never saw a trace of it." Relief shone in Ben's eyes and rang in his voice. "At least Prince came out of it without a scratch on him, else we'd have had a bit of a walk back into town."

Frank appeared in the doorway, holding Charlie in his arms. Jennie raced by him and ran to them. Ben leaned down and swept her into his arms.

"There's my best girl," he told her. "I was wondering where you were, Punkin."

The child beamed at him as Frank made his way over. He handed Charlie to Rebecca and he crushed Maggie in a bear hug. He turned and did the same with Ben.

"Don't ever scare us like that again." Frank warned them. "Else I'll have to arrest you."

"And where would you keep us since you don't have a jail any longer?"

Frank burst out laughing. "Leave it to you, Maggie, to look on the bright side of things." He sobered. "It's hard. Seeing my town torn asunder. My jail gone. Everything gutted in less than a minute." He paused, sorrow crossing his face. "We lost some good folks today, including the new Baptist minister and his wife. And poor Morton Joad. He died of a heart attack, God rest his soul. We were trying to get him out from under his collapsed livery building. His leg was crushed. Doc says his heart just gave out on him."

"Morton was a generous soul," Rebecca added. "Willing to lend anyone a helping hand. He'll be missed in Easton. They all will."

"What can we do?" Maggie asked, looking around. "It's so quiet, it's eerie."

"Most folks had left and gone back to their homes by the time the twister hit," Frank told them. "After it blew through, everyone poured out into the streets. We worked until dark, saving what could be saved, trying to find lost animals and account for everyone in Easton. We'll start again at first light tomorrow."

"Count Maggie and me in," Ben said. "We might not be permanent residents here, but I know we both care about this town. We'll do whatever it takes to help put things back together."

"Let's get you inside. You look like you could stand to clean up." Rebecca said. "Maggie, you'll need to stay here tonight. Mrs. Morrow's got a crowd at her place. She invited back several people who had nowhere to go. In fact, after she feeds everyone, some of them are coming back to the general store to bed down for the night."

"I'll run over and let her know that Maggie and Ben made it back in one piece," Frank added.

"I'll have supper ready by the time you get back," Rebecca said. "There's still cold chicken from today's festivities and a few slices of pie left that we can have."

"I could stand to eat," Ben said. "I guess even the excitement of a twister didn't kill my appetite." He looked over at Maggie and winked.

She felt the heat rise in her face. She knew exactly what had caused his hunger. By the twinkle in his eyes, he was hungry for more than food.

And so was she.

MAGGIE JOINED everyone who pitched in over the next few days to help clean up Easton. Families whose homes survived doubled up, taking in others who had nothing but the clothes on their backs. Optimism reigned, and she caught the spirit.

One afternoon when Rebecca lay down for a nap with the children and Ben was working downstairs in the store, Maggie drafted Frank to help her with the dishes. It provided an excuse to speak to him about her idea.

"You dry. Be careful with those plates. Rebecca got them from her grandmother. They came from England."

"Yes, ma'am." He rolled up his sleeves and picked up a dish towel.

"Frank, I want to talk to you about something."

He studied her a moment. "You've got a look in your eye, Maggie. A kind of gleam. Like that time you hid a frog in Marcus's boot. What are you up to?"

She laughed. "Oh, it's far beyond frogs. It's about my birthday."

He stopped and stared. "Dagnabbit! I forgot all about it, honey. It was last week. You should've said something." He chuckled. "Well, at least you got a good present from me. I handed over my shooting title to you."

"No, that's not what I meant. Frank, I turned twenty-five."

He shrugged. "So? I did that a few years ago and survived. Nary a gray hair on this head. Yet. I don't know. The twister may have put a few there that I haven't spotted. Worry will do that to you."

"You don't remember?"

"Turning twenty-five? Maggie, I'm lost. Just spit it out."

"My trust. The one my mother left me. I came into it last week once I turned twenty-five."

Frank's eyes widened. "That's right. It's been years

since I heard about it. She left you an inheritance so you could maintain your independence like she did."

"Exactly. I wrote Marcus last week and told him to bring Dudley Simpson to Easton with all the paperwork necessary for me to have total access to the funds. Dudley's been our attorney for more years than I can count. He sat me down ages ago and explained the terms of the trust thoroughly. I know there's quite a bit of legal work to accomplish before I take control and can handle the funds."

He smiled. "Marcus. Here. Finally. I'm so glad he's coming." He flushed.

Maggie knew what that meant. "I know you'll be happy to see him after so long a time. I'm sure you'll want to introduce him to your future wife."

His jaw dropped. "What did you say?"

"You heard me. Frank, you and Rebecca are meant to be together."

"But Adam's only been dead a short while."

"We all know that." She took a deep breath. "Rebecca also needs help with the children. She needs a man to look after her. And you're that man, Frank Stansel."

He fiddled with the dish towel nervously. "I'm crazy about her, Maggie. I've never felt this way with any other woman. And I already love those children so much."

"I know you do. Believe me, from everything I've heard about Adam, I know he would approve. You're a good man, Frank. You'll help rebuild this town and start a new life for yourself with a ready-made family. Marcus will adore Rebecca. She's sweet as the day is long and doesn't take sass off anyone."

He smiled slowly. "No, she doesn't."

Maggie finished rinsing the last dish and handed it

to him. "Back to my legacy. The sum of money is quite large. I've grown to love Easton. I want to make this my home. Put down permanent roots. Because of that, I intend to help fund everything and rebuild the town."

She grabbed the towel from him and dried her hands.

"Are you sure, Maggie? This is really what you want?"

"I have big ideas, Frank. I want to build a bank. A hotel with a restaurant. I'd love to see the general store expanded. Maybe add a feed store. When I was doing research in Abilene earlier, I heard talk about the railroad possibly expanding in this direction. They might place a depot here in Easton. Then things would really take off."

He nodded. "I can see that kind of growth happening, especially with our proximity to Abilene. I've also heard talk about creating some hubs in a few different directions and having them connect with the main line headed toward Chicago. We'll need a new smithy right away. One won't be enough. We should add a carpentry shop, with all the building and rebuilding that needs to occur."

She smiled at him. "Don't forget a school. I don't want children like Jennie and Charlie neglected. Building a school and hiring a teacher is a top priority. I was thinking about a post office and maybe a telegraph office, too. Or what if we could attract a newspaper editor? Wouldn't that be grand?"

He retrieved the towel from her and finished up the last plate, looking at her with pride. "You have big dreams, Maggie. If anyone can make them come true, I'd wager it's you." He brightened. "Of course, we could use a saloon. Easton hasn't been big enough to have more than a little drinking hole-in-the-wall until now. Speaking of wagering, maybe it could also have a gaming room."

She wasn't happy with that thought but knew every good-sized town in the West had one. "Spoken like a typical man. Naturally, we'll need a new jail. I'm sure you can tell me the particulars about it."

"Oh, I'd like to have five or six cells instead of the three from before, especially if the town grows. More people can mean more trouble, especially if you put in that saloon. How's about a town hall so we have a meeting place to conduct business?"

"That's a wonderful idea. I'd love to create a town square. Maybe have a gazebo, benches, and landscaping. Why, we could surround the square with all kinds of shops. A millinery. A bakery. I'm sure some lawyer would want to set up shop. Dr. Miller could have a proper office instead of working out of his two-room shack. Just think of all the things we can do."

"I'm thinking it's quite a bit of money, Maggie. You've never been in business like this before. You'll need an architect. A construction manager. There's a lot to consider."

"Well, I'll just hire a business manager to put a team together. It'll be his expertise but our town's vision. What do you think?"

Frank swept her in his arms and danced her around the room until she was dizzy. He put her down and kissed her soundly on the cheek. "I think the citizens of Easton, Kansas, will happily appoint you as their savior. Maybe even make you the mayor." He studied her a moment. "But what about New York, Maggie?"

She stiffened. "What about it?"

"Won't you miss it? The society? The finer things in life?"

She sat on the mohair sofa. "It's not in another universe, Frank. I can always reach New York in a few days by train, but to answer your question? No, I won't really miss it. Most of my friends are married with children now. I really didn't have a place in society anymore. Especially after jilting Richard at the altar."

"Why would they blame you for that? You did what you needed to do."

"That's right. When I came West, I came alive, Frank. Alive! I found a new life. I see things differently now. I'm my own person. I make my own decisions. I have friends. I don't think I'd ever run out of ideas for my books by living here. I belong in the West. I'm ready to sink roots deeply into Easton. It's home now. New York's a memory. Here is my present. And my future."

He sat next to her and put an arm around her, drawing her close. "Then I welcome you to your new home, Maggie Rutherford. I look forward to helping you make Easton a thriving community."

He offered his hand. "Let's shake on it and make it official." He grinned at her. "And I promise I won't even spit in my palm before we clasp."

She put out her hand and took his firmly. "This seals the deal, Frank Stansel. I'm going to use my inheritance for the good of the town of Easton. My new, permanent home."

"I promise that I won't ask for the floors of the city jail to be marble. Nor will I demand more than one rolltop desk. And one deputy to start. Two as we grow larger."

She heard footsteps coming. "I guess Ben needs a break. I might need to spell him. Not a word to anyone yet, Frank. I want to make sure all my papers are signed and the funds transferred before any of this gets out."

He motioned turning a key to his lips and tossing it away.

Ben entered the room. "Telegram came for you, Maggie. I thought I better bring it right up."

"Thank you." She accepted the envelope from him and tore it open. Her insides danced with glee when she read the message. "It's from Marcus," she shared. "He's arriving in Abilene on tomorrow's two o'clock train."

21

Ben agreed to accompany Maggie into Abilene. He needed to meet with two individuals who'd responded to his advertisement regarding the purchase of the general store. He'd set up appointments with both men. Ben wanted to meet them in person and judge their character before taking it further and having them come to Easton to see the premises.

Frank graciously offered to run the store for the day in his place. Ben hoped by the end of today he'd have a qualified buyer in mind. The sooner he could settle Rebecca and the children, the faster he could leave.

If only he wanted to.

He looked over at Maggie sitting next to him as Prince drew the buggy toward Abilene. She appeared lost in thought, a half-smile on her face. He knew how much she loved her brother and how long it had been since the two were together. He hoped Marcus Rutherford would stay a while in Easton. It would make things easier for Maggie when Ben left.

If he left.

He had to leave. He couldn't stay. Who knew where Black Tex Lonnegan was hanging his hat? How close had the outlaw come to Easton? Ben had re-mained far longer in Kansas than he anticipated.

Yet what else could he have done? Rebecca needed him to help deal with Adam's death and the birth of little Charlie. She was a strong woman, though, and he knew he'd leave her in good hands. His time in the little town drew to a close. He'd already pulled away from Maggie physically—if not emotionally—and that ate at his soul every day. He'd rather be off and tortured at a distance than having to see her trim figure and hear her voice and rich laugh every day.

"Penny for your thoughts?"

"Huh?" He snapped out of his reverie.

"I'm usually the one known for daydreaming," she said. "Although daydreams are my bread and butter. I've found at least half of writing is thinking about things. The *what ifs*? Walking through scenarios and devising half a dozen different outcomes until I hit on the perfect one. Why were you lost in thought, Ben Morgan?"

He couldn't tell her that he was torn between running from a gunfighter and staying in her sweet embrace.

"Wondering about the two men who answered the advertisement. What will they be like? Will they be suited for life in Easton?"

"You're a good judge of character, Ben. If neither of these men fit the bill, you'll find someone who does." She smiled, her hazel eyes up to mischief. "Maybe you'll even find someone who's single that can move to town."

"What the hell does that mean?" He glared at her, jealousy tweaking his bones.

"Oh, Mrs. Morrow might be in the market for a new husband. You know she can bewitch a man if he tries a single bite of one of her flaky, buttery biscuits. If the new owner is a man of mature years, he might be perfect for her." She paused. "Or perhaps I could be persuaded to squire about a younger owner, even if I don't have biscuits that bedazzle him."

Ben's heart skipped a beat. "Are you thinking of staying a while in Easton? I had the impression you'd be moving on with your travels."

She pursed her lips and he was ready to yank the horse to a stop then and there. He'd take her in his arms and kiss her senseless. Somehow, he managed to maintain control so he could hear her out, keeping his gaze steady on the road ahead.

"I've traveled for over a year and seen quite a lot. I may still want to journey to a few places in order to capture their flavor. While I waited for my wrist to heal, my time in Easton taught me I'm better suited to living in one place. I've been productive here, finishing my novel more quickly than any other previous work. I like the people in Easton and I've made friends."

He looked at her. "So, you're telling me you're staying."

She bit her lip and nodded slowly, as if she'd finally reached a decision in her head and heart. "Yes, Ben. I will be staying. I've found a home on the Kansas prairie." She looked into his eyes. "Maybe, you'll stop by and see me when you make one of your infrequent visits. That is, assuming you will always come back to visit Rebecca and the children."

"Of course!" He heard the harshness in his tone and tried to soften it. "They are my family, my blood. Even though Adam's gone, I am responsible for them. I'll never abandon them."

"That's nice," she said softly.

He heard the wistfulness in her words and pulled up on the reins. Prince came to a halt.

"Maggie, you know how I feel about you."

"No."

"No?"

"No. Not in words." She reached over and took his hand. "You're not one for flowery phrases, Ben. Your actions spoke to my heart. I will never forget the day of the tornado." Her eyes grew dark. "And our time together."

He swore under his breath, cursing the sweet memory of her lying in his arms. "I had a family before, Maggie. A wife. I almost had a son." He swallowed. "They were killed years ago, during the vicious Indian attacks that dotted the Great Plains.

"It changed me. Even more than fighting in the war did. In ways I may never be able to understand or express. I just don't think I can try that life again." He reached up and stroked his thumb against her cheek. "If only things were different, Maggie."

She gave his hand a squeeze and released it. "But they're not. I understand. I truly do. You need to move on. I've decided to stay. We want—or need—two different things, Ben. You've had a family. I may want one someday. If I stay in Easton, I can build a life. My kind of life. It may or may not include a man. He may or may not become my husband one day. I may even decide to have children. My future's unwritten—but it's mine to make. You need to go live your life. Your way."

"And not your way?"

She smiled at him, a genuine smile that reached her eyes and lit her face. "I'll always be grateful that you are my friend."

He felt helpless. He wanted her, wanted her desperately. She was the one thing he wanted and couldn't have.

"I'm lucky to call you friend, as well."

He flicked the reins. They covered the remaining distance to Abilene in silence.

The November day was sunny and had turned cold. The streets of Abilene appeared calm, with few pedestrians out at ten in the morning. It was a far cry from the days of summer and early fall, as thousands of cattle arrived daily, tended by wild cowboys starved for whiskey, women, and conversation.

"I'm sorry you're arriving much earlier than your brother's train," Ben told her.

"I knew you already had your appointments waiting. I've a few errands to run in town. I'll stop by and see Sam at The Alamar. He was so kind to me during my stay there. He's a wealth of knowledge."

"You mean gossip."

Maggie grinned. "Well, there is that. I don't think much goes on in Abilene that Sam doesn't know first-hand or hear about."

"Would you like me to meet you at the train station just before two?"

"No, you might not be through with your appointments by then. We'll head directly to The Alamar once the train arrives. Marcus is bringing our attorney with him. I've arranged for rooms there for us for a couple of days. The three of us have some business to attend to," she continued. "Especially with my being gone from New York for so long. Then, we'll put Dudley back on the train to New York and I'll bring Marcus to Easton. I can't wait for everyone to meet him."

"Is that why you had me put your valise in the

back of the buggy? You had already made all these plans?"

She nodded and eyed Ben hopefully. "If you have time, I hope you will stop by The Alamar. Marcus will be famished, as usual, so I'm certain we'll take tea in the lobby after we arrive. I very much would like the two of you to meet."

"If I don't make it to the station by the time the train pulls in, I'll head straight to the hotel when I've concluded my business, and deliver your valise. Where can I drop you now?"

Maggie directed him to a large bank and Ben escorted her inside before departing. He headed to the corner of Broadway and Second, where a brick and stone courthouse stood, and secured Prince to the hitch rail. He thought meeting at a landmark would be easiest, since neither man he was set to interview lived in the area.

Ben checked his pocket watch and headed up the steps. A thin, sallow man tapped his foot impatiently, staring at his own timepiece as he waited.

"Mr. Canning?" Ben asked.

"Arthur Canning. You must be Ben Morgan. You are forty-five seconds late, young man. I pride myself on being on time everywhere I go."

He laughed. "My watch tells me I'm two minutes early, sir." He looked up at the clock in the tower above them. "And that's about to chime the half-hour when we're due to meet. Let's not worry about the time. We're both here and have a lot to talk about."

Canning's face soured. "I don't like being corrected, young man."

Ben narrowed his eyes. "My name's Ben Morgan. Not young man."

Already, they'd gotten off to a bad start. It didn't

improve. Arthur Canning showed he was a huge know-it-all, a complainer, and a busybody. Ben tried his best to be polite but Canning dodged every civilized phrase and somehow turned their conversation combative.

He terminated their interview as soon as he could, not even promising the man he'd be in touch. He refused to unleash Arthur Canning on Easton. The next encounter with Clarence Granville must go far better.

It had to, Ben thought. He felt the clock ticking. He needed to secure the sale of the general store for Rebecca and get far away from Easton.

Before the pull of Maggie Rutherford staying kept him there.

MAGGIE FINISHED her business at the bank and set about on a few errands. Once she completed them, she walked directly to The Alamar. She saw Tim in front of the hotel when she arrived, sweeping the sidewalk. "Hello, Tim. How are you?"

He brightened. "Hi, Miss Rutherford. Papa said you were coming to stay for a few days. It's nice to have you back."

"Thank you. It's nice to be back. You look like you've grown a few inches since I last saw you."

He blushed. "It's a growth spurt. At least, that's what Mama says."

"I'll bet you're keeping your mother busy as she tries to alter the hem of your pants every week."

He shrugged. "I'm hungry all the time and my legs ache something awful. Papa tells me the best thing to do is to stay busy and not think about it."

"Are you in school?"

"Not anymore. I just turned seventeen. I'm ready to find a job. Mama won't let me be a cowboy. Papa thinks I should learn a trade. I'm not sure what I'm meant to do."

"From what I've seen, you're a smart boy, Tim. You'll figure out what you want to do and shine at it."

He offered her his arm and led her up the steps, opening the door to the hotel for her. "Papa will be happy to see you. He's still waiting for your next novel to be published."

"So am I."

Maggie walked across the lobby, noting how it sat empty. Unlike the crowds when she'd last been here, Abilene must slow down at this time of year. She moved to the front desk and rang the bell.

Sam emerged from a door behind the desk. He brightened when he saw her.

"Hello, Sam. Thank you for arranging rooms for my party of three. As I mentioned, my brother and our lawyer are coming in from New York. Marcus and I will only stay a couple of days before returning to Easton. Mr. Simpson may be here for up to a week. I appreciate you handling the details for me."

The desk clerk adjusted his pince-nez. "With pleasure, Miss Rutherford. You all have rooms directly next to each other for your convenience. Your suite has ample room for you to conduct your business meetings. If need be, I can move Mr. Simpson to it when you depart."

"I was hoping you could take a few minutes and visit with me, Sam. I've been in Easton for a couple of months now, but I'd love to hear what's been going on in Abilene. It seems much quieter than when I last stayed here."

He nodded. "It'll be slow for a few months. Things

will pick up in the spring. May I offer you something to drink? I have some coffee brewing in the back."

She removed her gloves. "That would be lovely. Could we sit in the lobby and have it?"

"I'll bring it out in a jiffy." He eyed her carefully. "You have a seat now and make yourself comfortable. We have lots to talk about."

Maggie ventured to a dark green velvet settee and took Sam's advice. It felt good to get off her feet. She hadn't slept much the previous night due to her excitement at Marcus coming to town. Between that and all of the plans she had for Easton dancing in her head, she'd doubted she'd gotten more than a couple hours of sleep.

The desk clerk arrived with the coffee on a tray. "I added a few cookies in case you might be hungry. Don't let Tim know, else he'll gobble them up before you lay eyes upon them."

She laughed. "He did mention he was quite hungry these days. What would you like him to do for a living?"

Sam snorted. "Anything but be a cowboy. Oh, I know some of them are good men. Most are uneducated and uncouth, though. Tim finished up through eighth grade. He's bright as a new penny. He's helped around here for a couple of years but his mother and I want more for him."

Maggie took a sip of the coffee. "Oh, this feels good going down. A brisk wind's come up since I've been in town the last couple of hours."

"Nothing on the prairie to stop that wind. No trees to break it up. It whips and whirls. I heard Easton got hit pretty bad by the twister."

She placed the cup down on its saucer. "Yes. One side of the town no longer exists. Everyone from the area's been so good about coming in and helping with the clean-up. I gather these tornadoes aren't unusual."

"Not by a long shot. I've seen 'em take out every-thing in their path, things flying this- and that-a-way, scattering to the four corners. No predicting when or where they'll hit. We were lucky to avoid it here."

"What has been happening in Abilene these past few months? I've missed our talks. You always seem to know what's going on, Sam."

His lips thinned. "Oh, there's definitely news to share with you, Miss Rutherford. I knew I had to tell you the minute I received your message." He frowned. "It's just so hard. I don't know where to start."

"Spit it out, Sam. I've found honesty up front to al-ways be the best policy."

He drew in a deep breath before letting it out slowly. "All right. I need to warn you to avoid someone while you're here in town. Everyone's giving him a wide berth."

Maggie sat up, interested. "Hmm. Sounds like someone I might want to write about."

Sam shuddered. "Not this one, you don't. Or if you do, I wouldn't get closer than a hundred yards to him. He's a dangerous one, that he is. Name of Black Tex Lonnegan."

She thought a minute. "I've heard of him. He's a gunfighter, isn't he? He is supposed to have killed dozens of men. Don't worry, Sam. I don't have any business being near someone like this Mr. Lonnegan. What's brought him to Abilene? Does he have a con-tract to kill someone here?" She shivered at the thought.

"It's personal, he said. At least that's what he told me."

"You *spoke* to him?"

Sam trembled slightly. "I wouldn't say spoke to him as much as listened. When men like Black Tex talk, you don't really hold a normal conversation."

"What on earth did he want with you?"

"He's looking for a man." Sam stared hard at her. "He's looking for someone you know, Miss Rutherford. That's why you've got to be careful. Sooner or later, someone's going to remember or let slip that you were seen with him. With that head of copper hair, you're noticeable. Folks remember how pretty you are. Not that many young women come to Abilene, pretty or not."

Chills ran down her spine. "What man, Sam? Who?"

He swallowed hard. "That man you visited with here in The Alamar. The one you asked me to help find a room for that one night. Ben Morgan."

Maggie clasped her hands together to still the violent tremors that began instantly at hearing the name. "Why does a gunfighter like that want to find Ben?"

The clerk's jaw dropped. He tried to speak but nothing came out. She reached out and gripped his arm. "Why?"

Sam's frightened gaze met hers. "Because he wants to kill him."

22

M aggie nervously paced the waiting room at the train station. As small as it was, she found herself turning in a loop. She sat on one of the two wooden benches available.

"Dammit!" she muttered to the empty room.

Her heart pounded. Her dry mouth made it hard to swallow. A headache had formed in her temples. No amount of rubbing soothed the ache or throbbing.

Black Tex Lonnegan had come to town to kill Ben.

Pretending wouldn't make that fact go away. She had no idea where Ben might be meeting the men interested in becoming the next general store proprietor in Easton. That meant she had no way to warn him of the danger.

What if Ben stumbled across Black Tex?

She shivered at the horrible thought. She knew Ben was more than handy with a pistol but he would have no idea that Black Tex had arrived in Abilene with a thirst to kill. Ben must have known all along that the gunslinger chased him. Sam didn't know why, only that the outlaw was bent on seeing Ben dead in the dirt.

Ben wasn't a violent kind of man. He'd been a

homesteader turned gambler after his family died on the prairie. He didn't strike her as the cheating kind. It couldn't be over a card game that Lonnegan had bet and lost to Ben. So, why was an infamous gunfighter looking to shoot Ben dead?

Maggie had gone directly to the post office after speaking with Sam at The Alamar. She found the wanted poster affixed to the wall. When no one was looking, she'd torn it down and slipped it into her reticule. She pulled it out now and studied it.

The man pictured on the wanted poster had soulless eyes. Black as midnight and deadly as a snake. His beak-like nose looked as if it had been broken on more than one occasion. His hard mouth bore a savage smile. The flyer stated that seventeen men had died at the hands of Black Tex Lonnegan. The possibility existed that he was responsible for the death of nine more. No witnesses would testify to that fact.

Sheer terror would keep someone silent. A criminal such as Lonnegan wouldn't think twice about shooting an innocent man, leaving his family with no means of support. She shuddered, knowing if the outlaw crossed paths with Ben, there wouldn't be a happy outcome.

She glanced out the window and saw the time on a large clock mounted on a steel pole. The train would arrive soon. She rose and stepped out onto the covered wooden platform that ran parallel to the tracks. Marcus would be here within minutes. He would know what to do.

He had to.

Right on time, she heard the iron horse before she saw it come around the bend. The sleek engine, painted a bright red, chugged merrily into the station. It slowed and the conductor appeared. He jumped down and placed a set of steps in place for passengers to disembark.

He caught sight of Maggie and gave her a jaunty wave, tipping his hat. She plastered a smile onto her face. She returned the wave, aiming for some semblance of normality before Marcus appeared.

Suddenly, her brother stood in the doorway, beaming at her. Maggie's heart burst with love and pride. She hiked her skirts and ran toward him, flinging herself into his arms as he reached the bottom of the stairs.

"I thought you might not recognize me. It's been so long since we've seen one another," Marcus teased, crushing her against him. He hugged her long and hard before pulling back and studying her.

Without warning, Maggie burst into tears.

"There, there," he soothed, taking her into his arms again. "I'm sure it will all be fine, dearest."

A wave of peace wash over her for the first time since Sam's dire warning. She knew it couldn't last. She pulled away.

"I'm in love with Ben Morgan," she blurted out. "He's a gambler. I know that gives you the totally wrong impression when you hear someone called a gambler. He fought in the war and was a homesteader. He's working at his brother's store now because he's dead. Adam. His brother. Not Ben. He's such a good man, Marcus. Trust me on this."

She took a deep breath and raced on, words pouring from her. Fear for Ben clenched tightly in her stomach. "Some gunslinger named Black Tex Lonnegan who kills people for a living wants to kill Ben. And he's here in Abilene. Lonnegan. Ben came into town with me so he's here, too, but I don't know where he is now. He doesn't know Lonnegan is looking for him. I mean, I suppose he must but Ben doesn't know Lonnegan's arrived in Abilene. I don't know what Ben did or what this Lonnegan character thinks he did but I love him. Ben. Not Lonnegan. Oh, Marcus, you have to do something."

Tears rained down her cheeks. She sobbed uncontrollably.

"Dudley? Will you see to our luggage?" Marcus said calmly.

She looked up and saw the family attorney standing there, his mouth agape. He had the good sense to close it when he realized she stared at him.

"Oh, hello, Dudley. I'm sorry I'm such a fright. I'm babbling like a crazy person because I'm in love with a man who's got an assassin gunning for him. But I know Marcus can fix things. He always does. And it's good to see you, by the way. I've missed our meals together and all your advice. You've always been like a father to me. I do appreciate you coming all the way here from New York. Despite the mess. Which I know Marcus will handle."

Dudley's usual composure had returned. "I am happy to be of service, Miss Maggie. It's nice to see you after such a long time." He smiled fondly at her.

She took the handkerchief her brother offered and mopped the tears from her cheeks.

"We're at The Alamar, Mags, correct?"

She nodded as she blew her nose loudly.

"Then we'll see you at the hotel, Dudley."

The attorney straightened his tie and smoothed his jacket. "I'll collect our bags and call at the bank first. I have a few things to set in motion there in preparation for certain transfers. That will give you time to discuss matters with Miss Maggie and come up with a solution to her problem."

Dudley marched off with purpose in the opposite direction, his bald pate gleaming before he set his hat upon his head.

Maggie wiped her nose. "I suppose you don't want your handkerchief back." She held up the damp square, now wrinkled and soggy.

Marcus sighed. "I seem to always run short of them whenever I come in contact with you." He threw an arm around her shoulder. "Come on, dearest sister. I'm certain someone as clever as Lud Madison is will be able to help your Mr. Morgan out of this situation."

She stopped in her tracks. "What do you mean?"

He laughed heartily. "Oh, Maggie, I figured out long ago that *you* were Lud Madison. I could hear your voice in the stories he told, just as you did constantly when we were growing up. Why do you think I sent Mr. Madison that contraption?"

"The typewriter?"

"Yes, that's what they're calling it. Haven't quite figured it out myself yet but I knew you would. It's supposed to make writing easier than putting pen to paper, I've heard." He chuckled. "I'm delighted you're using your imagination to make money. Lud's done quite well for himself. And of course, you had to survive somehow this past year without begging me for a wire transfer of money."

Maggie punched him hard in the shoulder. "I can't believe you knew and never told me. You know you do exasperate me at times, Marcus, but I am so happy you are here." She slipped her hand through the crook of his elbow.

He led her through the waiting room and out onto the street. "How far is it? Do we need to hire a carriage? Or can we walk from here?"

She sniffed. "We can walk. It isn't far." She let out a

long breath. "I'm calmer now. I can talk as we walk. I might even sound coherent."

"I'm glad you've composed yourself, Mags. All right. Start at the beginning. Tell me about this Ben Morgan and how you came to fall in love with the fellow. We'll figure out what to do. I promise you."

"I came to Abilene to do some research on men who worked the cattle trails. I had an idea for a book, but I wanted to see a cow town like Abilene or Dodge City and talk to real cowboys. I interviewed several, but Ben came across as the most articulate."

"And handsome?"

She blushed. "That goes without saying. If I'm going to fall in love, Marcus, I'm going to do it up right. Anyway, I found out he was a gambler who'd joined a cattle drive. I'm sure now that it was to hide from Black Tex Lonnegan, who is a most awful outlaw. That's saying a lot, seeing as how the West is full of such characters."

She stopped and dug into her reticule, producing the wanted poster. "See for yourself."

She watched Marcus study the picture and the crimes listed, committing them to memory. Being thorough was one of his best traits. He returned the flyer to her.

"I went to Easton to visit a few days with Frank. You know most of the rest. How I injured my wrist. That I stayed on while it healed. Oh, Marcus, I've made such good friends in Easton. I plan to stay on there. And keep writing."

"With Mr. Ben Morgan?"

"No. I wish. Ben arrived in Easton a few days before I did. He visits there each year with his brother. Adam was in a terrible accident just before Ben arrived. He died, leaving his wife with one child and expecting another one. Ben stayed on to run Adam's general store and help care for Rebecca until the baby was born.

"He's here in Abilene now interviewing applicants who wish to purchase the store. He brought me into town with him so I could meet you and Dudley. Ben will meet us at The Alamar once he's concluded his business."

She gripped his arm. "Marcus, he could stumble across Lonnegan at any moment."

"Why does Lonnegan want to kill your Ben? And does he love you back? He'd be a fool not to."

Maggie felt the tears well in her eyes. "I do think he loves me but he's not one to settle down. He did after the war, but his wife and child were killed in an Indian attack. He's never gotten over what happened to them. He's kept on the move. I'm not sure why Lonnegan wants him dead. He's a good man, Marcus. I know hearing he's a gambler sounds shady. It couldn't be further from the truth. Ben is honest. Hard-working. Kind and generous to a fault. I know he wouldn't have cheated at cards or swindled Lonnegan in any way."

She stopped in her tracks. "We need to find Ben. Now. We need to warn him."

"He could be anywhere in Abilene, Mags. I'll assume this Lonnegan character is the type to hang about in saloons. I wouldn't think Mr. Morgan would interview prospective buyers for his brother's general store in that type of establishment."

She couldn't help but laugh. "Oh, you have much to learn about the West, Marcus. Don't you read my books? Besides, I almost interviewed Ben in a bar."

Her brother's eyebrows shot up. He started to speak but held his tongue.

"I wound up interviewing him in The Alamar's lobby." She pointed across the street to the hotel. "And we've arrived at the very place."

As they entered, Sam called out a greeting and met them.

"I hold your sister in high esteem, Mr. Rutherford. She is a remarkable lady. I've got your tea ready to go. Be back in a jiffy."

They sat on a settee with a small table in front of it. While they waited for the meal she'd ordered, Maggie managed to smile. "I'm soothed for just having seen you, Marcus. I know your capable hands will create a solution to all my problems."

He frowned. "I'm not so sure. I'm afraid you're going to be angry with me."

She looked at him. "What mischief have you been up to? I can see it in your eyes. You might show the world a bored, blasé look, but you're definitely guilty of something."

"Richard might have followed me here. To Abilene."

"Richard? Richard as in my jilted fiancé, Richard? The man who wanted to marry me for my money and would have sucked the life and soul from me, as well as taken every dime to my name? *That* despicable Richard?"

Marcus flushed. "The one and the same. He swears he's not over you, Mags. That you totally misunderstood the situation. Oh, not him being just this side of destitute. He's about to join the church mouse in a contest as to which is the poorer. I'm afraid it would be a toss-up but the church mouse looks more a winner to me than poor Richard DeForest."

She glared at her brother. "Exactly what makes you think *poor* Richard might be coming to Abilene?"

"He came into the club when I was discussing my trip with a few of the boys. Frankly, I didn't even realize he'd slunk over and joined the group. As we ended our discussion and people went their own way, there stood Richard. He moped about as usual, frantic to speak with me. Apparently he heard most of what I said. That you were in Abilene. That Dudley and I were coming out to visit you. That we were ready to draw up all the papers to ensure you took control of the fortune Mama left you."

Maggie fumed. "He'll come out and try to sidle up to me and sweet talk me, when all he wants is access to my money! I won't have it, Marcus. I won't. I never wanted to see the likes of him again. I haven't forgotten what Patrick Kelly taught me, you know. I'd sooner punch Richard DeForest in the face and be done with it."

Sam interrupted them, bringing a teapot and cups on a tray laden with ham sandwiches and a variety of sweets. Maggie thanked him and allowed the clerk to get out of earshot before she continued.

"Richard is a phony. A fraud. I don't think he knows how to be a friend, much less a husband. He was ordering me about, right there at the altar, Marcus, telling me to pipe down and making sure I knew he was the boss and would handle the finances. *Especially* the money I brought into the marriage."

"Well, if the fellow shows up, either tell him to get lost, Mags, or box his ears. Or both. By the way, Patrick Kelly said to tell you hello. He recently won the middleweight boxing title for all of New York. He still speaks of you fondly."

She shook her head. "I have a mind to whip out my petticoat pistol and threaten to shoot him. Richard. Not Patrick."

Marcus sat up. "You carry a pistol now? You're becoming quite an interesting woman, Maggie Rutherford. A successful, published author. In love with a gambler chased by a gunslinger. Packing a pistol and ready to shoot an ex-fiancé. I'd say it has all the makings of a good dime novel." He smiled at her. "More tea?"

"You. Are. Infuriating. And I only said I'd *threaten* to shoot Richard. I don't think I'd actually carry through with it. Unless he infuriated me, that is. You know. Like a doting, older brother."

He gave up a good belly laugh. "How I have missed you, Mags. And Frank. I can't wait to see him. I can't believe we've gone so long without having seen one another."

"Be prepared. He's also in love."

"Our Frank?"

"The very one. I thought he'd be a bachelor for life, but he's taken a shine to the lovely Rebecca Morgan."

"The widow and friend you've written of?"

"Exactly. He's not only madly in love with her but also her children. Jennie and the baby, Charlie. Why, Frank even changes Charlie's diapers."

Marcus grimaced. "That's not the Frank Stansel I know. I shudder to think of him being domesticated. Much less changing a diaper."

"Well, he does it. And well. He's had quite a bit of practice at it. He doesn't mind at all."

"Then that's how I know it's true love. Frank wouldn't do something like that if it weren't. Rebecca must be a most remarkable woman."

"Don't say anything to him. He's yet to tell Rebecca. But she knows. She's not only a smart woman but she's very patient. She knows everything will fall into place in good time."

Maggie sighed. "Oh, where is Ben? I'm starting to worry again, Marcus. I'm ready to walk the streets until I find him."

"I don't think that'll be necessary."

She looked over and saw Ben approaching. Relief rushed through her, making her head spin faster than downing two brandies in a row. She leaped to her feet.

"Ben, we have to talk."

He gave a smile and her heart melted. He held out a hand. "Ben Morgan. You must be the man who sits atop the pillar. Otherwise known as Marcus Rutherford."

Marcus laughed. "Good to meet you, Ben. Have a seat." He sobered. "We do need to talk, though. Quickly and seriously. Time is of the essence."

Ben's brow wrinkled in puzzlement. Maggie reached and took his hand. Before they could sit, Sam appeared, wringing his hands.

"You can't be here, Mr. Morgan. You've got to leave at once. I can't jeopardize my life, my family, or the guests in this hotel."

Maggie saw Ben's face turn from confusion to enlightenment. "Black Tex Lonnegan must be in town."

Sam nodded nervously. "He aims to shoot you dead, sir."

23

B en nodded. "I'm sorry, Sam. I would never want to put anyone in danger. I'll be on my way."

"Well, then." The desk clerk adjusted his pince-nez nervously. "Thank you, sir. I have a back way for you to exit safely."

"May I have a moment to say goodbye?"

Sam nodded, his head bobbing up and down quickly. "I'll go stand on the porch and keep watch. I'll come back in two minutes, Mr. Morgan. Two minutes!" He scurried off.

He looked at Maggie. His heart felt lodged in his throat. He'd known it would be difficult to say goodbye to her, but he hadn't imagined it would be so hurried or under these circumstances.

"Excuse me," Marcus Rutherford said. "I think I'll keep our good friend Sam company." He inclined his head to Ben and exited the room quickly.

Ben searched Maggie's face with his gaze. He wanted to memorize everything about her. The shine of her copper hair. Those hazel eyes that changed colors so frequently, depending upon her mood. The lush mouth that begged to be kissed, even now.

And so he did.

He took her in his arms, his mouth coming down hard on hers. Her lips parted. He gained entrance into Nirvana. Their tongues mated in heat, in fire, in a desperate need born of longing.

And love.

Yes, as he kissed this woman in his arms, he knew —*he knew*—that he would love Maggie Rutherford for all time. With a depth and breadth and longing to the core of his soul. As she'd said, he was more a man of action than words. He tried to let his body tell her just how much he cared in the few stolen seconds left to them.

"It's time," Marcus said.

Ben held on a moment longer then pulled away. Maggie's eyes, dark green as a forest, blazed up at him.

"I can't... I won't... endanger you or anyone else I love. I'll go back and say my goodbyes to Rebecca and the children." He paused. "I doubt I'll ever see you again, Maggie. But know you'll always be in my heart. My mind. In every thought I have and every breath I take. Now. And until the end of my life."

Her lips trembled. She closed her eyes and nodded. "Go," she whispered.

He strode off, not looking back. He couldn't. If he did, he would rush back and take her in his arms again.

This time, he might not let go.

He refused to get her killed. He knew nothing would stop Lonnegan in his search for revenge. If Maggie stood in the way, Black Tex Lonnegan wouldn't think twice about mowing her down to get to him.

He passed Sam without a word. He headed in the direction the hotel owner pointed. Ben slipped out the back trade entrance and made his way down an alley to where he'd tied Prince and the buggy. He hoped no one had seen him enter The Alamar. Ben unhitched the gelding since speed was of the essence. He could make it back to Easton in half the time or less without the rig.

He kept a watchful eye as he mounted the horse and wove down a few back alleys, skirting the main thoroughfares of Abilene. Within minutes, he traveled on the open road to Easton. Incoherent thoughts swirled in his mind as he drew closer to the place that had become home, a place now ripped from him. He knew after today he might never see Easton again.

Or Maggie.

He pushed that thought aside as he swung off his horse. He hitched Prince to the rail in front of the general store, the one his brother built. His insides twisted at the way he was leaving. He didn't want Lonnegan to make the connection between him and Rebecca.

Ben hurried inside the store. He locked the door and put the closed sign into place. He turned and saw Frank standing behind the counter, a questioning look on his face.

"Come upstairs with me," Ben said. "It's important."

The lawman followed him silently. They found Rebecca darning socks at the table.

She smiled as they came in. "Charlie's asleep in his cradle. Jennie's gone off with Mrs. Morrow to–" She stopped mid-sentence, setting her needles aside. "You're white as a sheet, Ben. Tell me what's happened."

He pulled out a chair and sat, taking her hands in his. He took a deep breath, wondering how much he should reveal.

"I killed a man. Back in Texas." He paused. "He was

cheating at cards. When called out, he tried to shoot me and killed another player. It was self-defense."

"Why are you worried about this today?"

He took another breath and looked her in the eye. "There were fifty witnesses in the bar when it happened. I think to a man, they would've testified on my behalf. Nothing would've come of the incident. But right after it happened, the man's brother walked through the saloon doors. I shot and killed Black Tex Lonnegan's little brother."

Frank whistled low. "I'm surprised you're here now."

"Who's this Lonnegan, Ben?" Rebecca asked worriedly. "You're making me nervous."

"He's a gunfighter, Rebecca. He kills people for a living. Some are contracts. Some he shoots for fun. He swore revenge on me. It's complicated, but I got away from him that night. I've been looking over my shoulder ever since."

"He's found you?" Frank asked.

Ben nodded. "He's arrived in Abilene and is asking around about me. I don't know when he got there, but the fact is he's there and must know he's close." He squeezed Rebecca's hands. "I never meant to stay this long. I never wanted to put anyone in danger. But when I got here, Adam was so bad off. Then he passed and I knew I couldn't walk out."

"Of course not," Rebecca said. "We needed you. I needed you, Ben."

He stood, raking a hand through his hair. "I've been living on borrowed time. I've got to leave, Rebecca. Now. The risk is too great to stay. I found a buyer for the store this morning. A really nice, decent fellow. Name of Clarence Granville. Has a wife in

Cincinnati and two kids, twins that are five. He knows his stuff. We agreed on a purchase price and drew up the papers at the First National in Abilene. He plans to take over. Starting tomorrow. You'll need to meet him at the bank tomorrow morning at ten to sign the papers and receive his payment."

"All right, Ben."

He sat and took her hands again. "I was going to stay a few days and show him the ropes, but you'll have to do that now. Arrange for him to stay somewhere until you can use the funds and build something for you and the kids. He's aware of the situation and won't press too hard until you're settled. Then he'll send for his family."

"Thank you, Ben."

He gave her a long look. "I promise I'll stay in touch, Rebecca. I may never come back, in order to keep you and the children safe, but I will send you money on a regular basis. I just have to get out of town as fast as possible so Lonnegan doesn't know we're linked in any way."

"Oh, Ben. I don't want your money. I only want you to be safe."

"I want the same for you."

Frank came and stood next to them. "I'll take care of Rebecca and the children, Ben. I aim to marry Rebecca. Build her and the children a home. She'll have a roof over her head and plenty of love, I promise you that."

She beamed at Frank's words and then placed a hand on Ben's shoulder. "Lonnegan is bad news, Ben. You'd best be going. Put as much distance as you can between him and you. It's what you have to do."

His sister-in-law hugged him tightly. "Oh, Ben. We

love you so much. Everyone in Easton does." Tears spilled down her cheeks.

"I've already said my goodbye to Maggie back in Abilene. She understands the situation."

"It doesn't mean her heart won't break any less," Rebecca said frankly.

"No, you're right. The feeling's mutual," he replied.

He brushed her falling tears away. "Tell the two little ones I love them." He glanced over at Frank. "I'm sorry I'll miss your wedding. I would've looked forward to giving this bride away."

He held a hand out to the sheriff. They shook solemnly. "Take care of them, Frank. Take care of them." He stopped speaking before his voice broke.

"I will. For you. And for Adam. Godspeed, Ben."

He hurried down the stairs, blinking hard. He'd leave with the clothes on his back and the gun he'd strapped on to go to town. And he'd leave behind the one person who mattered most.

Maggie Rutherford.

MAGGIE SAT in a chair in the lobby of The Alamar. Dudley had arrived shortly after Ben departed. She'd told him she was in no mood to discuss business today. She sent both him and Marcus to the suite of rooms upstairs, wanting nothing more than to be alone with her thoughts. Marcus had bent to retrieve her valise that Ben had brought in with him. She told him to leave it. She brought it over and placed it next to the chair.

She reached out again and touched the handle, knowing Ben's strong fingers had wrapped around it only a short time ago. She looked around the room and found she couldn't leave. It was the last place they'd been together. The place he touched her. Held her close. Kissed her with both love and regret on his lips.

Maggie leaned against the chair back, resting her eyes, but all she saw were pictures of Ben. Dancing with her. Laughing. Swinging Jennie into his arms. Placing items in a basket for a customer. Singing to Charlie. Smiling at her.

She wished she could throw a vase, smashing it against the wall into a thousand pieces. But what good would that do? There'd only be broken glass to collect, shattered into nothingness. Just like her heart.

She had never known love until Ben came into her life. She'd discovered it to be many things. Physical, when they touched. Very physical when they'd made love, joining together as one. Emotional. Spiritual. Incandescent. Fragile. This longing, this hurt inside, caused a pain so great that she didn't know how she'd make it through the rest of this day and the long night —much less the rest of her life—without Ben by her side.

Intellectually, she understood why he left. Where her heart joined her soul created a gap so large, it could never be filled or replaced. She had no interest in eating. Sleeping. Talking. Even writing. She had no interest in living at all.

She balled her fists and squeezed her eyes shut. She wished she had a punching bag in front of her now. She'd pummel the hell out of it.

Or Richard. That would even be better. She hoped he did come to Abilene because she intended to give him an earful.

"Maggie?"

She opened her eyes to the too-familiar voice.

"Well, speak of the devil. Richard DeForest. What on earth has brought you to Abilene, Kansas?"

"Good afternoon, Maggie." He crossed the room and bowed to her, oh so properly.

She almost laughed aloud. She studied him, wondering at how little he'd changed since she'd jilted him at the altar over a year ago. As always, every fair hair on his head seemed perfectly in place. His moustache, always neatly trimmed, had a few new gray hairs in it, which secretly delighted her. Always a clotheshorse, much more so than Marcus ever dreamed of being, Richard stood before her in an immaculately starched shirt and dark blue suit. She recognized the suit. Apparently he hadn't the money to update to the current year's fashion as he once had.

"You're looking ever so splendid," he complimented her.

"Of course, I don't," she snapped. "I've been crying and I know I look like a raccoon when I do so. Some women cry so prettily, Aunt Harriet in particular, but I'm not one of them. My eyes get puffy and I stay red in the face for hours." She glanced down. "Even my blouse is still damp with tears."

"Then I hope they were tears of joy at being reunited with Marcus," he said smoothly.

She arched her brows. "How would you know I've recently seen Marcus?"

Richard smiled. "I could never lie to you, Maggie, and I won't try to now. I know Marcus has already told you that I found out you were here. I'll admit it. I followed him and Mr. Simpson, slinking about as one of those Pinkertons I've read about. I shadowed their every step, making every transfer they did, until we all arrived in Abilene."

She studied him. "Then why didn't you make

yourself known at the station? Or did you know I would humiliate you in public if I saw you, so you've come to take your beating in private?"

"Maggie. Maggie." He shook his head, as if placating a child. Without waiting for an invitation, he took a seat in the chair next to her. "I'm here to win you back."

24

Ben decided two minutes outside of Easton that he would be making the biggest mistake of his life if he didn't go back to Abilene for Maggie. He couldn't leave her behind. He didn't know how to live without her.

Every step Prince took was one that sent him further away from her. He would ride back to Abilene and see her at The Alamar. He couldn't offer her much. He was a farmer turned gambler with a cutthroat killer hot on his trail. Every fiber of his being needed her. She was as essential to him as air.

He plotted what to say as he rode hard toward Abilene. They could go out West to San Francisco. Or even back East. He'd love to show her Boston. He doubted the likes of Black Tex would travel there. Europe? He'd always wanted to see the exotic places he'd read about. London. Rome. Paris. Athens.

He had some money saved, wrapped in the money belt about his waist for safekeeping. They could marry in New York and set sail anywhere they desired. She could write. He always could find a game of chance. Maybe they'd find somewhere to settle down. He didn't care what they did, as long as they spent the rest of their lives together.

Of course, she might not want to go with him. Pick up and leave with nary a goodbye or a packed suitcase to slow them down. Ben banked on the fact that she loved him. If she loved him even a tenth as much as he loved her, she'd run away with him. Tonight.

Determined now, he rode even harder. He'd sneak in the back way at the hotel again and hope to avoid Sam. The desk clerk was right to be concerned about Black Tex finding out Ben had been there. But he'd only visit a few minutes to plead his case. He hoped to leave with Maggie in tow, as they were meant to be.

He hitched his horse just outside the back entrance and glanced in every direction. Luck was on his side. Not a person darkened a doorway. Ben hoped his good fortune continued. He passed a few workers in the kitchen. They gave him a cursory glance, probably thinking he was a lost guest who'd made a wrong turn.

Peering around a corner, he saw Sam talking with a tall, lean gentleman at the front desk. He waited until their conversation ended. The man crossed to enter the parlor while the desk clerk opened the half door to go to the room behind the counter. Ben slipped down the corridor and started to go up the stairs when he heard Maggie's voice coming from the parlor. He turned and made his way there.

Just as he started to round the corner, he heard a man say, "I'm here to win you back."

Ben stopped in his tracks. He leaned slightly and saw the parlor empty, save for Maggie and the stranger. She smiled at him. It hit Ben that the man must be Maggie's ex-fiancé. He'd come all the way from New York.

To win her back.

His stomach dropped to his heels. Bile rose in his throat. Ben stepped back, just out of sight. He knew no good came from eavesdropping but he was powerless to move.

"You've come from New York. All the way from New York to Kansas, Richard? To win me back?"

"Yes, my darling. I haven't had a decent night's sleep since you left. You're constantly in my thoughts. Not a day goes by that I don't think of you. What you might say. How you might react. How you always gave your honest opinion, never censoring anything. I've missed you. So much. I love you, Maggie. I am utterly, desperately, madly in love with you."

Ben's pulse beat wildly. He stumbled back a few steps back. He understood exactly how this man felt. He'd tracked Maggie down, even after she'd abandoned him at the altar. Ben once asked Maggie about her wedding day and if she'd loved the groom. She told him she'd panicked and run away, all the way out West.

But they'd been interrupted by Mrs. Morrow's broom—and Maggie had never answered his question.

What if she *had* loved this stranger but the idea of marriage frightened her? Her fiancé had traveled a very long way and wanted her back.

Ben hesitated. On one hand, *he* was the one that wanted a life with Maggie—but what kind of life could he give her? If he marched into that parlor right now, what was his best offer? To run away while a bloodthirsty outlaw chased them, a man who would kill them—both of them if they were together—on sight. No questions asked.

He loved Maggie enough to give her up. He couldn't ask her to leave with him when a gunslinger hunted him. She deserved more, much more, than a life on the run. He'd been selfish to think to ask her to come with him. She'd be better off either staying in Easton and building a life there or returning to New York with a man who obviously loved her. He'd heard enough of their conversation. There wasn't any sense allowing the knife to slip in more deeply.

With painful regret, Ben turned away without a goodbye and retraced his steps. He climbed on his horse. He pushed down the bitter sadness that welled up and rode away as dusk fell over the plains.

MAGGIE KEPT a big smile on her face despite the load of rubbish Richard fed her. She nodded while he declared his undying affection and commitment to her. He finally finished his long soliloquy, a satisfied look on his face. Then he had the audacity to reach for her hand. Even worse? He stroked it.

She almost threw up all over him.

Maggie jerked her hand back. Fury vibrated through every bone in her body. She tried to tamp down the anger so it wouldn't explode like a volcano. After all, she was a modern Western woman. She could tell this insane fool just what she thought of him in a ladylike—yet deadly—tone. No sense in upsetting Sam or any of the guests at The Alamar.

Exercising what felt like was impossible control, she said, "You. Are. *The* most despicable. The *most* vile. The most slimy, unworthy, worthless, wretched excuse for a man that I have ever had the displeasure of knowing. You are the *worst* ignoramus who ever walked this earth."

It astonished her when he had the audacity to look

surprised at her words. Even innocent. He wasn't some wronged man. He was a fool.

"What part did you not understand about my leaving you, Richard? I would think telling you that I had no intention of marrying you and then rushing out of our wedding and straight into a cab that took me to a train station so I could leave the state to get as far from you as possible *might* have been your first clue. Or that anyone of the upper echelon in Manhattan society who heard my declaration loud and clear that *I didn't want to be married to you.* That might have been explanation enough. At least for most morons."

She stood. "But the fact that you're here tells me how truly desperate you are. You *still* want my money. Especially now that I've come into Mama's inheritance." She glared at him. "Admit it, Richard. Be a man. You might want me, or think you want me, but what you really want is what comes with me. All that lovely, cold, hard gold."

"Maggie, darling—"

She shook a finger at him. "Don't *darling* me, Richard. Look at me. Tell me to my face that you want my money. You want. My money. Say it." She gritted her teeth. "All of it. Say it."

The mask of earnestness dropped from his face. A cold, hard look glittered in his eyes. The real Richard revealed himself.

"Yes," he hissed. "Yes. God help me. I still *do* want you. Be it love or lust, I want you. But I also want your money. Even more."

Maggie staggered back at his ugly words as if he'd slapped her.

"I'm tired of owing everyone in town. Father's gambling debts ate us alive. We're running a skeleton staff in the Fifth Avenue mansion. The country estate is all but abandoned. A single caretaker resides there. That's simply to let prospective buyers in to see the property. Mother and I have sold off every piece of art, every antique, every stock—and we still owe more than we can ever repay. My father's dead, Maggie."

She started. He grabbed her elbows and yanked her close, his face inches from hers.

"Yes. Dead. *He shot himself*. That was the last straw. The weasel escaped and will never have to pay the piper. My mother will probably become a common seamstress. I'll have to go into trade." He turned and spat in disgust. "Marcus actually offered me a job as if I were a common wage slave, not a DeForest who attended school with him."

"That was kind of him," Maggie said, amazed by her brother's generosity. "What could you do at Rutherford House?"

Richard glared at her, not answering her question. "Father kindly shot himself in the bathtub. The clean-up for his valet was minimal. If push came to shove, I'm sure he held more affection for his valet than he did for me."

She gasped. She'd never liked Richard's father. Mr. DeForest's attitude toward his only child reminded her too much of her own father and his lack of affection for her. Yet hearing Richard voice such enmity shook her to her core. "How can you say such things?"

He snorted. "I didn't even stay for the funeral. I have no idea how Mother might pay for that. There are no more candlesticks to sell, or silverware, or china, or Aubusson rugs. I was desperate enough, after overhearing Marcus share where you were, to go from viewing my father's bloodied head to packing a quick bag and running to jump on a train to head

West and find you. *You* are my golden ticket out of this mess. Yes, Maggie. I desperately need saving."

She lifted her chin. "Find someone else to do it."

He grabbed her shoulders and shook her until her teeth rattled. "I can never go back to New York. Not to the gossip and innuendo. We can stay in the West, though God knows there's nothing in this cow town. Perhaps New Orleans or San Francisco will be more to our liking. You *will* marry me, Maggie. You *will* rescue me from this hell hole. After you embarrassed me in front of all of society, you *owe* me.

"I owe you nothing."

"I love you. I need you. But I need your money more. You're rich as Croesus now, and money buys what I need. Does that answer your question? I've freely admitted it. Are you satisfied now? Have I groveled enough before you?"

She stared at him, not knowing how or where to begin. She'd told him off, humiliated him, and he still wouldn't leave.

Richard DeForest stood before her in abject misery. Little did he realize that she was miserable, too. The thought of Ben softened her anger. Maggie took a deep breath. "No, I'm not marrying you."

"Ah," said Richard. "I finally understand your reluctance. There's someone else. Miss Independent Maggie has fallen in love. What is he? A rancher? Some cattleman? Maybe a small town physician or banker?" He looked at her in disdain. "Come on, Maggie. No one knows you as I do. I know the lost little girl inside you. The one whose father never loved her. I'll give you all the love you need, Maggie. Just say the word. Marry me. We'll go somewhere new and grand and build a life together. We can become whatever we want."

She blew out a long breath. "You are so full of yourself, Richard. Yes, there is someone else. We met in Easton. He's a better man than you could ever imagine being. Unlike you, he's a true gentleman. He respects me. He values my opinions and my work. He is kind, loving, and chock-full of integrity and courage. He is your exact opposite. He works hard to support his family. You aren't even fit to shine Ben Morgan's boots."

"But I'm the one willing to show you the world."

Maggie shoved Richard hard, wanting his hands off her and him as far away as possible. "I never, ever want to see you again, Richard. Ever! Don't stay in Abilene. Don't come looking for me in Easton or anywhere else. You disgust me. I loathe you. And just for the record? No, I don't want to marry you."

She threw a hard left punch straight into his nose. She didn't know what gave her greater satisfaction— the loud crunch or the astonished look on his face as she escaped out the parlor door.

25

R ichard DeForest numbly lifted another whiskey to his lips. The sting of Maggie's parting words hurt as much as his swollen nose. His shirtfront still bore the blood that spurted after she struck him unexpectedly.

Damn the bitch to hell!

He drained the remaining amber liquid. The fire from the alcohol trailed down his throat to his belly. He'd lost count of how many drinks he'd downed. All he wanted was to block out the pain. He had nowhere to go. He didn't even have enough money to get back to New York. Nothing good awaited him there anyway.

He slammed the heavy tumbler to the table. All he wanted now was revenge. He wanted Maggie Rutherford to suffer as much as he had. But, how?

He leaned back in the chair, dizzy and nauseated from all he'd drunk. He tried to breathe slowly. The last thing he needed was to empty the contents of his stomach onto the sawdust-covered floor in front of all these roughneck strangers. He could only imagine the ridicule and scorn that would follow. He'd had that in spades from the hoi-polloi of New York society. To be mocked by drunken cowboys in a bar that barely qual-ified as civilization would be the ultimate insult.

He listened as the saloon fell silent. Even the piano player paused. A man sauntered in with purpose. His hat was pulled low on his brow, a pair of pearl-han-dled guns slung low on his hips. Whipcord thin, the stranger's gaze scanned the bar long after he entered. He took a seat at an empty table.

Slowly, conversation picked up again. It flowed in lower tones this time around. Curious, Richard leaned over to the next table and tapped the closest occupant.

"Who's that man?"

"Quiet!" The cowpoke forced down Richard's arm. "Don't point. You don't ever want to draw attention from Black Tex Lonnegan."

"Is he someone important?"

His new acquaintance studied him. "You really are from nowhere near here." The cowboy shook his head. "That man is one of the most infamous killers this side of the Mississip. Kills for money sometimes. Pleasure the rest of the time. Give him a wide berth, greenhorn."

Richard looked over at the gunfighter. "Why is he in Abilene? Is he here on a job?"

The cowboy snorted. "It's personal, I've heard. He's looking for the man who shot his brother during a card game. Black Tex aims to bring his own version of frontier justice to the fellow. Rumor has it the un-lucky sum-bitch surfaced here in Abilene. Black Tex plans to find him and gun him down like a rabid dog."

That image made Richard's queasy stomach roil. "If I were this man, I'd have vacated the premises long before now."

"Tex'll find him 'fore he can hightail it outta here.

It's just a matter of time before someone knows and tells where Ben Morgan's hiding."

The cowboy turned back to his companions. Richard thought a moment. Ben Morgan. Ben Morgan. *Where have I heard that name?*

Then the answer dawned on him through his alcoholic haze. *That was the name Maggie uttered. The man she loved. She claimed he, Richard DeForest, wasn't worthy enough to shine the man's boots. Well, at least he didn't have some gunfighter trying to kill him.*

He stood, swaying unsteadily. He gripped the table for support. He waited until the spinning sensation passed, and then consciously put one foot in front of the other until he stood at the table where Black Tex Lonnegan sat sipping whiskey.

He tipped his hat. "Mr. Lonnegan? I hear you're searching for Ben Morgan."

The outlaw swallowed and calmly set down his glass. Only then did he raise his gaze to meet Richard's.

A ghost of a chill raced down Richard's spine. Black eyes—flat, cold, and deadly—stared back at him. Suddenly, talking with this man didn't seem like such a good idea.

But before he could step away, Lonnegan pushed the chair opposite him, nudging it nearer with a foot. "Sit."

Richard sobered instantly as the bar patrons ceased speaking. Everyone turned to stare at him, waiting to see what fool dared to address Black Tex Lonnegan and just how long the gunslinger would let him live. Would the outlaw kill him before he sat, or after a few moments?

Perspiration broke out across his brow, but he was smart enough to follow the order and sit. "I thank you for your hospitality," he said politely. Years of good manners controlled him, despite the fact that he might only have seconds to live.

"What do you want?" Lonnegan demanded.

Richard placed his elbows on the table, needing to brace himself physically as much as he needed to fortify himself emotionally. "I have some information regarding the man you're looking for. Ben Morgan."

Lonnegan considered him, his features giving nothing away. He nodded and reached for his whiskey again, draining the glass. Calmly, he refilled it from the bottle sitting on the table. No one in the bar spoke, much less breathed, as all present strained to hear their conversation.

The gunfighter looked around. "Clear the bar."

The command was spoken softly but every patron heard it. A rush of chairs scooting back across the wooden floor occurred almost in unison. Men hurriedly filed from the saloon without backward glances. The piano player, barkeep, and half a dozen painted ladies followed. Within less than a minute, only the two men remained.

"Tell it slow. I don't like a man who repeats himself. Get it straight the first time. I want to know everything you know about Ben Morgan. Then I'll decide whether or not to kill you." Lonnegan looked around. "No witnesses make that an easy decision."

Richard fought his fear. Sweat flowed freely down his temples and his back. He focused on the man in front of him. His next few words would determine his fate. And Maggie's.

Knowing that gave him the courage to begin.

"My name is Richard DeForest. I'm from New York City. I came to Abilene with my fianceé's brother, Marcus Rutherford, and his attorney, Dudley Simpson. We arrived on the two o'clock train this afternoon. I'm sure you can easily verify this. Maggie, my fiancée, booked rooms for everyone at The Alamar. She has turned of age and is coming into quite a nice inheritance from her deceased mother."

He found his mouth had gone dry. He swallowed and licked his lips nervously.

"Wait."

The gunslinger stood and went behind the counter, where he fetched a glass. He brought it back to the table. He poured a drink. He motioned for Richard to take it.

He wanted to down it, but kept his head and only took a small swallow. "In my conversation with her, Maggie confessed that she was in love with another man. Ben Morgan."

A light came into Lonnegan's eyes. Richard stopped speaking a moment to let the gunman digest this bit of information.

"Go on."

"She's done with me. Tossed me over for this man. I don't know a thing about him or what he does. I do know she met him in Easton, which I gather is a small town near here. She's been visiting with a family friend there, Frank Stansel. I'm sure if you go there, you'll easily find this Morgan fellow."

Lonnegan traced a finger around the rim of his glass, lost in thought. Finally, he took the drink and finished it off.

"You said her name was Maggie. Rutherford, like her brother?"

"Yes," Richard said, his nerves on edge. "I gathered from Marcus that she'll be in town several days completing the business at the bank with her lawyer regarding her inheritance."

"A Mr. Simpson? Dooley?"

"No, Dudley."

Lonnegan picked at a fingernail. "Ah, yes. Dudley. Simpson. And they're staying at The Alamar, correct?"

"Yes."

"And you don't know if Ben Morgan was with them there or back in Easton?"

"I do not, sir. I haven't laid eyes on the worthless scoundrel."

Lonnegan snorted. "I'll bet he's laid your woman."

Richard felt his eyes widening. He bit back a retort regarding insults and propriety. He remembered how Maggie wronged him. It pushed him to be brash.

"Why should I care anymore? She's not worth my time. I consider myself lucky to be rid of her. I do find it very ungentlemanly of this man to have become involved with my fiancée. A man should respect a commitment such as that. Obviously, this Morgan chap has no manners at all. I simply heard you were looking for him. I thought I would give you a bit of information so that you might find him more readily."

Lonnegan sat quietly, still picking at his dirty nails. It sickened Richard to watch it yet he couldn't look away.

"You know why I want him. Don't you." It wasn't a question.

He threw back his shoulders and puffed up. "I heard a rumor but it's none of my business. I'm simply passing along information. I'm ready to wash my hands of the whole affair and be done with it."

Lonnegan looked him squarely in the eye. "I don't know about any rumors. The fact is Ben Morgan shot and killed my brother in cold blood. My baby brother. I had to go home and break that news to my mama. Never a sweeter, more charming boy was born than little Jimmy Lonnegan. I swore I would see justice done. So however long it takes, I will find Mr. Ben Morgan. I will send him to his Maker. I will dance atop his grave with glee after his blood runs hot through the dusty street."

He took in everything Lonnegan said. All of a sudden, it seemed so real. Was he actually helping send a man to his death?

"You can go now. Don't go back to The Alamar. Find another place to stay. I'm going to be having a little talk with Miss Rutherford about her new beau. You don't want to be around for that."

Richard stood shakily. His legs wobbled as he walked away. He fought the terror that rushed through his veins.

Would this man kill Maggie, too? Or torture her?

All his grand schemes of revenge sat cold in his stomach. His lips trembled. Tears filled his eyes. He walked out of the saloon. Men stared at him in disgust as he pushed through the crowd.

Oh, God. What had he done?

Suddenly, he understood his father's way out might be the only choice left to him.

26

While Marcus and Dudley discussed business over breakfast, Maggie listlessly played with a piece of buttered toast. Today would be the first in an endless march of days empty of Ben. Knowing he would be leaving Easton soon had been one thing. Knowing he was gone forever from her life felt quite different.

She hoped he remained safe from Black Tex Lonnegan's long reach. She fought to hold back the tears. She wondered where he was and where he would roam in the future. At least he'd been warned of the danger and left yesterday. Hopefully, Lonnegan would search for Ben for several more days, giving him the advantage of a head start.

"Chicago, with all its railroads and businesses, is growing into a true mecca," Marcus said. "It also has more culture than I would have expected. That's why I'd like to locate a branch of Rutherford House there."

Dudley sipped his black coffee, nodding in agreement. "I think it's the right time to expand, especially with several of our authors doing so well in the current market. You're right, Marcus. You could establish a few local offices in different cities located throughout the country. Have New York retain dominance as the home office and site of physical production. It might be wise to look into Atlanta or New Orleans for the south. Definitely San Francisco for the West."

"I've heard that's a wonderful city, as if you'd stepped into the world of Europe right here on American soil." Marcus looked at her. "Maggie? Would you be up for a trip to San Francisco?"

She shrugged. "I don't think this is a good time, Marcus."

"Why not?"

"Because I have plans." She tore off a portion of the toast and ate it, chewing thoughtfully.

"I'd like to hear what those plans are. Especially if it involves your inheritance."

"It does, Dudley. Quite a bit of it, in fact." She set down the toast and pushed her depression aside. She'd determined to make Easton her home. She needed to look to the future and not the past. "A tornado recently came through Easton. It destroyed a large portion of the town. I have plans not only to rebuild what was lost but to add on more. Much more."

"That sounds interesting," her brother said. "Tell us more."

She sat back in her chair. "I've discussed this with Frank. He's the only one aware of what I have in mind. Since I've been in Abilene, I've been able to confirm rumors I'd heard when I first arrive a few months ago."

"What was that?" their lawyer asked.

Maggie stood and walked to the window, pulling the curtain aside to look out as she spoke. "The railroad will be expanding, building spurs in several directions from Abilene. It will come through Easton.

The town will grow from a sleepy hamlet to something that could be much more substantial."

"You intend to make Easton your home?" Marcus asked.

She dropped the curtain and faced them. "I want to build everything a healthy, prosperous town needs. A bank and a school. A town square surrounded by thriving businesses. A hotel. I've made a list of businesses to start with and we can expand as we go."

"Your circumstances have changed recently." Marcus pointed out.

"If you're referring to Ben leaving, the answer's still *yes*. I'd decided to stay even before that, because I knew he would be leaving soon."

She went and stood by her brother, laying a hand on his shoulder. "I love it here, Marcus. It's as if I searched the whole world over and finally found my place. I want to put down roots. I've made friends. I want to see my money put to good use. Helping to build the new Easton would be a lasting legacy for Mama's money. I want to make her proud."

Maggie turned to Dudley. "I'll need your help in finding a business manager to oversee the entire project. Frank says I need an architect and a construction manager, as well. You'll know more about hiring the proper professionals. I'll also need to buy some land in and surrounding Easton. I definitely want to purchase the right-of-way near the future railway station." She smiled. "I hope you're in for a good stay, Dudley. You might be here a while."

He returned her smile. "It sounds like a worthwhile project, Miss Maggie. I actually have a few people in mind but they're back in New York. Would you be willing to allow non-Westerners to become involved with this project? I'll also need more help. I will recommend a man or two from our firm that would have the vision and stamina for this type of prolonged project."

She thought over his words. "I haven't really planned that far ahead. I'd have to speak with them to see if they share my vision. I'll leave it in your hands, Dudley. If you choose to send for them, I'll be happy to meet with anyone you recommend. We can also search for the appropriate people here. I think some of the cowboys coming off the cattle trails next summer and fall might be willing to stay on as construction workers."

"This will take a lot of planning and preparation. Don't forget, we have a ten o'clock appointment at the bank this morning."

Marcus consulted his pocket watch. "That still gives us an hour. The bank isn't far from here, is it?"

A knock at the door, followed by a giggle, halted the conversation.

"Are you expecting anyone, Maggie?" Marcus asked, as he walked to the door and opened it. "Frank! It's about time."

The two men fell into each other's arms. They pounded one another on the back. As they separated, they grinned at each other like seven-year-old boys proud of the mischief they'd just created.

Seeing that Frank wasn't alone, Maggie crossed to greet Rebecca as she and the children entered the room. They embraced and Maggie turned to her companions.

"Dudley, you already know Frank. I'd like to present Rebecca Morgan. Her daughter, Jennie. That sweet sleeping child in her arms is our very own Charlie, whom I helped deliver." She brushed a finger across his soft cheek. "Rebecca, this is my dear brother, Marcus, and our family's attorney and good friend, Mr. Dudley Simpson. Please, come in and sit."

Jennie came and stood next to her, still giggling. Looking directly at her so Jennie could understand the words on her lips, Maggie said, "I'm so happy you and your mama decided to come see me, Jennie. I've missed you and I've only been gone one whole day."

The little girl gave her a sweet smile. Maggie picked her up, tweaked her pigtail and then led everyone to the sitting area of the suite.

"I hope you don't mind us surprising you like this, Maggie," Rebecca began tentatively. "Ben came and said his goodbyes yesterday, so I thought you might be a bit lonely."

She reached over and squeezed Rebecca's hand. "I am grateful for your company. And your support."

Frank cleared his throat. "We know you have business to do while you're in Abilene." He raised his brows at Maggie in question.

"Yes, Frank, I was just sharing my plans over breakfast. I believe it's a wise way to invest my inheritance."

"Dudley and I agree," Marcus said. "It means we'll probably extend our stay somewhat. I may come back and forth a few times from New York and Chicago. I'm thinking about opening a division of Rutherford House there."

"That's a splendid idea, Marcus. Your father would be so pleased. I know you're proud of Maggie. Did you get to tell him?" Frank paused, then added, "You know? The other thing?"

She shook her head. "Oh, Frank. Our Marcus was much more clever than we thought. He's known for quite a while that he has a famous author in the family." She shot her brother a glance. "That doesn't mean

Lud Madison will work for a family discount, though. In fact, this latest book will be his best yet. I do believe he might need to negotiate a fat fee since sales for the previous books have gone from good to outstanding."

Everyone laughed. Maggie shared her plans for Easton with Rebecca. They spent a good half-hour expanding on what she and Frank had discussed.

"The town will be grateful, Maggie, but they'll especially be happy that it's coming from one of its own." Rebecca gave her a fond smile. "I'm so glad you're staying." She turned to Marcus. "I'm happy you've arrived, Marcus. Frank says that no one would stand as his best man save for Marcus Rutherford, even if we had to drag him kicking and screaming from the civility of his New York mansion."

Maggie beamed. "It's official?"

Frank flushed at the attention. "I wanted to send Ben off with the reassurance that he needn't worry about Rebecca. Or the children. I plan to take care of them for a long, long time."

"When's the wedding?" she asked. "Have you set a date?"

"We haven't gotten that far," Rebecca told them. "The whole idea is new. We're getting used to it." She glanced over at Jennie. "A certain young lady seemed awfully pleased when we shared the news with her."

Maggie patted Jennie's hand. "I think the occasion will call for a new dress, Jennie. It's time for you to have your first hat. After we do our business at the bank today, why don't you and I call at the millinery shop this afternoon? It's never too early for a lady to build her collection of hats and reticules."

"I don't think we're going to be staying that long, Maggie," Frank said. "We've got to meet up with the new owner of Morgan's General Store at the bank this morning. We need to run a few errands before we head back to Easton."

"Why don't you let Jennie stay the rest of the day with me?" Maggie suggested. "She can sleep over and then we can bring her back to Easton in the morning. I'd like Marcus and Dudley to see the town as soon as possible. We could come out early tomorrow morning. Maybe call first at Mrs. Morrow's for breakfast and her delightful biscuits."

"That's a fine plan," Dudley said. "I'd like to see Easton before I wire my firm and ask for a few of our people to join me. If I see the town, I'll have a better idea who needs to be sent for and what should be accomplished."

"Maggie can walk us around and show us exactly where she wants things to be," Marcus added. "You mentioned buying some property. I know Dudley will want to see exactly where this might lie before we make an offer on the land."

"Are you sure you don't mind?" Rebecca asked.

"Not at all," she replied. "It'll be an adventure for Jennie. I know you and Frank might appreciate some much-needed time alone. You can conduct your business with the new owner and then all come back to The Alamar for luncheon. We'll try to join you, but if not, we'll return shortly afterward. I'll take Jennie shopping with me. Dudley and Marcus have mentioned business appointments they will keep. Then we'll all reunite tomorrow morning."

Frank stood. "It sounds like we should be off to the bank then. We can stroll over together. I'll be sure to stop by Mrs. Morrow's when we return to Easton and tell her to expect company for breakfast."

Maggie allowed Marcus to escort her back to The Alamar while Dudley wrapped up things with the local bank manager.

"I'm sorry we missed luncheon with Frank and his new fiancée," Marcus said, as they walked against the brisk wind. "I was afraid we would when all the paperwork started coming out from Dudley's briefcase. When he lifted a second case to the table? I knew food with friends was a lost cause."

"That's all right," she assured him. "You're the one going back to look at some numbers and other interesting things."

"Do I detect a hint of sarcasm, Mags?"

She waved a hand. "Oh, you've always liked business, Marcus, whether you're fiddling with numbers or wording contracts. I do believe you would have made a fine attorney."

"Oh, Papa would have loved that." He chuckled. "No, I followed the path he set for me. I've been happy running Rutherford House, whether focusing on the business side or the literary division. Mags, I do enjoy Lud's stories. Since I've confessed to you that I know your secret identity, I may have to occasionally pull rank and beg to read pages before you send them in to your editor. After all, I should be able to take some advantage for being related to Lud."

"I'll think about it. You know, I'm actually quite relieved to have you know I'm Lud. I kept it from you because I didn't want a pity-publish simply because I was your sister. I didn't want you to feel obligated to buy my work."

"There's no pity on my part. You're a fine writer, with a keen imagination and wonderful twists in your stories. Readers clamor for Lud Madison stories." He paused. "I want you to think seriously about stepping out of Lud's shadow and proclaiming from the high heavens that you are responsible for his work."

"Why?"

"Partly because I'm selfish. I want my little sis to receive the credit she's due." He grinned. "And partly because I think it would be a huge sensation. Just like when it became public knowledge that Currer and Ellis Bell were in fact Charlotte and Emily Bronte. You are a woman who writes dime novels as well as—no, even better than—a man. I think it would stir up quite a bit of press, which would only increase sales. Think about it."

She shrugged nonchalantly. "I think I'll leave that decision up to Rutherford House to make. It's a business decision. I'm a writer. If it were me, I'd wait till the next book is in print. Then, after it's doing so well, that would be the time for your big reveal."

He studied her. "I do believe you have more of a head for business than you let on, Maggie Rutherford."

They reached the hotel and entered, glad to be out of the November chill. She spied Tim behind the desk, helping Sam, who waved at them.

"Your friends just finished up luncheon. They're waiting for you."

"Thank you for taking care of them." She paused, eyeing the younger man. "Sam, you said that Tim was an excellent student, didn't you?"

The desk clerk beamed broadly. "Oh, he is, Miss Rutherford. He read from a young age. Always was a whiz with numbers. He's terrific at solving all kinds of puzzles. I don't think there's anything my boy can't do. Except figure out what he wants to do for a living, that is."

She nodded as she watched Tim blush at both his

father's praise and mild rebuke. "I think I have an idea."

She looked over at Marcus. "With what we have planned for Easton, I'm sure Dudley could use an assistant to help organize everything. The people we hire. Schedules. Payroll. Architect plans. Someone who could help coordinate the general process and know what was going on and with whom on any given day."

He nodded slowly, taking in her words as he looked Tim over. "I think that's an excellent idea, Maggie." He thrust his hand out. "Marcus Rutherford, Tim. A pleasure to meet you. How would you like to accompany me back to the bank and meet with our attorney? I could tell you along the way about the project Maggie has in mind and see if you might be interested."

Tim's face lit up. He looked at his father eagerly. "May I go?"

A smile tugged at Sam's mouth. "Of course, Son. Go comb your hair and put on a jacket."

Tim hurried away toward the family quarters.

"I don't exactly know what this opportunity is but I thank you both kindly for considering Tim."

"Oh, I think he'll be perfect, Sam. He's young. Eager to learn. Of course, he'll probably need to come live in Easton for the duration."

"And I may have need of him when I travel to Chicago. Or back to New York," Marcus added.

Sam looked flustered. "Well, my stars!"

"Let me go tell Frank and Rebecca goodbye, then I'll take young Tim under my wing," Marcus said.

They greeted Frank and Rebecca. Maggie told them what they had in mind for Tim. "I know Dudley will love him," she said. "He never married nor had children. I think he'll take to Tim like a duck to water."

"If Tim is as good as Maggie thinks he will be, maybe when this project is complete, I'll simply steal him away to work for Rutherford House," Marcus added.

When they were ready to leave, Rebecca and Frank both kissed Jennie. Rebecca reminded her daughter to be a good girl for Maggie.

"She'll be fine," Maggie said. "You two enjoy a quiet evening. Hopefully, Charlie will settle down early and sleep through the night."

They all walked out of the lobby together, everyone going separate ways. Maggie took Jennie's hand and led her to the millinery store. They tried on a dozen hats and posed in front of a large mirror. They looked through several different reticules, spending hours trying to decide what to buy.

She purchased a new hat for herself and a reticule for each of them. The shop owner promised that the hat for Jennie would be ready in two days' time. She didn't keep any children's hats in her stock. Maggie made a mental note to inquire that goods for children be included in whatever stores opened in Easton. That would be simple enough once the railroad spur came through and new shops began opening.

Carrying her hatbox and package, she took Jennie's hand as they exited the store. It was just after four. The wind had picked up since they'd arrived for their shopping excursion.

Maggie shivered as the November breeze ran through her. "Let's hurry back to the hotel, Jennie, before this cold front arrives in full stride. Your mama said snow comes quickly on the prairie. I hope we don't see any tonight."

She turned to walk toward the hotel but stopped abruptly. A man dressed in black from head to toe, except for the pearl-handled guns strapped to his hips, stepped out from the alleyway in front of them.

"Excuse me," she said politely. She started to go around him, thinking he should be the one apologizing for blocking their path when the sidewalk was empty around them.

"No excuses required," he said in a low, deep voice. "Maggie Rutherford?"

She turned and looked at him. "Yes. Whom am I speaking with?"

His smile chilled her more than the sharp wind. "Black Tex Lonnegan, ma'am." He touched the brim of his hat with a finger. "I hear we know someone in common."

Maggie froze at his words. Her gloved hand tightened around Jennie's protectively. The girl started squirming. Maggie tried to loosen her grip. She didn't want to call attention to Jennie or let Lonnegan know that she was Ben's niece. After reading the crimes listed on his wanted poster, she knew he would use whatever leverage he could find. She had to keep Jennie safe.

The gunslinger crouched down and gave a wintry smile to the child, one that never reached his eyes. "How are you, little one? What's your name?"

Jennie's eyes rounded as she stared back at him. She looked up at Maggie, trying to hold her trembling bottom lip in place by biting down on it.

"She's deaf," Maggie said flatly, setting down her purchases and smoothing Jennie's hair in a comforting gesture. "She can't hear what you're saying."

Lonnegan glanced up at her from where he knelt. He reached out and stroked Jennie's cheek once and then rose quickly to his full height. "Is that a fact? I didn't know you had a child. I really don't know much about you. Other than you came to Abilene a while back asking a lot of questions about cattle. After that, you moved on to Easton. I did hear Ben Morgan might be sweet on you."

Maggie always thought fast on her feet. The trait helped make her a good writer and boxer, the ability to think quickly, several steps ahead. Her priority was to protect Jennie. Everything else came second. "Frankly, I thought he was more than sweet on me. Mr. Lonnegan, you said?"

He nodded.

"I found Mr. Morgan to be quite charming and I'm not easily charmed. When I decided to make my home in Easton, I sent for Jennie. She'd been staying with my husband's family after his death."

She paused, frowning, setting her mouth and shaking her head in disgust. "But once she arrived? Ben Morgan lost interest in me. I suppose it's one thing to be taken with a young widow. It's entirely another matter if that widow comes with a child."

Lonnegan's brow creased. "So, is he in Easton now?"

Maggie harrumphed in a manner imitating her father. She'd met with his disapproval many times. She knew exactly the tone and pitch to take. "Not anymore. It's a small, family-oriented community, Mr. Lonnegan. I was the only unattached female. That is, except for the Widow Morrow and she's old enough to be my grandmother."

She pulled a handkerchief from her sleeve and dabbed at the corner of her eye. "Once Ben Morgan realized I was a mother, he uttered a few paltry excuses and left town. I don't know where he went. I really don't care."

His eyes narrowed as he took in what she said and she knew he carefully assessed her words. She prayed they rang with emotion, if not the truth.

Waving the handkerchief for effect, she added, "It's certainly for the best. I learned that he was actually a *gambler*." She gave what she hoped passed for a horrified look. "It was already a bit of a struggle for me to imagine settling for a cowboy, though he is very handsome indeed, but to learn he's a degenerate gambler? I was appalled. In no circumstances would I ever have exposed Jennie to him if I'd known that fact." She sniffed. "One he conveniently left out from all our discussions.

"So if you'll excuse us, sir. I've about had my fill talking about Mr. Ben Morgan. I'm sorry if he's a friend of yours, for he's certainly no friend of mine."

Maggie leaned down for the hatbox. As she rose, Lonnegan began clapping. Slowly. Steadily. Loudly.

She took a step back, pulling Jennie with her.

He finally stopped, his eyes boring into hers. "Miss Rutherford, you belong on the stage. That was one of the most magnificent performances I've ever had the pleasure to watch unfold. If I hadn't spoken to Richard DeForest at length and learned that you'd tossed him over because you were in love with Ben Morgan, I would have believed every word you uttered. You were that sincere. And I know if you love him, you're protecting him. From me."

Maggie's insides coiled in fear. "If you've met Richard, then you know what a sniveling weasel he is. Of course I preferred Ben to Richard. I told him to his face. I broke things off with Richard and he's anxious to cause mischief for me. But what I told you is true. Ben Morgan is a gambler. A scoundrel. I'm finished with him and he's left Easton. Probably Abilene, as well, though it doesn't really concern me. He may swindle and sweet-talk anyone else, as long as I never have to lay eyes on him again."

Lonnegan cocked a head and studied her. "Either you're a consummate liar—or you're actually telling me the truth."

She met his gaze. "Why would I lie to you? I don't even know who you are."

"But you will."

BEN WOULD'VE LAUGHED ALOUD if the situation weren't so fraught with danger. He rode toward Abilene.

Again.

All this back and forth caused his head to spin. He'd left Abilene to tell Adam's family goodbye and headed in the opposite direction. Then, he turned around and rode back, hoping to convince Maggie to come with him. After overhearing her conversation with her fiancé yesterday, he'd stormed away. He'd ridden Prince until late at night, only stopping so the poor beast wouldn't keel over dead.

Yet he found himself pointed to the cow town today. Ben had only ridden a short distance this morning when he realized he didn't want to live the rest of his life on the run from an outlaw like Black Tex Lonnegan. He'd rather die at Lonnegan's hands than look over his shoulder from now until eternity. That was no kind of life.

Actually, any kind of life without Maggie in it was no kind of life at all. Ben headed to the railhead a final time. It was a kill-or-be-killed situation. He'd find Lonnegan and confront him. Or try to reason with him. Maybe he could outdraw him. Or simply hold his hands up and let the gunfighter shoot him dead.

Whatever the outcome, it would be settled. Either he would come out of this situation alive or he wouldn't. If he lived, he'd approach Maggie's fiancé and talk it out with him. If this man were truly the right one for her, Ben would walk away and never look back. If he discovered the man wasn't good enough for Maggie, he'd pursue her like Billy Yank did Johnny Reb during the war.

And if he died? Well, problem solved.

Ben had no idea where to find Lonnegan, but he knew someone who might. He headed for The Alamar. Sam knew everything and everybody's business. He was bound to know where Lonnegan might be staying.

Hitching his horse to a post in front of the hotel, he strode into the lobby. A quick scan showed the desk unattended, but Sam might be working in the small office located behind it. Just as he went to ring the bell on the counter, he heard someone call his name.

He turned and saw Marcus Rutherford hurrying down the stairs, a look of worry across his brow. Ben had only known Marcus a short time but the other man seemed unflappable. If he was visibly upset, he must have good reason.

"Marcus. What's wrong?"

"It's Maggie. And Jennie. They aren't in the room." Marcus took a deep breath. "I've been with Dudley and the bankers. Afterward, I had some other business to handle for the remainder of the afternoon. Maggie took Jennie shopping for a hat. I've only arrived but they should be back from their excursion by now."

"And they're not," Ben said, worry beginning to fill him.

"No." Marcus hurried to the counter, where the desk clerk had just emerged from behind closed doors. Ben saw Sam's eyes widen when he caught sight of him.

"You can't be here, Mr. Morgan. You just can't!"

He joined the two men. "I came back to see you, Sam. I'm not going to run. Neither will I stick my head in the sand. I need to know where Black Tex Lonnegan is staying to end this business, one way or the other." He glanced over at Marcus. "And I may need to look for Maggie."

Marcus looked grim. "The two may be connected."

Ben nodded. "I had the same thought."

Sam fiddled nervously with his tie. "Miss Rutherford took the little girl shopping. I'm not sure if they've returned or not."

"They haven't," Marcus informed him. "I've been to our suite. There's no trace of them or of them having been there."

Sam removed his pince-nez and rubbed his nose before replacing them. "Mr. Lonnegan is usually at one of the many saloons along the main thorough-fare from late afternoon until the wee hours of the morning. I swear to you, Mr. Morgan, I don't know where he's staying. He's stopped by here twice, looking for you. Just appears out of thin air, he does."

"Was he aware that Maggie knew me?" Ben questioned.

Sam shook his head. "He did. I don't know how, but he knew there was some connection between you. As did the other gentleman."

"Other gentleman?" Ben and Marcus echoed.

"Yes. The one who stopped by late yesterday after-noon. It was after you left, Mr. Morgan."

"Was it Richard DeForest?" asked Marcus.

"It was, indeed, Mr. Rutherford. He spoke with

Miss Rutherford. I gathered their meeting was not successful."

Ben's heart started racing. "How do you know that, Sam?"

Sam looked flustered. "I shouldn't gossip but seeing as how Mr. DeForest is not a paying guest of The Alamar..." His voice trailed off.

"Then I don't see any harm imparting the information you might have, Sam," Marcus injected smoothly.

"She *struck* him! In the nose. Mr. DeForest had blood all down his shirtfront. On his vest. His frock coat, too. Miss Rutherford may have broken the man's nose. I came in from collecting the mail just as Miss Rutherford emerged from the receiving room. She wore a satisfied look on her face, but I noticed she cradled one hand in the other in front of her. She greeted me cordially and then sailed up the stairs as if she hadn't a care in the world."

Marcus started to smile. "And Richard?"

"Mr. DeForest stepped out and immediately told me, well, I can't repeat what he said in polite society. But he made it clear that Miss Rutherford was the culprit who'd bloodied his nose. He was none too happy with her."

"Do you know where he went?" Ben asked.

"He mentioned something about drowning his sorrows. I assumed he'd go get liquored up."

Ben glanced at Marcus. "Do you think it's possible DeForest could've run into Lonnegan while at a saloon? Is he the type that would be indiscreet if drunk?"

Marcus nodded grimly. "I'm afraid that's typical of Richard. If Maggie mentioned your name and he found out Lonnegan's looking for you, Richard is petty enough to think telling this outlaw about the two of you would somehow even the score. His pride's been bruised not once, but twice now. Maggie jilted him in front of hundreds of guests at their wedding. This time she stood up to him and bloodied his nose."

Ben adjusted his hat. His hand slipped to the gun now worn in a holster, making sure it was ready for use. "Stay here, Marcus. I'll hit the barrooms and see what I can find out."

Before Marcus could reply, the front door opened. Jennie came running in, aiming straight for Ben's leg. She latched onto it, burying her face in his thigh. Ben watched a stylish, plump woman rush over.

"Are you Ben Morgan?" she asked, clearly out of breath.

"I am." He lifted his niece into his arms.

Jennie looked him squarely in the face. "Miss Maggie's in trouble, Uncle Ben. The bad man took her."

28

Hearing Jennie speak stunned Ben into momentary silence. Fear seized him and held him like an iron vise. Jennie had been with Maggie.

And now the bad man had her.

The woman looked visibly relieved. "I'm Sybil Johnson. I own a millinery store here in Abilene. I'm so glad to find you. Jennie said you'd be here." She looked at the other two men. "I suppose one of you is Miss Rutherford's brother?"

"Yes. I'm Marcus Rutherford." He looked at Jennie and gave the trembling girl a smile. "Hello, Jennie. I'm glad you remembered where we were staying. You're such a smart girl. Can you tell us how you met this nice lady? Why isn't Maggie with you?"

"Uh-huh." Jennie turned to Ben, jamming a thumb into her mouth as she had when she was a baby. Ben wanted nothing more than to find out how Jennie had been separated from Maggie, but he understood he needed to exercise patience.

He looked over at the desk clerk. "Sam. Maybe you rustle up a cookie. Jennie loves her cookies."

Ben hoped the sweet treat would help his niece re-lax. He needed as much information as he could get from her and the woman who'd returned her, before he set out to get Maggie back.

Sam nodded in understanding. "Coming right up, Mr. Morgan. I'll bet I can also find a glass of milk to go with it." He scurried off.

Ben stroked Jennie's hair, hoping to soothe her. He sensed her relaxing in his arms as he turned to the woman. "Thank you for returning my niece, Mrs. Johnson. I need to ask if you saw Maggie or the man who took her. No detail is too small, ma'am."

"Miss Rutherford spent time in my store this afternoon with Jennie. They had a fine time trying on hats and posing in front of the mirror with different reticules. She eventually purchased a hat for herself. Oh, dear. I saw the hatbox on the sidewalk in front of the store."

"Don't worry about that now, ma'am. Please continue."

"They left the store a good hour before I closed up. It's a slow time of the season. No customers came in after they left." She glanced at Jennie, who still sucked her thumb noisily and had her head on Ben's shoulder.

"I found Jennie sitting on the curb about half a block from my store as I left for the evening. I close up before Mr. Johnson does. He runs a haberdashery next door to my shop. I walk a couple of blocks home to get supper started each evening so it's ready by the time he gets home. Frankly, it startled me to see an unattended child left alone on the street, especially with it growing dark. When I recognized Jennie, I went straight over to her."

Ben nodded and waited for the woman to continue.

"I asked her where Miss Rutherford was and that's

when she began telling me about the bad man, her Uncle Ben, and how she needed to go to The Alamar. I knew Miss Rutherford had stayed here in the past. She told me to send the bill here for her purchases today, along with the bonnet I was to make up for Jennie."

Ben tamped down the anger that threatened to surface, wild thoughts racing through his brain as he wondered just what Jennie had seen. And where Lonnegan might have taken Maggie.

He needed to remain calm despite the tension coiling within every muscle in his body. He didn't want to frighten Jennie. He glanced at Marcus questioningly, who nodded in return. It seemed both men were in agreement that Sybil Johnson had told them all she knew.

"Mrs. Johnson, I can't thank you enough for returning Jennie."

Her face softened. "Oh, Mr. Morgan, I wouldn't have left the poor girl stranded on the street."

"Would you be willing to speak to the sheriff if he has any questions for you?"

Her eyes widened. "I suppose so," she said thoughtfully. "But I don't want any trouble. Mr. Johnson wouldn't like that."

"We can't thank you enough for taking the time to see Jennie safely to the hotel." Marcus reached into his pocket and removed a money clip. "Would you please accept a small token of our appreciation?"

The milliner's eyebrows rose. "Your thanks is enough, Mr. Rutherford. And seeing this sweet girl in good hands." She paused. "I just hope you're able to find Miss Rutherford."

"We will," Ben said, steel in his voice. After he did, he would take pleasure in tearing Black Tex Lonnegan into bite-sized pieces that he would grind under his bootheel until nothing but dust remained.

The milliner said goodbye and left the hotel. Ben smiled at Jennie while he walked over to a nearby chair. He sat with her still in his arms. "I'm happy you're talking again, little one. Can you hear as well as you could before you got the mumps?"

She pulled her thumb from her mouth and nodded eagerly. "I got scared when I couldn't hear. My cheeks hurt. My ears hurt. Mama and Papa were so sad. Mama cried. But I can hear you, Uncle Ben. Real good."

Jennie thought a moment. "I heard Mama and Mr. Frank talking the other night. It sounded funny. Like when Mama washes my hair and talks to me."

"You could hear noise? But not their words. Like it was muffled?"

"Uh-huh. And then they popped and hurt more, but then my ears got all better." She brightened. "I could hear Mrs. Morrow yesterday. She talks. A lot. I could hear everybody today." Her face fell. "Even that bad man."

She snuggled closer to Ben. "I was gonna tell Miss Maggie I could hear her but then the bad man got in the way." Her bottom lip trembled. "He scared me. I didn't want to talk or hear him or see him anymore."

Marcus knelt beside them. "Jennie, the bad man isn't here. Your Uncle Ben and I will protect you from him. But we also want to protect Maggie. She is my sister. I love her very much. I want to find her and help her come home so we can all be together again. Anything you remember about the bad man—or what he said—might help us do just that."

Jennie worried her lip and frowned in concentration. "He had shiny guns. And a black shirt and black pants. He smiled but I don't think he knows how. It looked like it made his face hurt. And he said he knows you, Uncle Ben. He said he wanted to be friends with Miss Maggie like you are."

Ben gritted his teeth and kept his composure. Scaring Jennie wouldn't accomplish anything. It wasn't her fault Lonnegan took Maggie.

"Where did they go, Punkin?"

Jennie shrugged. "I don't know. They talked. Miss Maggie told me to sit myself right down and be her good little girl. I'm not really her little girl. I'm Mama's little girl, but I didn't say that. She told me not to worry. To stay there and wait. Then someone would bring me back to The Alamar. And they did!" She yawned. "I'm sleepy."

Ben cradled her in his arms. "Just shut your eyes, love." He kissed her forehead. Within seconds, she fell asleep.

Marcus rose to his feet. "We need to send for the sheriff. This Lonnegan is guilty of kidnapping Maggie at the very least. And Frank. We need Frank here. He's always kept his head in a crisis."

Ben was about to tell him they didn't have time to wait around for Frank when Sam returned with a plate of cookies and a glass of milk. A middle-aged woman with gray streaks running through her brown bun accompanied him. He introduced his wife and she volunteered to watch over Jennie.

"My husband told me what happened to Miss Rutherford. You need to act fast and not worry about this precious child. I can take her up to your suite and sit with her until her mama comes."

"I sent Tim for the sheriff," Sam explained. "Then I told him to head to Easton. He's to bring back Jennie's mama and Sheriff Stansel."

"Thank you," Marcus said.

Sam accompanied his wife and Jennie up the stairs. The two men began tossing around ideas of where Lonnegan might have taken Maggie. Ben knew the longer the gunfighter held Maggie, the worse it might be. Marcus promised he would spare no dime in seeing her returned if it came to a ransom needing to be paid.

Ben shook his head. "He doesn't want money, Marcus. He wants me."

"My sister is being used as a pawn. All because of *you!*" Hands balling into fists at his sides, Marcus glared at Ben.

"Don't you think I know that?" Ben ground out. "Maggie is my heart and soul. Dammit, Marcus. I *love* her. Why do you think I came back?"

"How should I know?" Marcus demanded. "My sister is in danger. And it's your fault."

"I returned to Abilene of my own free will, knowing I was walking into a death trap. *Because I love her.* I couldn't imagine my life without her. Lonnegan's using her as a hostage. To get to me. He doesn't have any use for her. I'll gladly trade my life for hers in a heartbeat."

He strode to the door, wanting to escape the hotel and blow off some steam while he thought. Instead, he stopped in his tracks as a man with a dusty white hat and a star pinned to his chest entered the hotel.

He held a hand out to the lawman. "I'm Ben Morgan, Sheriff. Thank you for coming." He ushered the newcomer over to Marcus and made a quick introduction.

The sheriff looked him over. "So, you're the famous Ben Morgan? Seems everyone in town's been looking for you the last couple of days."

"To give Black Tex Lonnegan a heads-up to where I am?"

"Nope." The lawman shook his head back and forth slowly, pursing his lips. "To steer as clear from you as possible. No offense, Mr. Morgan, but nobody wants to tussle with a wild card like Lonnegan."

"Well, you'll have to start now, Sheriff. He's kidnapped Maggie Rutherford, a local citizen from Easton," Ben explained. "You don't have any choice but to get involved."

The peace officer gave him a slow once-over. "Is that a fact?" he drawled. "Actually, I do have a choice. And I choose not to get involved with any business concerning Black Tex Lonnegan."

"Are you joking, man?" Marcus asked. "You're the law. It's your obligation, sir, to do your job and find my sister!"

The sheriff gave them a patronizing smile. "Well, Mr. Out-of-Towner, I have no obligation to you. My first and foremost duty is to keep myself alive. Tangling with Lonnegan ups the odds from a long shot to a sure bet that that ain't gonna happen. Personally, I prefer living to dying. I aim to stay alive for another day."

"You're a chicken-shit," Ben told him.

The sheriff had the decency to shrug in agreement. "Maybe so. But I'm paid to keep order in this here town. Lonnegan ain't been disorderly with any of my citizens."

"I'm sure his wanted poster hangs in your office, detailing the many crimes he's committed. Including murder. Isn't it your responsibility to protect Abilene from wanted criminals?" Ben demanded.

"Yes, it is. Unless they're the likes of Black Tex Lonnegan. I'll admit it. I'm scared shitless of him. I don't know anyone who isn't. If you say you aren't, then I would judge you to be a very foolish man, Mr. Morgan." He tipped his hat to them. I'd best say goodnight. Good luck if you find Lonnegan. Or if he finds you first." He paused. "You're gonna need it."

They watched the peace officer mosey out of the lobby and through the hotel's exit as if he hadn't a care in the world.

"I am dumbfounded," Marcus said.

Every moment that went by, Ben feared for Maggie's safety. He may have tried to reassure Marcus that Maggie was a lowly chess piece in the game Lonnegan played, one easily traded for him in return.

He knew the truth. Every moment Maggie spent in the company of Lonnegan exposed her to imminent danger. Injury would be the least of it. By the end game, Maggie would be dead.

The doors opened. A slender boy of about eight hurried through them. Without a glance at Ben or Marcus, he ran straight to the desk. He slammed an envelope he carried onto the counter and then zipped back through the doors again.

Somehow, Ben knew that letter carried his name.

He moved to the desk and saw his name scrawled across the front of the envelope in bold letters.

29

Maggie watched in disbelief as an entire bar emptied. Granted, it was only about six in the evening. She knew from her research that the action and clients picked up later but it still amazed her how the crowd dispersed with but a few words from a fairly soft-spoken Black Tex Lonnegan. An entire saloon full of men and painted ladies cleared out without a single complaint. It showed her just how much fear Lonnegan elicited.

No one questioned why the gunslinger held her arm in a death grip. Nobody looked her in the face. They'd have seen most of the blood had drained away if they had. She must be as white as snow. She certainly felt as cold.

Lonnegan released her arm. It immediately tingled with pain.

At least with pain, you knew you were still alive, she thought. She could try to run but she knew she wouldn't make it a foot away before he'd pulled those pearl-handled six-shooters. He'd gun her down in cold blood. She wasn't ready to die just yet.

She was the bait to attract Ben into a trap. As long

as she might have one more glance at the man she loved, Maggie planned to stay still. And keep thinking.

As a writer, she put her characters into impossible situations all the time. She also learned quickly that she had to get them out of trouble, too. Well, this was one of those circumstances. The high point in a novel. When Ben walked through those swinging doors, the climax would have arrived.

In writing, she made her climax fast, furious, and fun. The scene resolved itself in mere paragraphs—or in seconds, to her characters. She didn't know how long it would be until Ben arrived. She desperately begged her brain to spin out a solution. She wanted a life with Ben Morgan. Children by him. A home they'd share together. She wanted what at this moment seemed to be the impossible.

But she refused to give in.

"Let's have a seat, Maggie," the gunman said. "Pick a spot in the middle if you would."

Anger flashed through her. "That's Miss Rutherford to you. I reserve Maggie for my friends and family. You are neither." She lifted her chin, daring him to say anything to differ with her.

He nodded, a gleam of respect dancing in his black eyes. "Miss Rutherford, it is."

Despite her trembling legs, she walked as calmly as she could. She sat in a seat at a table in the dead center of the room. She knew Lonnegan wanted to face the door. She sat in the chair that would be to his left. Now, her hidden gun would be on the side facing away from him.

Maggie didn't know how she'd get to the pistol. Placing herself in a position to work on getting it free to use was a start. She looked him squarely in the eye when he took the seat she expected. He drew his guns from his belt and set both on the table in intimidation, daring her to reach for one. She wouldn't have the speed or temerity to be successful.

She decided to engage him in conversation. Maybe she'd learn something, anything about him that she could use.

"Is it your business to go about kidnapping innocent women and using them to lure equally innocent men to their deaths? Or do you just commit felonies for pure enjoyment?"

He guffawed, startling her. She hopped her chair back a space. Immediately, she thought it a good move. She'd put even a little more distance between them. She needed to have her hand in her pocket. She'd try to tear a seam somehow and create a hole. If she could do that, she might be able to slip the gun into her hand, while she kept it hidden in the pocket.

Or even hold it through her skirt. Now there was an idea. If she could get to the trigger, she could manipulate it through the cloth. He'd never expect some fancy eastern woman to shoot him from a hole through her skirts.

"Oh, Miss Rutherford. Ben Morgan is far from what I'd term innocent."

She arched her brows at him. "Why do you wish to punish him with death? I'd be interested to see what crimes you think he's committed."

He raised a hand to his chin and stroked it thoughtfully. "I wish I'd had a champion like you in my corner. Maybe things would've turned out differently for me." He gazed out across the room, lost in thought a moment.

"Well, if you didn't insist on going about shooting people for a living, you might have found a decent young lady to love and be loved by. I can't understand a man who'd be so greedy that he'd take lives for money."

Lonnegan nodded. Smiled at her, which looked odd on his features. She doubted he ever had a much of a chance to smile in his line of work.

"It wasn't my first choice. Nor my second or third. A man falls into this sort of business. He doesn't aim to start out in it." He narrowed his eyes at her. "But a man's gotta do what a man's gotta do."

She looked at him in amazement. "But you don't *have* to kill Ben. At least, I'm assuming it's Ben we're waiting to see. You invited him here, via the letter you paid that little boy to deliver to The Alamar."

"We are. And it did. Invite him here. I know he'll come. If only to see you. One last time."

She shook her head furiously. "I told you before. Ben's gone. He left Abilene. He won't be back."

He studied her. She didn't like the look in his eye as he did. It made her feel even dirtier than when he'd held onto her so she wouldn't run. She'd left with him in order to put distance between him and Jennie. As they'd walked away, he'd latched onto her and hadn't let go until a few moments ago.

"If I were a betting man, and I'm not, but if I were? I'd bet my last dime that Mr. Ben Morgan will walk through those doors before the night is out."

Maggie frowned. "Why are you so sure? I know he left town. He told me goodbye. I could taste it in his kiss."

Black Tex Lonnegan shook his head and waved a finger around, as if making a point with a small child. "The way you talk about him? There's love there, *Miss* Rutherford. It runs deep and wide and strong. And if a pretty little thing like you loved me? I'd sure come back. Even if I had said my goodbyes. Morgan will show. Because he loves you."

Her despair grew. Of course, she hoped Ben would come back. She would've left with the clothes on her back if he'd returned and asked her to leave with him. That was before Lonnegan grabbed her. As a hostage, she was merely being used to lure Ben to this place.

If Ben had returned to Abilene, he *would* come for her. She hadn't a doubt in her mind. The bond between them was too strong. He wouldn't sacrifice her to save himself. He'd walk headfirst into the bar and try to save her. He'd die if she couldn't think of a way to stop Lonnegan. Soon.

She slid her hand into her pocket. Time to get to work. "You never answered my question. *Why do you want Ben dead?*"

"Because he killed my little brother." Lonnegan's jaw tightened. "Jimmy was the sweetest kid in the world. A charming scamp. Women loved him and wanted to mother him at the same time. He had this air about him. Like no one else. I helped raise him. He was like my own son."

The gunfighter met her gaze. "Morgan shot him dead. Over a card game! If that's not the most ridiculous thing to die over. Little pieces of pasteboard with silly shapes and numbers on them. They're meaningless. And Jimmy died."

Realization dawned. Maggie knew Ben well enough to know he wouldn't have cheated at cards. It must have been Jimmy Lonnegan who swindled Ben. But for Ben to shoot another player over that? It didn't seem like the man she knew.

The gunslinger continued his bitter tirade. "Morgan had the nerve to claim Jimmy not only cheated at cards but he tried to kill other players. Not my Jimmy! Never!"

His words formed the final piece of the puzzle. Jimmy Lonnegan had been careless and got caught cheating. When called out by Ben and someone else, he'd probably drawn and fired on them. She'd seen Ben's skill at the gun shooting contest. She was certain he'd shot the younger Lonnegan in self-defense.

Something like that wouldn't matter to a dishonorable outlaw such as Black Tex Lonnegan. He would see it one way—his way—and act accordingly.

Maggie began to laugh. She knew it was partly the hysteria building in her. And she laughed some more. Marcus called it her giggle box turning over. She'd done it as a child, getting tickled at something inappropriate at an inopportune time. The laughter would bubble within her and spill out, unstoppable, until she finally wound down like a spinning top.

Lonnegan hauled a hand back. She gasped, holding her breath in, trying to stop, even as he struck her hard. She fell from her chair to the floor, her palms sliding out as she tried to break the fall. She sucked in her breath in pain, as much from her knees hitting the hard wooden floor as from the splinter driven into her right hand.

At that moment, Ben thrust open the swinging doors to the saloon. He stepped through with his revolver in hand.

BEN ENTERED INTO THE SALOON. His eyes went straight to Lonnegan, whose back was turned from the doorway. The gunslinger stood over Maggie, his hand still poised in mid-air from the vicious slap that knocked her from her chair. She'd fallen to the floor, slightly behind the gunman. Fury erupted as Ben raised his Colt to fire. Lonnegan sensed him there and turned. A black-clad blur, he swiveled to go for his guns sitting on the table.

Even as he did, Ben watched Maggie yank her skirt up with her right hand. She pulled the petticoat pistol from her garter with her left. She jammed the gun into Lonnegan's unprotected kidney.

"Don't move, you son of a bitch!"

The outlaw froze, exposed, both arms stretched out, hovering inches from his weapons.

Maggie crouched next to him, the gun steady in her hand. "This is what the sporting gals advised me to carry once I came out West. My own pistol. Just in case I ran into the likes of swine such as yourself."

Lonnegan started to move. She jabbed him with the gun. "You may not think much of it but it's quite accurate at close range. And I am at very close range." She paused. "I have two shots. If you even think about blinking, the first will be reserved for your gut. The other? I'd have to think about where to place it while you were writhing in pain. Either between your beady little eyes or in your balls. I can debate those choices with Ben for several minutes while you're wasting away in agony."

Ben walked cautiously toward them, his own gun aimed at Lonnegan's heart as the gunslinger watched him approach.

Suddenly, Marcus stepped out from doors behind the bar. He was also armed, his gun trained on the outlaw as he casually strolled closer. "Mags," he admonished playfully. "What would Aunt Harriet say if she heard you spouting such filthy language?"

Ben saw a slow smile touch her lips.

"Oh, Marcus, I do believe she'd disapprove heartily. Of my language. Of my carrying a pistol. Of my willingness to use said pistol if this piece of vermin dares to breathe wrong."

Ben reached the table. He swept the gleaming, pearl-handled guns to the far side of the table, away from the famous gunslinger. He handed one to Marcus and took the remaining one himself. Now, both men possessed a pistol in each hand.

Maggie eased away from Lonnegan and rose, her own gun still pointed at the outlaw. She remained near enough to shoot if needed.

Marcus inspected the new six-shooter he held. "My, this is impressive. I think it will be quite the souvenir to take home to New York." He gave Lonnegan a nasty smile.

The gunfighter started to speak, but Maggie brought her gun down hard on the back of his head. He slumped against the table in front of him, out cold.

She placed one hand upon her hip and waved her gun around with the other. "*That's* what he gets for messing with Maggie Rutherford."

Ben closed the gap between them and holstered his gun and Lonnegan's. He gingerly lifted hers from her hand and placed it on a table. He yanked her hard against him.

And seized her mouth with his.

It was a kiss he would remember until his dying day, searing with all the pent-up passion he held for this remarkable woman. Her lips, so long denied to him, now became his possession as he ruthlessly plundered every bit of sweetness from them. He thrust his hands into her magnificent copper hair, the pins spilling to the floor as he worked his fingers through the lush waves.

Ben kissed her until nothing existed but Maggie. Her taste. Her vanilla-scented satin skin. Her ripe breasts pinned against his chest as his hands worked their way down her back and gripped her small waist, his thumbs massaging her through her skirts.

"Ahem."

From the fog of passion, he realized that Marcus stood but a few feet from them, his gun trained on Lonnegan. He tore his lips from Maggie's. He saw the dazed expression in her hazel eyes, which had gone green again, with the little gold flecks that he loved when she was aroused.

"I love everything about you, Maggie Rutherford. Everything. From your beautiful eyes to that sashaying walk to your fine mind and wicked mouth."

"Wicked in that it's sinfully wicked to kiss? Or that wicked things come out of it sometimes?"

He grinned and kissed her hard again. "Both." He looked at her as the love poured from every pore he possessed.

"I came back because I couldn't imagine a life without you. I'd rather die in agony a thousand times than live one lifetime without you by my side. Marry me, Maggie Rutherford. Marry me and make me the happiest man on earth."

Her eyes twinkled with mischief. "Only if you promise that this one lifetime will be a long, long, very long one. I won't settle for anything less."

Ben swept her up and twirled her in his arms as he kissed her over and over.

Marcus cleared his throat. "I'll consider that a *yes* from Mags. By the way, someone needs to go for the sheriff. Although I don't think that cowardly oaf should get any credit for this arrest."

"He won't. I'll take charge of the prisoner."

They all turned and saw Frank standing in the doorway, both guns drawn and ready to light up the room. He strode across the saloon and came to stand in front of Lonnegan, who began to stir. Frank whipped out a set of handcuffs. He slapped them on as the criminal moaned.

"What took you so long, Frank?" Marcus teased. "Ben and I didn't have time to wait around for you with Maggie's life in danger." He glanced over and gave her a fond smile. "Not that she needed our help. By the time we arrived, she just about had the situation in hand."

Frank snorted. "I rode like the devil once young Tim arrived. I'm just sorry I missed out on all the fun."

Ben reluctantly released Maggie to slap Frank on the back. "I hear there's a huge reward for Black Tex Lonnegan. Alive or dead." He gave his friend a smile. "A reward that would go a long way to establishing a new household with a bride who happens to come with a ready-made family."

Frank sucked in a breath. "I can't take credit—"

"You're the arresting officer, Frank," Maggie interjected. "I'd say the reward is all yours. To do with as you see fit." She grinned. "Maybe even to have a wedding before Marcus ups and leaves for Chicago."

"Or Denver," her brother added. "Dudley seems to think Rutherford House should expand there. And to San Francisco. And New Orleans." He looked at Frank. "But if Frank chose to get married soon, I'd certainly be interested in standing up with him."

Ben added, "Don't forget about our wedding, Marcus. I'm sure you'll be needed to give away the bride."

"I wonder if Rebecca would agree to a double wedding," mused Maggie.

Ben pulled her into his arms. "I can't waste another minute, Maggie. Women take too much time planning weddings. I don't want to spend another night without you by my side. I know you did the fancy ceremony once before. The gown. The church. The guests. Could I talk you into something right now? This minute? Say the word. I'll round up a preacher. Marcus and Frank can be witnesses."

She cupped his face in her hands. "Are you that eager to marry me, Ben Morgan?"

"To start my life with you? I thought I'd lost you, Maggie. Now that you're back in my arms, I doubt I'll ever let you go."

She looked over at Marcus. "Go find us a preacher, Big Brother. It looks like I'm getting married tonight." Her eyes shone with love as she said to Ben, "I thought I'd simply interview some random cowboy about cattle drives for research. I had no idea that love would be written in the cards. Funny how love can bring about a change of plans."

Ben looked at the love of his life as tears filled both their eyes. He leaned down and kissed her, murmuring against her mouth, "Maggie Rutherford, soon to be Maggie Morgan, I'll love you until the end of time. And a thousand years beyond that."

She whispered, "Make it a million and you've got yourself a deal."

ALSO BY ALEXA ASTON

THE HOLLYWOOD NAME GAME

Hollywood Heartbreaker

Hollywood Flirt

Hollywood Player

Hollywood Double

Hollywood Enigma

Lawmen of the West

Runaway Hearts

Blind Faith

Love and the Lawman

Ballad Beauty

DUKES OF DISTINCTION:

Duke of Renown

Duke of Charm

Duke of Disrepute

Duke of Arrogance

Duke of Honor

MEDIEVAL RUNAWAY WIVES:

Song of the Heart

A Promise of Tomorrow

Destined for Love

SOLDIERS AND SOULMATES:

Return to Honor

Season of Honor

NOVELLAS:

Diana

Derek

Thea

The Lyon's Lady Love